Jacob's Trouble

A Story of the Tribulation

Jacob's Trouble
A Story of the Tribulation

Michael Pennino

Jacob's Trouble
by Michael Pennino

Printed in the United States of America

Library of Congress Control Number: 2003102348
ISBN 1-591605-42-3

Scripture taken from the HOLY BIBLE, KING JAMES VERSION. Public Domain.

Xulon Press
10640 Main Street
Suite 204
Fairfax, VA 22030
(703) 934-4411
XulonPress.com

To order additional copies, call 1-866-909-BOOK (2665).

Acknowledgments

With appreciation to:

My wife, Brenda. You believed in me when others gave up. The Lord made me whole when He brought you into my life. I love you.

Pastor Mark Evans and his wife, Vivian. Both of you were there when I accepted the Lord and you gave me encouragement and spiritual milk. You treated me as your own son.

The Lord Jesus Christ, my Savior. I am continually amazed by Your forgiveness and Grace upon my undeserving soul. I am a blessed man.

TO

My Wife and My Children and to the
Memory of our Son and Brother
Matthew Michael
The Lord has Truly Blessed Me

Prologue

The early morning darkness had found Tracey Fredricks alone and kneeling at the foot of her bed, praying for her husband's salvation. The nightmare that had awakened her from her sleep had left her shaken with beads of sweat dripping from her brow. The dream was a warning from God that the end of time was near. The Holy Spirit had been moving, stirring within her soul. *"Be ready. The hour of your Savior's return is near."* She knew. From deep within she knew the end was near-very near.

"Have courage." Again she sensed the Spirit's urging, *"The hour of salvation has come to those who believe on the Lord Jesus Christ."*

"My husband-" she prayed almost pleadingly, "-does not know you. I pray for a little more time."

Again the Holy Spirit spoke, *"The time is ripe. Let him who does wrong continue to do wrong and let him who is vile continue to be vile."*

Overcome with emotion, she fell to the floor. Face down, her arms extended past her head with her palms held upward, she continued her prayer, "Lord, surely in your righteousness you can change the heart of one more in the time left."

"Am I not the Creator of the Universe? Am I not the God of the impossible? Have I not predestined the chosen ones who have been called to salvation since before time?

Trembling, Tracey Fredricks answers, "Yes, Lord."

"Then have faith my child. Be still and know that I am God."

Chapter 1

The view of the Sierra Nevada Mountains was spectacular with its snow-covered peaks and Lake Tahoe directly below. In his fifteen years of flying, he had never witnessed anything as beautiful. Mark Twain's description of the lake as "the emerald in the sky" gave little justice to the true splendor of this large body of water that lay almost seven thousand feet above sea level. Her crystal-clear water was as smooth as glass, and it mirrored the mountains that formed her boundaries, magnifying them against the lake's dark blue color. The melting snow along her shores sparkled in the midday sun like thousands of polished diamonds waiting to be scooped up by anyone lucky enough to find them. The lake was truly majestic and, as with all royalty, she had a crown, not made of gold and rubies but from the snow-capped peaks and purple mountains that surrounded her.

Streams formed by the receding snow pack snaked their way down the slopes toward the lake, drawn to her like a salmon is drawn to its spawning place, stopping at nothing to reach its final destination. The largest stream flowed uncontrollably over a cliff, forming a towering waterfall. As it catapulted over the edge the water changed color from a greenish-blue to a frothy white, making a thunderous roar on the jagged rocks below, creating a small rainbow in the cool mist at the bottom.

No God could create anything this beautiful. Angry that God was invading his thoughts again, Captain Jacob Fredricks stared out of the window of the airplane trying to forget about God, at least for a little while. He had wrestled with the idea of God and His existence ever since his wife had "found Jesus" a year earlier. Captain Fredricks did not believe in God, or so he would say, but the truth was that he did not want to believe in Him.

An only child, Jacob Fredricks was raised in a Christian home. When he was thirteen years old his parents were killed in a car accident, leaving him with his maternal grandmother, who was more devout in her Christian faith than his parents. Although a fire and brimstone type individual, she was a good woman and he had learned well from her about Holy Scripture. After living with her for a few years, he could practically recite the books of Daniel and Revelation, and he knew end-time Biblical prophecy. But he remained angry at God for the death of his parents, even questioning His existence. *How could a loving God take his parents, leaving him orphaned?* His answer was that there was no God and that is how he lived, until a year ago when he was forced to confront the issue when his wife accepted Christ as her Savior.

As fate would have it, Jacob's wife was obsessed with the end of the world and end-time prophecy. He had grown weary of listening to her talk of the Anti-Christ and the return of Jesus Christ. He tried to get even with her-the more she talked of Christ, the more he talked of evolution. He didn't necessarily believe in evolution, but it at least allowed him to explain away God, believing instead that science and technology would find answers to the problems that the world faced.

The difference in their beliefs had put a strain on their marriage, and he longed to have their relationship return to the way it once was-back to the oneness that he had felt with her and the ease of mind of knowing his wife completely. He wanted to share his innermost thoughts with her again, but this "Jesus" had alienated him from her, and he was bitter for His invasion in their lives. The Word of God had become a double-edged sword that had split their inseparable union and had threatened the life that he had known and the bond that he once had with the woman he loved.

Known as Jake to his friends, Captain Fredricks was a stocky man with broad shoulders. His once black hair, now with a touch of gray and not quite as thick, was combed back and accented by his black mustache. His brown eyes were striking. The right eye, slightly darker than the left, often caused second glances from those close enough to notice. He was a handsome man; a chiseled jaw line and high cheekbones gave him a rugged, yet pleasant appearance. The dark circles under his bloodshot eyes and the salt and pepper stubble on his face caused him to appear older than his forty years.

A pilot for Pan World Airlines for the past eleven years, Jake had finished piloting flight 437 from Tokyo to San Francisco just three hours earlier and was exhausted from his grueling schedule that had kept him away from home for the past three and one-half weeks. He was relieved that, on this flight home to Boston, he could relax in the first-class section of the plane as a passenger. The section was two-thirds full of passengers, and he was pleased that the seat next to his was empty.

All he wanted to do was sleep; however, he could not get the thought of his wife's conversion to Christianity out of his mind, so sleep escaped him. His thoughts brought him back to the previous year and to the day that his wife told him of her conversion.

Up until that time, as he remembered it, life had been normal. Normal, the way he defined the word, was a life not bogged down by religion or any specific moral code of conduct. That's not to say that he wasn't a moral man, by societal standards that is exactly what he was. He took pride in giving to charities with his time and money, on being a good husband, and on forsaking all others as he promised his wife on their wedding day. He and Tracey had been happily married for three years and were expecting their first child. He could still feel that nervous excitement of becoming a father, remembering as if it were just yesterday-the giddy feeling and anticipation of having a new mouth to feed. Tracey, despite being seven months pregnant, was a petite woman with long brown hair and brown eyes who had a radiant smile and olive brown skin. She was never more beautiful than when she was carrying their child. Pregnancy tends to bring out inner and outermost beauty in a woman, and Tracey was no exception. She and Jake owned their dream home, a humble home despite his six-figure income, and lived in a quiet well-to-do neighborhood. Every year they would vacation in Florida, spending a week with Tracey's parents, Sam and Joyce.

But the life he knew and loved changed when Mark and Vivian Daniels moved into the house across the street. Mark and Vivian were very active in their church and hosted a Bible study every Wednesday night. After Tracey accepted an invitation from Vivian to attend church, the two had quickly become close friends. Jake didn't mind much at first; he wanted Tracey to have friends since his job forced him to be away from home for weeks at a time. He worried about Tracey's well-being and was glad that she had Vivian close by to keep her company. But Tracey was spending more time in Bible studies, and Jake resented the time Tracey was dedicating to church and the hours she spent reading the Bible.

He remembered that morning during breakfast when Tracey first told him of her decision to accept Christ and how nervous she was. *And why wouldn't she be nervous?* She knew the way he felt, about the anger that he had toward God for the death of his parents.

But she had to tell him, he knew how she was, there was no other choice for her.

Jake closed his eyes as his mind flashed back to that morning and to the conversation that he had with his wife.

———————

Jake noticed that Tracey had not been herself. Breakfast had been served, but she couldn't sit still. She kept getting up from the table to get things that she didn't need. Yet again she stood up, this time to get more coffee for Jake to pour into a cup that was still almost full.

"Tracey, are you all right?" Jake grabbed Tracey's hand and looked up at her. "Do you feel okay?"

She couldn't hold back any longer. Now was the time to tell him. "I've accepted Jesus as my savior," Tracey poured Jake more coffee, spilling some of the hot drink onto the table.

Jake slid quickly from the table to avoid the spilled coffee that was now dripping from the edge of the table. He looked up at Tracey, surprised at what she had just told him, "Oh, come on, Tracey. Do you really believe that stuff?"

"I didn't know what to believe at first. I just went to church and listened. But after going a few times, I was drawn to it more and more. It was as if someone or something was urging me, compelling me to accept the Lord. But now I feel convinced that God does exist." Tracey reached for a wash cloth and wiped the table. "Jake, I would love it if you came with me and found out for yourself."

"No way," Jake responded quickly. "I don't want to be some Jesus freak-do you really want me to go to church and worship a God that took my parents away? I can't believe that you've really fallen for this."

"I'd be lying if I told you I fully understood it too, Jake, and I know you're angry, but believe it or not your parents are in Heaven. I bet they're praying that you'll reach out to Jesus."

"And you think that if I go to church that it's going to make me feel better about everything?"

Jake's sarcasm did not escape Tracey. "Well, it makes me feel good when I go-I feel His presence there every Sunday. I know you blame Him for your parent's death, but if you give God a chance-"

"Just leave me out of it," Jake's objection was clear to Tracey, "God has been no friend to me, and I want nothing to do with Him."

That's how he felt the day that he lost Tracey to God and the life that he had grown accustomed to. He still loved Tracey with all his heart, but she continued to change in the weeks that followed. He wondered, as he reflected back to that morning, if he could have done anything different to change her mind or, at least, to ease his mind. Over the next few weeks Tracey's continued attempts to get Jake to go to church and Bible studies were unsuccessful. She would talk to him about Jesus and His sacrifice on the Cross of Calvary, but he would not listen, angrily avoiding the discussion.

"Will you come to church with me today?" Tracy grabbed the keys to her car. "Jesus is coming again, Jake. I don't want you to be left behind."

"Coming again?" Jake was sarcastic. "I'm getting tired of being asked to fall for something I don't believe in. Tracey, Jesus has been dead for two thousand years, and He's not coming back."

"But Christ is alive, and I think deep down you believe it too."

"What I believe is that Christianity is nothing but a crutch-something to hold on to for those who can't handle life and for those who are afraid of what happens after they die, and they need something, even illogical reasoning, to make them feel better about it."

Tracey was hurt, "Are you telling me that I can't handle life?"

"No, I'm not saying that. All I'm saying is that Christians want to brainwash your thoughts, and they do that by trying to scare people with doom and gloom, end-times and tribulation. I'm not sure that you have thought this through."

"So now I'm brainwashed?"

Jake had dug himself into a hole. "What I mean to say is that there is no proof of the existence of God. Science and technology are proving the Bible wrong. Why believe in God when man and his advancements will be able to solve any problems that come along?"

"Science and technology proving the Bible wrong?" Tracey replied. "Science is only creating more problems. Weapons for war and-"

"What are you talking about?" Jake interrupted, "Weapons for war? The world has never seen a peace as it has now, and there will probably never be another major war now that the leaders of Europe are talking about uniting to make one country. The economy has never been better for both the United States and Europe. Fire and brimstone won't scare me into going to church with you. I'll be on my deathbed before I convert." Jake shook his head, "At least that way I'll enjoy life until then."

"That's just what the Bible predicts Jake. That Europe will unite and that a powerful leader will rule the world. You're just too stubborn or angry to realize that. The world will have a false sense of security during the end time-the kind of security that you have in science and man-made governments. I've told you what the Bible predicts and how the governments will fail. The peace now is only a temporary peace, Jake. I believe we're close to the end and to the Rapture. I don't want you to be fooled by what is happening in the world. Don't wait until your deathbed to accept Christ into your life because it may be too late."

"Don't you think I know what end-time prophecy says? My grandmother forced me to know all of that. Daniel and Revelation-hell, I probably know more about what prophecy says than you do. The only difference is that you believe it and I don't."

Tracey sighed then shook her head, "Salvation is now. There will be no second chances to be Raptured." Tracey leaned on the counter, feeling weak, and her knees buckled. Her face paled as the blood drained from the surface of her skin. She appeared white as a ghost, and she grimaced in pain. She reached to hold her belly; the cramping left her breathless and barely able to speak, and she collapsed into Jake's arms.

"Tracey, what's wrong? What's happening?" Jake grabbed Tracey, keeping her from falling to the floor.

"I don't know; it hurts. It's the baby. Oh, God no!" Tracey screamed, then slipped into unconsciousness.

The plane shook hard, jerking Jake's mind from the events of last year, causing him to gasp out loud. He could smell the aroma of the freshly brewed coffee and feel the vibration of the planes engines as he looked around first class to see if any one had heard his cry. The stewardess turned to Jake, smiled, then approached.

"Captain Fredricks, are you okay?" asked the stewardess. "Would you like something to drink?"

"No, thank you, Mary." Jake looked up at her then out the window again.

Mary Johnson was tall and slender with shoulder-length blonde hair. Her fair skin and rosy cheeks highlighted her piercing blue eyes. The competitiveness of her job forced her to keep trim and in good physical shape, which was obvious by the fit of her dark blue uniform. She had been the senior stewardess on Jake's maiden flight with Pan World Airlines eleven years earlier, and they had become close friends. Mary's husband, Randy, had also become friends with Jake, being introduced five years earlier on a hunting trip. Randy was a career military man, a captain in the army, and was presently assigned at the Pentagon as first assistant to Brigadier General Russell Kemp. Jake liked hunting with Randy because of the survival skills that he had learned when training as a commando in the army's elite force of the 20th Battalion. The two hit it off right away and had hunted every year since.

"Sure is a beautiful view, Jake." Mary stretched to look out of the window.

"Yes it is," Jake replied, his mind still occupied by the thoughts of his wife. "My wife tells me that the glory of God is revealed through such beauty and is proof of His existence." Jake stared out the window again then back at Mary. "Do you believe that?"

Mary gave a cynical smile, "I don't have much time for God or religion. I've had too many tragedies in my life to believe that a loving God would allow them to happen. It's a beautiful place, but I need more proof than that to believe in God. I wouldn't tell that to Bill Peters or Sam Waters," she said with a chuckle, nodding her head toward the cockpit. "They're practically having a Bible study in there now. We've nicknamed them *God's crew*. As long as they don't preach to me, I'll be fine. Got to go, Jake, have to get *God's crew* some coffee."

"I'll talk to you later." Jake smiled and stared out the window, once again reflecting back to his wife and the events of a year ago.

———————

Tracey's Doctor, Mike Wills, was a big man with silvery white hair. He had a full face and wore tight-fitting glasses, the lenses resting on his puffy cheeks made his face appear larger than it actually was. He was tired and smelled of coffee; his eyes were blood shot, and his tie and collar were worn loose around his neck. He had practiced medicine for twenty-two years and was considered an expert in his field. He smiled as he walked into the hospital room which, to some extent, gave Jake and Tracey some comfort.

Tracey's room was cold and dreary, and the elm trees just outside the window allowed only a small trickle of sunlight in. There were two beds in the room, separated only by a thin curtain which could be drawn closed for privacy. A television, mounted on the wall in the center of the room opposite the beds, was turned off. Next to each bed was a portable table designed to position over the beds to be used by the occupants for eating and storage. The bed next to Tracey's was empty, covered with a light blue blanket, perfect in its appearance and without a wrinkle.

"Well, Tracey-" Dr. Wills sat on the foot of the bed, "-you and your son gave us a scare last night, but I think you two will be fine. We were lucky we didn't lose you both. You lost a lot of blood."

"What happened? I thought everything was fine?" Tracey was drained and fighting back tears.

"I can't tell you why it happened, but for some reason your placenta got partially detached from your uterus and started hemorrhaging. Sometimes overexertion or undue stress can cause that to happen. We'll probably never know what caused it for sure. But when you arrived here unconscious and bleeding, I had no choice but to perform an emergency cesarean section." Dr. Wills pulled back the bandage off of Tracey's abdomen and took a looked at the incision then felt the wound for inflammation with his fingers. "I'm surprised that we were able to save you. It was touch and go for a while, but the baby is doing fine. We have him in a special care unit now for observation, but I suspect that you will be able to have him here with you soon. Well, everything looks great," he said, putting the bandage back over the scar, "For now I need you to get your rest. If you need anything, let the nurses know and I'll be back to see you in the morning." As Dr. Wills left the room he turned to Jake and Tracey and asked, "Do you have a name for your baby?"

"We named our son John," Jake replied, and for the first time since Tracey's arrival at the hospital, he was unable to hold back his tears.

"I'm so thankful," Tracey allowed herself to smile. "Jesus truly watched over John and me last night."

"How can you still believe in God after what has happened?" Jake replied angrily, his eyes still moist. "You and John almost died last night, and if it weren't for Dr. Wills, you'd both be dead. I can't believe that you're not blaming God for what has happened."

"John and I are alive because God wants us alive. I'm convinced of that. I'm not going to be like you and blame God for every bad thing that happens to us. Bad things do happen to good people, even Christian people. I know that you're still angry at God for your parent's death, but you need to put that behind you and stop blaming God for every little thing that happens." Jake sat silently. Tracey had struck a nerve and she knew it. She reached out to grab Jake's hand but he pulled it away. "Jake, God has a purpose for us, and I believe our purpose is to convince you of His existence and of His Son, Jesus. Last night was a test of faith, and Jesus was faithful to John and me. He saved us-and you should be happy about that. Please give church a chance and come with us when we get out of the hospital." Jake leaned his head back in the chair and sighed. "Jake, it's not like any other church that you might think of. It's a non-denominational church and very informal. The church is called Cross Roads Ministries and they meet at an old Lutheran Church, which was bought by our pastor after the Lutheran congregation built a new church and moved. Pastor Morgan is planning to renovate the whole inside and remove the altar so that he can replace it with a platform or stage for the band to perform on and for him to speak from. It's very informal-something I think you'll like."

"Okay! Okay! I'll go to church with you but that's it." Jake replied, "I'm too tired to argue about it any more. And you don't need any more excitement today, so I won't argue with you. But I'm only doing it for you and John." Jake shook his head and frowned, "I still don't believe in God, and your forcing me to go to church with you won't change that."

"That's okay, Jake," Tracey said with a smile. "We'll work on that, John and I."

Springtime was Jake's favorite season of the year. Unlike the hot, humid days of summer, the air was fresh and the ocean breeze cooled the heat of the day. The birds, carefree and full of life, sang their songs to welcome in the new morning and collected material to build their nests. The sun was shining, and a light breeze whistled through the oak trees as Jake and Tracey walked up the steps to the church. John, wrapped in a blanket so as to be barely seen, was held tightly by Tracey. It had been four weeks since John was born and it was now time for Jake to deliver on his promise to Tracey.

The church building was a traditional-looking structure with a high A-frame roof and a large wooden cross placed at the apex toward the front. The outside walls were made of red brick surrounded by a tightly trimmed hedge of phytonia. A blue cobblestone walkway lined with yellow and white daisies made its way to the two large oak doors that opened to the sanctuary. Jake stopped and took a deep breath.

"Are you okay, Jake?" Tracey asked.

"The last time I was in a church was the Sunday of the car accident." Jake stared at Tracey then straight ahead, "We were on our way home when the other car came out of nowhere. My parents never knew what hit them."

"I know it was hard for you." Tracey reached to caress Jake's cheek, "but you don't have to be afraid to go inside."

"I'm not afraid." Jake glanced at Tracey and smiled, "Let's go."

The doors opened to a center aisle that was bordered on each side by a large single row of wooden pews, and continued uninterrupted to the altar. The altar was covered by a white cloth bearing the insignia of a red cross on its front. Set upon the cloth at the center of the altar were placed a large gold chalice and golden candlesticks on either side. Flames flickered atop the short candles. Jake remembered what Tracey mentioned about Pastor Morgan's idea to replace the altar with a stage, and Jake thought that that would better match the informal feel of the congregation. Behind the altar, a large stained glass cross extended from the floor to the ceiling, allowing the glow of sunlight to enter and illuminate the altar. To the right of the altar, the band of two guitarists, a drummer, and a pianist were performing a modern version of "Amazing Grace" to which the congregation sang along. The sanctuary echoed in praise and song, and it was not difficult to understand why Tracey felt so comfortable here. It had been a long time since Jake had been to church, and he'd never been to one like this. The band and the informal dress of the members didn't seem to match the formality of the way the building looked. But Tracey did say that Cross Roads Ministries was informal, which concentrated more on what the Bible taught versus outward appearances, unlike Jake's opinion of what churches were. Nonetheless, Jake felt uncomfortable.

"Let's sit here ... ," Jake pointed at the back pew, "... that way we can make an easy exit if John gets a little fussy."

Tracey smiled and knew that Jake would probably feel better sitting there, so they found a spot next to the aisle.

Tracey leaned into Jake. "Jake, just sit back and relax and listen to Pastor Morgan's message," She wanted so badly to have Jake accept the Lord Jesus as his personal savior, but she was fearful that if she pressed too forcefully, she would scare him away.

"I'll try." Jake let out a long, slow breath. He had been hoping that John would get loud so that he could take him outside, but today he would not be so lucky.

The service opened with a few hymns and an opening prayer led by Pastor Morgan. Pastor Morgan was a heavyset man with broad shoulders. His stomach hung over his belt, which was partly hidden by his unbuttoned tan tweed blazer. The dark brown patches in his graying hair and beard belied his age. There was a scar at the bridge of his crooked nose, a trophy of a onetime football star. He looked nothing like Jake thought he would. He wore no formal vestment or robe indicating his position as a man of the cloth. When he spoke, he positioned himself in front of the altar, not behind, so that he was easily visible to the congregation. He was a seemingly meek man, that is until he spoke, and his southern drawl could not be mistaken as he started his sermon.

"The Lord is coming soon," roared the pastor, "Don't be left behind. For today is the day of salvation."

Just what I wanted to hear, Jake thought, rolling his eyes, *more end-time folly. Is this all these people think about? I've been invited to a pep rally for the end of the world.* The pastor continued his sermon for what Jake thought was a lifetime. Jake did not want to be there and fidgeted uncomfortably in his seat, causing Tracey to grab his arm like a mother disciplining her child to pay attention. He thought of his next scheduled trip, of his son's birth, and of hunting with his friend Randy Johnson-anything but what he was there for. The sermon ended soon enough with the pastor asking for those who wanted to accept Christ to come forward.

"Salvation is now." Pastor Morgan shouted out. "Don't wait another moment. There will not be any second chances! Don't deny the urging of the Holy Spirit. Come to the front and stand with me. Accept the Lord Jesus as your Savior and I will pray with you. Don't wait another moment." The pastor bowed his head and waited. A handful of people got up and walked to the front and waited with the pastor.

"These people are brainwashed," Jake said to himself softly shaking his head. Jake knew what Tracey wanted him to do, but he could not get himself to stand and walk to the front. Tracey had her head bowed praying for that to happen, but Jake remained seated, staring straight ahead and not altering his gaze fearing that his eyes might meet Tracey's.

"Tracey-" Jake got up from his seat, "-I really don't want to come back. I felt very uncomfortable and I didn't get anything out of it. If you and John want to continue coming to church, then that's okay, but please don't ask me to fall for this. I'm just not ready, I don't know if I ever will be."

"I can't make you go to church, Jake-" Tracey was hurt, "-but don't fool yourself into thinking that I won't continue to talk to you about Jesus and His salvation. I love you Jake, and I want all of us to be in Heaven together someday."

The shaking of the plane once again interrupted Jake's thought and brought him back to the present. Jake knew that he had hurt Tracey by not giving church a fair chance and it ate at him.

He loved Tracey dearly and hurting her was the last thing he wanted to do. *I'll talk to her when I get back. Maybe if I can get her to stop talking of the end times I'd be more willing to go. But I doubt that will happen.*

"Would you like a pillow, Jake?" Mary asked handing it to him.

"That would be great. Mary, are you going to be able to spend some time with Randy after this flight?"

"I'm scheduled with *God's crew* on flight 237 to Miami at 6 A.M. tomorrow. I think I can get out of it, but I won't know until we get to Boston. Randy is driving up from Riverside to meet me there-he has a week before he has to get back to Washington. Hopefully I'll get someone to fill in for me."

"Let me know if you can't find someone to relieve you. Randy can stay with us if he wants."

"Thanks Jake. I'll have Randy call you tomorrow morning to let you know."

Jake could no longer see Lake Tahoe as he peered out of the window. The plane had put considerable distance between him and the lake while he was thinking about his wife. Jake placed his head on the pillow and reached up to close the window cover. He closed his eyes and tried to sleep, but his mind was still racing with thoughts of God and his wife's faith. It was as though his mind was daring him to believe in God and wouldn't allow him to sleep until he had done so. He could hear his wife now, "*It's the Holy Spirit urging you,*" she would say. He found himself thinking more and more about God and it continued to anger him. Jake sat there, deep in his thought with his eyes wide open and unable to sleep. It was going to be a long trip home.

Chapter 2

Tracey Fredricks loved springtime in Boston. The sweet smell of star jasmine mingling with the salt air brought back memories of her childhood in Florida and swimming in the family pool with her cousins while their parents drank lemonade. She, like Jake, was also an only child but never felt alone with the dozen or so cousins that all lived within a half-hour drive away. The view of Boston Harbor from her balcony and the many fishing boats that were buoyed there reminded her of day trips that she and her parents made to the Florida Keys. Those were good memories for her, and at times she missed the innocence that that period in life held for her. She was comforted by the sound of the foghorn that repeated its never-ending warning to those who had courage enough to brave the sea, and she loved the harmonization that the screeching sea gulls added to the sound. The harbor was known for the many gulls seeking to snatch any last morsel of food that they could find by swooping in and around the fishing boats that entered the harbor after days on the water with their fresh catch of fish.

Tracey and Vivian stepped out onto the balcony and paused at the railing to witness a flock of gulls circle above incoming vessels before sitting at the patio furniture to share a glass of iced tea. It was going to be a warm day, evident by how quickly the fog had burned off earlier in the afternoon, leaving only a receding cloud bank that extended the entire horizon over the cold waters of the Atlantic Ocean.

John was playing in the living room just a short distance away and visible behind the sliding screen door. He was thirteen months old now and showed no ill affects of his traumatic birth. In fact, he was quite healthy and above normal in both height and weight for a child his age. A true mixture of his parents' characteristics, he acquired Jake's black hair and light-skinned complexion while obtaining Tracey's smile and brown eyes. His chubby, pink cheeks were smooth to the touch with deep dimples, which were made more pronounced when he smiled. He had been talking more the last month or so, ever since he uttered his first word, "Daddy," although it sounded more like "Dada." His gait was unsure, stumbling most of the time, but he was able to muster enough energy to run and greet his father and scream "Dada" when Jake walked through the door. The special welcome from John never failed to melt Jake's heart.

Leaving for flight duty had become emotional for both father and son. The two were shadows of each other, never apart, and constantly bonding. Tracey would chuckle when they played. She didn't know at times which of the two was really the little boy, but she was pleased that the two had grown close, and she loved to hear them laugh. Tracey could not remember a time when Jake laughed so much. It was a deep-belly laughter, spontaneous and without reservation; one brought about only by a deep-seated understanding shared between a father and his son and appreciated only by them. But Tracey was concerned. Jake hadn't gone to church for over a year now and showed no sign that he wanted to. John would cry when Tracey would take him to church, not because he didn't want to go, but because he didn't want to leave Jake. Although still young, Tracey did not want John to be influenced by Jake's disbelief in God. The seeds of faith had been planted, and Tracey prayed daily that they would take root, hopefully sooner than later, before John got too much older.

"I don't know what else I can do Vivian," Tracey looked through the screen door at John. "I've tried to get Jake to go to church with John and me, but he just doesn't want to go. He's tuning me out when I witness to him about the Lord." Tracey shook her head and sighed. "I just feel like giving up."

Vivian had been a good listener over the past year. Their age difference allowed her to become more of a mother figure than a friend to Tracey. Vivian was fifteen years older than Tracey and it showed. She had shoulder length hair which she pulled back and tied into a ponytail. The streaks of silver and gray in her hair and the fine lines in her skin caused Vivian to look older than her fifty-three years; however, there was a glow about her and a contagious charisma that caused everyone that met her to feel comfortable in her presence. But there was something about her-whether it was her blue eyes that seemed to penetrate Tracey's soul and exposing her very "inner being," or the love that emanated from her spirit forming a bond as with her own mother, Tracey couldn't tell, but, whatever the reason, Tracey grew close to Vivian and relied on her wisdom.

"You've prayed about it, haven't you?" Vivian sipped her tea and set the glass down on the table.

"Of course I have." The question had taken Tracey by surprise. "I pray everyday that Jake will accept the Lord before it's too late."

Vivian leaned forward reaching to hold Tracey's hand, "Then let it go and give it to the Lord. There is no better place to put your concerns than in the loving hands of Jesus. Continue to pray and be a good example, and the rest will fall into place." Vivian smiled at Tracey and patted her hand. She seemed so sure of what she was saying and believed that it would come true. Tracey loved that about Vivian, the confidence that she always showed. Vivian sat back into the chair. "Jake has been away awhile. When is he coming home?"

"I have to pick him up at the airport at seven tonight." Tracey glanced at her watch then gestured toward John. "John is going to be so excited to see his Daddy. I'd like to take him with me to the airport, but it's a bit late for him. Would you mind watching him while I pick Jake up?"

"Of course I'll watch him, I'll take him with me when I leave," Vivian replied. "I think Mark will have fun with him too."

"Thanks Vivian. That will make things a lot easier."

"Did you have a chance to read the paper today, Tracey?" Vivian asked changing the subject. "There is an article about a man in Rome who is gaining political power in the movement to create a United States of Europe."

"No, I haven't had a chance to read the paper yet. What did the article say?" Tracey turned her chair to face Vivian, "Well, what did it say?" she asked impatiently.

"His name is Alexander Christos. Apparently he was a vital force in stabilizing the economy of the European Common Market with the development of the common European currency. A new United States of Europe is next in line which has been in the works since the formation of a united European Army a few years ago. The countries of Europe are voting on the resolution this week and he is supposed to become its first president. The article goes on to say that he has some clout with the Vatican and personally knows the Pope."

Startled by a crashing sound coming from the living room, the two women stared in the direction of the noise. Tracey got up quickly to see what had happened and found John standing and crying over a fallen lamp that he had just knocked off of an end table.

"Let's continue this inside, Vivian. I think John needs a little attention." Tracey stretched her arms out toward John urging him to come to her, picked him up, and sat in a rocking chair located in front of the television. Vivian placed the lamp back on to the end table and sat down on the sofa.

The vaulted ceiling in the living area made the entire room appear larger than it actually was. The dark traditional furniture stood out against the white Berber carpet and the family portraits added color to the light tan walls. A mounted deer head, shot on one of the many hunting trips that Jake and his friend Randy Johnson shared, hung at the center of the room just above the mantle of the fireplace. Its large, ten-point antlers reached towards the ceiling and were illuminated by the receded lights just above. On either side of the fireplace were solid oak cabinets were Tracey kept one of her Bibles and most of her Bible commentaries. Also built into the cabinets was the entertainment center were the stereo and television was located. Tracey sat on the rocking chair with

John on her lap and gently rocked him until he could no longer keep his eyes open and he fell asleep.

"The article went on to say-" Vivian continued, not missing a beat from were she had left off, "-that he is pushing for the creation of a unified 'world church' and is trying to get the Pope's help in making that a reality."

"What are you suggesting? Do you think this Alexander Christos is the Anti-Christ?" Tracey asked, gently stroking the top of John's head, "We've been hearing about the possibility of a United Europe for a few years now; why is this man getting all of this attention?"

"Apparently he is the main reason that all of this has finally happened. Plus, he has a tremendous following and support from the citizens of Europe. You have to remember they've been hearing more about this and are more aware of his prominence than we are here in the United States. He also has caught the attention of a lot of world leaders, including our president. He is in the process of proposing a peace plan for Israel and all the Arab countries, and thus far, it has been met with great optimism from both the prime minister of Israel and from the leaders of the Arab confederation. When the countries of Europe do unite, and it sounds like it will be voted on this week, I believe that he will be elected as the new country's first president. He's already a major leader in his home country of Greece and seems to be gaining more and more support from the voters. They love him there. We'll have to wait and see what happens."

"Vivian-" Tracey hesitated, not knowing if she should continue, "-the end is near. The Lord told me."

Vivian recoiled slightly. "What do you mean?"

"A nightmare had awakened me early this morning. I got to my knees and started to pray, and I could feel the Holy Spirit encompass me. And I knew that time was short. He didn't tell me when, just that His return was soon."

"Then remember the name Alexander Christos. He may be the Anti-Christ."

There was an awkward silence and Vivian sensed that Tracey was feeling a little anxious about the conversation. Tracey was worried about Jake's salvation and Vivian knew it. If Alexander Christos was truly the Anti-Christ, then time was running out for Jake, and he might be left behind. The Rapture could happen at anytime; no one really knows when, but they both knew that the time was close.

"I better try and convince Jake of the significance of it all." Tracey took in a deep breath and let it out slowly. "It's going to be tough though. He's a stubborn man."

"I'll be praying for Jake." Vivian looked at the clock, "Time's slipping away. It's almost five o'clock and I know you need to get ready to pick Jake up. Don't worry about John. I'll feed him."

"Great. Let me get you John's pajamas." Tracey stood and handed John over to Vivian, "Jake and I may get a bite to eat, if that's okay, but we shouldn't be too late."

"That's fine. I think John and I can manage."

Tracey gathered up a few toys and John's pajamas and placed them in a bag. She gave John a kiss and waved goodbye to them as Vivian carried him out the front door. Tracey stood in the doorway and watched them walk across the street to Vivian's home, then closed the door and went to her room to get ready.

The ten-minute drive to the airport was uneventful; however, Tracey couldn't stop thinking about the conversation she had with Vivian about Alexander Christos. What if he was the Anti-Christ? Could she ever convince Jake of that? And if he wasn't the Anti-Christ, Jake would surely never let her forget it. She could hear him now with that touch of sarcasm in his voice, *"Just some more Christians trying to make a mountain out of a molehill."* Regardless, she would have to tell him; there was too much at stake.

The plane taxied up to the gate and Tracey could see the pilots through the airport window. She waited as the passengers trickled out of the airplane onto the ramp and up the gate. Jake was the third passenger out and Tracey ran up to greet him.

"Hi, honey, how was your flight?" she asked, giving Jake a hug.

"Long," he replied looking around for John. "It's good to be home. I missed you. Where's John?"

"I didn't want him out too late. He was tired and I didn't know if you would want to get a bite to eat, so I asked Vivian if she would watch him."

"I'd rather just go home if that's okay with you." Jake replied. "I'm tired, too, and my own bed sounds great."

"That's fine, I'll fix you something when we get home."

On arriving home Jake took a quick shower and Tracey walked across the street to pick up John from Vivian's house. To Jake's disappointment, John was sleeping and Tracey put him in his crib. Jake had missed his son and was looking forward to seeing him, but that would have to wait until tomorrow.

"I'll get you something to eat," Tracey walked towards the kitchen. Jake followed behind and sat at the table.

"Jake?" Tracey said, reaching into the refrigerator to get the leftover meatloaf. Closing the door, she turned to Jake and took a deep breath. "I want to tell you something and I don't want you to say anything, just listen."

"Okay." Jake shrugged his shoulders. "Shoot."

"There's a man by the name of Alexander Christos who-" Tracey forced out the words nervously, hesitating to collect her thoughts, "-who is gaining a lot of power in Europe and who-"

"Well go on Tracey," Jake said impatiently. "I'm listening."

Tracey looked at Jake still a little nervous about what she was about to say, "-who I think might be the Anti-Christ and-"

"I don't want to hear it!" Jake said angrily, interrupting Tracey. Instantly his face was beet red, the veins in his neck bulging. The expression of anger on his face was one that she had never seen before. He had finally had enough. It was bad enough that he was going to try, once again, to go to church with Tracey, but he just didn't want to hear about the end of the world. All he could think about on the flight home was how God and religion had tormented him with the never-ending thoughts. The last thing he wanted to hear about now was more of the same. The look in his eye revealed his deep hatred, not towards her, but towards her belief and how it changed Tracey and their marriage.

"I'm tired and hungry. Please don't put me through this tonight!" Jake's breathing was heavy. "Couldn't you've at least let me relax for a day or two before you started harping on me about your belief. Oh, forget it, I'm going to bed."

"But Jake I-"

"Goodnight, Tracey, I'm too tired for this right now." Jake pushed the chair out from underneath the table and stood looking at Tracey with a penetrating stare then turned and went to the bedroom.

Tracey stood there dumbfounded, not knowing what to do. Her knees were shaking and weak, and she was barely able to walk to the sofa and sit down. She sat there in the dark for an hour before she had the strength to get up. She was still numb from Jake's outburst. She had never seen Jake that angry and it scared her that he could show such anger. He was sleeping when she walked into the bedroom, and not wanting to wake him, she changed into her nightclothes without turning on the light. She felt emotionally drained as she got into bed next to Jake, and knew she wouldn't be able to sleep.

"Dear Jesus," she prayed. "I thank you for the blessings that you have given me, and I praise you for your sacrifice on the cross for the forgiveness of my sins. May your Holy Spirit be upon me and guide my thoughts and actions so that they may bring glory to your name. May your Spirit come upon Jake and show him what he needs to do to obtain your gift of salvation. I give him to you and leave him in your mighty hands. Show him the way to life and guide him in his decision to accept you as his God. In the name of Jesus, I pray. Amen."

She lay there, lost in her thought, wanting to sleep so she wouldn't have to think anymore. She was afraid to talk to Jake anymore about the Lord, and she was afraid not to. Her thoughts were tormenting her as she lay there and unable to hold back her emotions, she started to cry.

The next morning the bright orange rays from the sunrise glowed through the window of their bedroom as it slowly appeared above the clouds and stretched its rays across the horizon. It was 6 A.M.., and Tracey hadn't slept all night, too emotionally affected from Jake's tirade of the night before. Jake was sleeping no more than two feet away, but in her mind he seemed a million miles away. He had a restless night, dreaming most of the time and letting out an occasional moan and involuntary jerk. It seemed that he was trying to get away from someone or something. *Vivian was right*, she thought looking down at Jake. *I'll just have to give it to the Lord and have faith that Jake will accept the Lord before it's too late.*

Chapter 3

A powerful explosion coming from the direction of Logan International Airport shook the house, vibrating the structure violently enough to drop the family portraits from the living room wall and to break the glass in the frames when they hit the floor. The shock waves, not unlike the sonic boom created when aircraft exceed the speed of sound, knocked Jake out of bed and to the bedroom carpet. Half asleep, he shook his head and smacked his lips, then stood up, slowly rubbing his eyes. *What was that?* Jake walked to the window and looked outside. What he saw frightened him and his heart pounded. In the distance Jake could see black smoke billowing up from yellow-orange flames that darted skyward, feeding the dark plume that was now blanketing the entire area.

"My God, Tracey, come take a look at this!" Jake continued to stare out the window. "Tracey?" Jake turned and looked at the bed. Tracey wasn't there. Wondering where she had gone, Jake walked quickly to John's room, thinking that Tracey might have gone there to see if the shaking of the house had awakened the baby.

"Tracey?" he said in a loud voice as he entered John's room. There was no sign of her, and the crib was empty. Jake picked up John's blanket, which was still warm. He must have just missed them.

"Tracey?" he yelled out again, this time walking towards the kitchen. "John? Is there anyone here?"

"Great!" Jake said out loud, throwing his hands up in disgust. *I really did it this time. She probably took the baby to Vivian's to get away from me.* His heart was still racing as he once again looked out the window toward the airport. The black smoke was now rising high enough to touch the sky and was being carried away by the wind current. He knew that there was only one thing that would cause that type of explosion; it could have only been a plane crash. Torn between getting his family from across the street or going to the airport, Jake decided that he was needed more at the site of the explosion and opted to go there to offer his assistance. He would get his family on his return.

Jake quickly changed from his pajamas to his street clothes and left a short note to Tracey telling her he'd be back soon. It was 6:10 A.M. when he glanced at the clock on his way out the door. The high-pitched sound of sirens reverberated through this usually quiet time of the day, catching everyone off guard. Jake's neighbors gathered outside, most of them in nightclothes, all of them trying to get a glimpse of what was happening. There was something odd, he could feel it. It wasn't just the explosion, but he couldn't put his finger on it. There were many more pedestrians on the street, far more than normal for this time of the morning, some of them hysterical, and he wondered if the explosion would have forced this many to go outside of their homes in such fear. A car accident just ahead, with the car in the roadside ditch and an ambulance along side, slowed traffic to a trickle. A woman with a large bump on her head and blood running down her cheek was screaming and throwing her arms about hysterically, while the paramedics tried to calm her. She was yelling something, but Jake could not understand it until he came closer to the scene.

"He disappeared right in front of me!" Her voice cracking and tapering off as she started to sob. "He's gone. He's gone." By the time Jake had driven by, she had become too weak to stand and collapsed into the arms of one of the paramedics.

Jake reached the airport, his stomach churning with emotion, afraid of what he might see. The airport obstructed the source of the smoke and he would have to go into the building and to the other side to catch the glimpse of the destruction. Inside, mass confusion and chaos permeated the panicked crowd. He had to force his way to the door that would lead outside to the runway. He paused there for a moment, trying to collect himself, summoning enough courage from deep within to face what he was about to witness. Pushing open the door, he could see the wreckage of the plane approximately five hundred yards in front of him. He could feel the heat of the flames as it radiated towards him, and he could smell the choking fumes of burning jet fuel. The fuselage was broken in half, just behind where the wings once were, and the cockpit area was completely destroyed, charred, and spewing flame and smoke. The tail section was not visible from his vantage point, obstructed by the larger portion of the plane. Emergency vehicles, with their red lights flashing and sirens wailing, encircled the area, getting as close to the wreckage as the heat of the fire would allow them. A large debris field, at least a half-mile in diameter, probably more, consisted of twisted metal and objects thrown from the plane. It was interspersed with the bodies of the dead and injured. Running toward the wreckage, Jake's heart was pounding and he felt short of breath. Despite the roar of the flames and the screeching sirens, he could hear the pleadings of injured passengers begging for help and the faint moans of the dying taking their last breath. The mingled smells of putrid burning flesh and jet fuel was unmistakable, stopping Jake in his tracks and dropping him to his hands and knees with nausea. Looking up he could now see the charred and twisted tail section of the plane with its logo of a globe with PAN WORLD AIRLINES encircling it.

Forty minutes had elapsed since the plane had crashed and its ensuing explosion that rocked the city of Boston. Jake had to find out which Pan World flight had gone down, remembering that Mary Johnson was scheduled to work flight 237 to Miami and that *God's crew* were to pilot the flight. *Was she able to get someone else to cover her flight?* The office of the regional flight manager for Pan World Airlines was located in the airport. If he could get to it, Jake could find out which flight had crashed and whether Mary Johnson was on board. Still in a daze, Jake got up and ran towards the building wanting to get to the office as quickly as he could. He had been to the office many times and knew Richard Alexander, the regional manager, very well. The door to the office was closed when he got there and Jake, out of breath and sweating, pushed the door open without knocking. The back wall of the office was actually a large window allowing anyone in the room to view the entire runway. Richard Alexander, his back toward the door of the office and looking out at the carnage, didn't move when Jake entered the room. Stunned and in a trance-like state, he stood motionless, oblivious to anything else other than the wreckage.

"Rich?" Jake asked walking closer. "Rich, are you all right?"

Richard Alexander was a tall, thin man, sharply dressed in a dark blue suit and wire-rim glasses. He was a young man, in his early forties, and clean-shaven.

Richard turned slowly toward Jake. He had blank stare and tears in his eyes. "I can't believe this, Jake," he forced himself to speak. "I've been in this business for twenty years and have never seen anything like this. I hoped I never would." Rich stared back out at the wreckage and slowly shook his head. "I knew the pilots Jake...I knew them well. How am I going to break this to their families?"

"Rich, what flight was it? Jake asked. Deep down he knew the answer but hoped he was wrong.

"What flight was it?" Rich repeated the question.

"Yes, Rich," Jake grew impatient. "What flight was it?"

Rich Alexander took a deep breath, trying to find the energy from inside to say the words. "Flight 237 with Bill Peters and Sam Waters piloting the plane. Did you know them, Jake?"

"God's crew," Jake said softly. His heart sank and the nausea that he felt earlier had returned. Mary may be one of the dead.

"What's that?" Rich replied.

"Oh, nothing-" Jake replied, "-do you know if Mary Johnson was on board?"

"I have the crew log here." Rich reached for some papers that were on his desk and paused to read the log. "It says that she was the senior stewardess on the flight. Were you two friends?"

Jake ignored the question. "She told me that she was trying to get someone to replace her so that she could spend some time with her husband. Would there be any chance of that happening and not being reflected on the log?"

"It's not very likely because-" Rich looked at the wreckage of the plane through the large window, "-because of what you see now. If a plane goes down, we need to know who's on board. We can't afford to guess who might be there. We need to know. I'm sorry, Jake."

Jake hung his head and leaned on the corner of the desk to give himself support. The two men gazed out at the burning plane, neither wanting to speak, both dealing with the grief of losing close friends. Jake turned and walked away slowly without saying another word. He needed to get away from the scene and get back home. He thought of his wife and son, how he had missed them both and how he needed them now. Except for a brief time the night before, he hadn't seen either of them in almost four weeks. He remembered his anger. He would apologize when he got back and hoped that Tracey would understand.

It was 8 A.M. when he drove into his driveway, hoping that Tracey and John were at home. Jake loved it when he walked through the door to John running to him and screaming "Daddy, Daddy." That is just what he needed now.

"Tracey?-John? Is there anyone here?" Jake said out loud, his voice echoing throughout the house. Jake took a deep breath. *I'll just have to go over there and get them myself.* He headed across the street to Mark and Vivian's home.

Some of the neighbors were still mingling outside as Jake crossed the street. Peering through the front window, he could see the television but could not see anyone inside. Jake paused at the front door for a moment before ringing the doorbell; he wanted to collect himself and to think of the right words to say. He needed his wife and son more than ever, and he didn't want to blow it now. His emotions were still running high when he rang the doorbell anticipating greeting Tracey and John. He waited there a few moments before he rang the bell again. In another few minutes he checked to see if the door was locked. The door popped opened when he turned the knob.

"Hello, Mark?" Jake walked through the door and entered the

living room. "Vivian?-Tracey?" Jake paused for a moment before realizing that there was no one in the home and worry for his wife and son set in. *Where could they be?* His mind was racing, filled with the images that he saw earlier at the airport but now added was worry for his family. Leaving the front door wide open, Jake crossed the street thinking of any place that his wife and son may be. Butterflies were swirling in his stomach; he was anxious about his family, and he was sickened by the loss of his good friend Mary in the plane crash. *Where would Tracey go?* he wondered. There was only one other place that Tracey might be, and he'd have to go to Cross Roads Ministries to find out.

It was only a ten-minute drive to the church, but to Jake it seemed a lifetime. He couldn't stop thinking about his missing wife and son and he feared for their safety. He left the car door open and ran towards the entrance of the church, wanting to find Tracey and John as quick as he could to relieve the anxiety that was building inside him. He rushed through the large wooden doors, seeing a handful of people sitting in the first few pews. A brown-haired woman was sitting at the very front. He noticed, surprisingly enough with all that was happening, that the altar was no longer there, replaced by a platform just as Tracey said it would.

"Tracey?" he said out loud walking towards the woman, relieved that he had found his wife. He placed his hand on her shoulder. "Tracey, I've been looking all over for you." The woman turned and stared. Jake's relief turned back to worry in an instant, realizing that the woman was not Tracey but another woman who resembled her.

"I'm sorry. I thought you were someone else," he said, not able to hide his disappointment.

The woman had tears in her eyes, and her cheeks were puffy and swollen. She had been grieving, and Jake was sorry for his intrusion. She continued to stare at Jake for a moment. With one look she knew that he was searching for someone she didn't know who.

"If you're looking for someone who accepted Jesus Christ as Savior-," the woman said as she looked down at a crucifix she held in her hand, "-then you won't find them, not here anyway. Jesus has taken them home."

"What?" Jake thought the woman was mad. "Where's Pastor Morgan? I need to talk to him. I'm looking for my wife and son. They have been missing all morning and he may know where they're at."

"Didn't you hear a word I said?" retorted the woman, looking Jake straight in the eye, "They're gone, all of them. Haven't you heard of the Rapture? Pastor Morgan is gone, my daughter is gone, and I suspect that your wife and son are gone too. The only way we'll see them again is to accept the Lord Jesus as our Savior. My daughter warned me about this but I wouldn't listen. We were having breakfast together this morning, and she disappeared right in front of me as I was looking at her. But now I know that she was telling the truth. I've accepted the Lord now, but too late to make the Rapture." The woman broke down and sobbed uncontrollably.

Jake gazed at the woman, dumbfounded and not knowing how to respond to her. Tracey had warned him that the Rapture may be close, but he never took it seriously. *Could it be true?* His heart was racing and beads of sweat trickled down his face as he tried to make sense of everything. He felt weak in the knees and he was unsure whether he would have enough strength to make it out of the church and to his car. The events of the day left him exhausted; all he wanted to do was to go home and sleep and maybe he would wake up and it would all be a bad dream.

"If you want to see your wife and son again," the woman screamed out as Jake exited the church, "then you better accept the Lord and pray that He gives you strength to last the Tribulation. The Anti-Christ is alive and well. Beware and don't fall into his trap."

The words of the woman echoed in Jake's ears the entire drive home, and as he processed them in his mind, they began to make more sense to him. He still wasn't completely sure, still doubting the Rapture had actually occurred. Were the prophecies that he had been forced to study as a child, the same ones that Tracey had been warning him about, being fulfilled? His wife and son were missing and the pieces of the puzzle were starting to fit into place. The first piece of the puzzle was the plane crash piloted by *God's crew*. The Rapture would have snatched the two out of thin air, leaving the plane without a pilot and causing the carnage that he saw at the airport. The second piece of the puzzle was that his wife and son were missing, along with his neighbors Mark and Vivian, and the pastor of Cross Roads Ministries. The third piece of the puzzle was the woman at the church. He thought her mad at first, but she was so sure of what she was saying; everything started to make sense to Jake. Jake was shaking with fear by the time he reached the house and drove into the driveway. The realization of all that was happening was now upon him, and he started to believe that maybe it was all true.

The phone was ringing when Jake entered the doorway of the house, and he rushed to answer it, hoping that maybe Tracey would be on the other end.

"Hello-Tracey?" Jake answered quickly.

"Jake?-" the voice on the other end asked, "-is that you?"

"Yes," he said with a deep sigh, recognizing that the voice wasn't Tracey's but her mother's, "Joyce, are you all right?"

"We're okay here. Is everyone okay up there? Everything is going crazy. CNN has been reporting that millions of people have disappeared-"

"What?" Jake felt faint.

"People have disappeared, Jake. Thousands of prisoners have just vanished from their prison cells. There is rioting and looting everywhere. There have been reports of five different plane crashes in the States alone and one is a Pan World Airlines flight out of Boston. I was hoping you weren't on it."

"Oh, my God." Jake's heart pounded, and he fell to his knees, too weak to stand, "Then it's true. My God, it's true."

"What's true?" Joyce responded.

"Joyce-Tracey and John are gone, too."

"Where? ... What do you mean?"

"We had an argument last night, and I thought that she might have taken John to be with a friend. I've been looking for them all morning."

Jake realized that all that Tracey had told him over the last year was true, and Joyce's comments brought it all crashing in on him. He started to cry, but his attempt to hide his emotion from Joyce was in vain.

"Jake, are you okay? Don't worry ... Tracey would never leave you."

"She didn't leave me, Joyce, she was taken away."

"Taken away ... what do you mean?"

"Look, I'd rather talk to you in person. I want you and Sam to come here right away. Tracey and John are gone, and we need to do something very important if we ever want to see them again. When can you be here?"

"We can be there tomorrow if we can get a flight ... Jake, you have me worried," Joyce replied, her voice cracking. "You think that Tracey and John are among those that have disappeared, don't you?"

"I'd rather talk to you about it tomorrow in person ... and try not to worry about Tracey and John. I'll make arrangements for you and Sam getting a flight here to Boston. All I have to do is make a phone call. I'll call you back later with your flight information Just stay at home until I call you. Okay?"

"Okay, Jake. But I'm worried."

"I know." Jake interrupted. "Everything's going to be all right if you listen to me. I've got to go, I'll call you later."

Just as Jake hung up the phone, he picked it up again to call Rich Alexander. If anyone could arrange a flight, it was him. Jake knew that it would be difficult to get a flight to anywhere without help, especially with all that was happening. The circuits had been busy, and Jake had to dial a few times before he finally was able to get through.

"Hi Rich?-This is Jake Fredricks. I was hoping you could help me out."

"I'll try, Jake. What do you need me to do?" Rich sounded more composed then earlier.

"I need you to arrange a flight out of Miami tomorrow; my in-laws need to fly in. I know that it may be difficult, but I really need your help on this one." Jake paused. He heard Rich sigh on the other end of the line. "Rich, I wouldn't ask you if it weren't important."

"I know," Rich replied thinking for a moment. "Okay, I can get them here by noon on flight 732. It's going to take a little explaining though. Flights are being limited, but you tell them to be at Miami-X at 9 A.M. and talk to Peggy Stewart. I'll call her and tell her to expect them."

"Thanks, Rich. I won't forget it."

Jake hung up the phone and sat, thinking of the day's events. He could no longer contain his emotions; his tears erupted from his eyes and flowed down his cheek, persistent and unstoppable. The Rapture had occurred, and he was left alone to face the future without Tracey or John. He had never felt so alone than at this moment. Jake was drained, having run the gauntlet of emotions from anger and fear to sadness and depression. He was angry at God for taking his wife and son, but he was more angry at himself for not believing Tracey when he had the chance. Tracey had warned him that there would not be any second chances, how he wished he had listened to her. He'd be with them now if he had. The fear that was building inside him, the fear of the wrath of God, of not knowing what lay ahead, and not knowing whether he could survive was too much to bear. Jake felt an empty sadness and loneliness, realizing that he would not be seeing Tracey and John again. It was though they were dead. Tracey would tell him, "*You can always rely on Jesus. He'll get you through.*" At that moment, a moment of deepest despair, his soul yearned for comfort, and Jake truly realized that he needed Jesus. If he were to survive the Tribulation and to obtain the strength to continue, then he would have to seek the Lord.

He had been struggling with the existence of God his entire life, especially in the past year. He preferred to believe that mankind had the power of controlling their own future, but he knew now that no human could explain away the disappearance of millions of people around the world, despite advancements in technology or the ability to create lies. God and His Divine Plan would be the only way to explain the Rapture. Anything else, at least for him, would not be logical. Deep down he realized that he always knew of God's existence but was too stubborn to give his life to the

Lordship of Jesus Christ. If he were ever to see his wife or son again, he would have to accept the Lord Jesus as his God; and now, finally, he was willing to do so.

Jake got on his knees and asked Jesus into his heart. As he did so, a white dove, as white as freshly fallen snow, landed on the railing of the balcony, and as Jake gazed at the dove, a calm fell upon him. It was God that had sent the dove to give him strength, he was convinced of it. Jake had finally accepted the Lord as Savior. It was not a death-bed confession of faith that he had told Tracey he would do, but one taken alone with an uncertain future. He knew that he would probably have to die a martyr's death before he would see his wife and son again. Only a small number of Christians would survive the Tribulation, and that fact did not escape Jake. He knew this because of Tracey's witness to him over the last year. If only he had listened to her, he wouldn't be here now, alone and tormented by his thoughts. He was thankful for Tracey's persistence in her witness to him, for the seed had been planted and he could understand what was happening. The dove was gone when Jake looked up again towards the railing.

If he were to survive the Tribulation, Jake knew he would have to keep one step ahead, and the Bible would be the key that would allow him to open the door to the future. If he knew what was coming next, he thought, then he could prepare for it; but he would need help. He found Tracey's Bible and started to read Revelation. He hadn't read the Bible since he was eighteen, but the words seem to jump off the pages at him. He hoped that Tracey had witnessed to her parents and that they would be receptive to the message of the Lord that he would soon be telling them. They would need to help each other if they were to survive until the Lord's return.

Jake picked up the phone to call Joyce to let them know of the flight arrangements for the next day. Rich Alexander said that he could get Sam and Joyce on the morning flight, but Jake did not feel very confident. He would leave it in the Lord's hands and he was satisfied to do so.

"Hello." Sam answered the phone.

"Hi. Sam?-this is Jake. I arranged a flight for you and Joyce tomorrow morning at 9 A.M.. Go to the Pan World terminal and ask for Peggy Stewart. She'll be able to get you on board."

"Ok, Jake, we'll be there. What the hell has been going on? It seems that the world has just gone crazy."

"I know, but I think I know what happened. Did Tracey ever talk to you or Joyce about the Rapture?" Jake knew that it would be easier to witness to them if Tracey had discussed end-time prophecy with them.

"Yeah, but we thought that she was going through a phase or something. You don't think that all that's going on has to do with the Rapture, do you?"

"Yes, I do. I think that John and Tracey have been Raptured and that's why I can't find them." Jake took a deep breath, trying to keep himself from crying. "Sam, you and Joyce will have to accept the Lord as Savior if you ever want to see them again." There was a long silence, and Jake thought that Sam was trying to absorb what he was hearing. "Sam, did Tracey ever talk to you about accepting the Lord? That's what I was talking about earlier when I told Joyce that we needed to do something if we ever wanted to see Tracey and John again. Sam?-"

"I understand," Sam replied. "Joyce and I did get a Bible and started reading through it together, but we didn't really know what to believe. I mean, it sounds so weird."

"I know. It didn't make a lot of sense to me at first either-" Jake thanked God that Tracey had witnessed to her parents, "-but after today there is no other explanation."

"Look, Jake, we'll talk more about it tomorrow. Joyce isn't taking this well. I need to go. She needs me."

"Okay, Sam. Try and rest and I'll see you tomorrow."

Jake was relieved that they had been reading the Bible; it would be a lot easier witnessing to them and convincing them to accept the Lord if they had some knowledge of the truth. It was 4 P.M. when he looked at the clock. It seemed years since the explosion that had instantly changed his world. He looked out of the window towards the airport and he could see only a small amount of smoke, a fraction of what he saw earlier in the morning. As the smoke of the plane crash was diminishing, he could see smoke originating from other areas of the city, and he wondered what could be happening.

Joyce mentioned the reports of looting that were taking place around the country, and he was sure that was the source of the smoke he had been seeing. Sirens were still echoing in the air and an uneasy feeling started to invade his thoughts.

Jake sat down and turned on the television to CNN and was appalled at what was being reported. The scene was reminiscent of the Los Angeles race riots of the 'sixties and the Rodney King incident of the early 'nineties. Lootings and beatings were rampant in all the major cities of the country and of the world. Churches were being set on fire as parishioners and clergy were being dragged out onto the streets and beaten to death. The perpetrators of these crimes seemed to know the significance of the disappearance of millions and were taking their vengeance out on those left behind, those that spoke of the Life, and yet revealed as hypocrites by being left behind. In horror, he watched the slaughter of these people, and Jake knew that from this time forward, life would not be easy.

Jake remembered that Tracey mentioned a man that she thought might be the Anti-Christ. He was surprised that he remembered the name, Alexander Christos. From this point on he would have to do his "homework" and keep himself abreast of what was happening in the world and of this man that Tracey was so convinced of being the Anti-Christ. There was no other way if he wanted to survive the coming Tribulation. The time was now to start planning his survival strategy for the next seven years and the first thing to do was to make himself an expert on the end-time prophecies. He would have to be able to interpret any significant developments that pertained to what the Bible predicted. He knew it wouldn't be easy, but the only other option was to sit back and wait for his martyred death and that, he thought, wasn't an option. The ringing of the doorbell startled Jake; his heart skipped a beat, and he got up to answer the door, wondering who it could be. Jake turned pale-white with surprise when he opened the door.

"Jake, are you okay?"

"Mary, I thought you were dead," Jake embraced her and tried to hold back his tears. "Rich Alexander said that you didn't get a replacement for the flight. Your name was still on the crew log."

"I almost didn't," Mary wiped tears from her eyes. "As I started to board the plane, Janet Sexton asked me if she could get the flight. Her mother lives in Miami and she wanted to make a surprise visit. We bent the rules a little by not reporting it to Rich. That's why my name was still on the crew log. Jake, that should have been me on that plane."

"That's not true. I don't think you were supposed to get on that plane. I think you have a purpose for being here. I'll tell you what I mean in a while. I'm so relieved to see you." Jake put his arms around Mary, giving her another hug. "I thought you were going to be with Randy. Where is he?"

"He drove back to Riverside. At the time, we thought that I would be off to Miami. I called him on my cell phone and told him to meet us here. I hope that's okay."

"Of course, I think he needs to be here too. We all need to discuss some very important matters."

The two stood there, staring at each other with tears in their eyes. It was going to be a long day, and both of them were relieved to be in each other's company. Mary did not know yet that Tracey and John were among the missing, but Jake would wait to tell her. Knowing Mary was alive was a relief for Jake. She was a close friend and if he could convince her of God and the Rapture, then the better chance of developing a survival strategy for the tribulation.

"Mary, I know that you don't believe in God, but I think you better listen to me."

"Ok, Jake," Mary replied, not sure where the conversation was heading.

Jake paused, thinking of the right words to say. "I think flight 237 went down because there was no one piloting the plane."

"What?" Mary replied quickly. "I saw Bill and Sam with my own two eyes. They boarded the plane just before Janet and I agreed that she would go to Miami."

"No, that's not what I mean. They were Raptured during take off. They disappeared into thin air, leaving the plane without a pilot-that's why the plane crashed."

Mary sat there just staring at Jake, and he felt that she must have thought he was crazy. He didn't want to push too hard yet, but he had to try and convince her. He needed her more than ever to believe him.

"Mary, I know it sounds strange, but millions of people all over the world have disappeared, and I know that's what happened to Bill and Sam." Jake paused briefly. His lips were quivering in an attempt to hold back his tears, and he turned his head to hide his emotion. "That's what happened to Tracey and John."

"Oh no, Jake, I'm sorry. I heard on the car radio that many people have disappeared but-"

"Mary-" Jake interrupted, "-the people that have disappeared are Christians. Think about it, Bill and Sam, Tracey and John. The pastor of Tracey's church. I would bet that everyone who disappeared were Christians."

"But that can't be. The radio had interviews of clergy and pastors giving their explanation of what happened. It even told of some violence against churchgoers. If it were only Christians missing, then why are they still here?"

"Those are the people that never truly accepted the Lord Jesus as Savior, even though they claimed to be Christians. I don't know how else to explain it, or what else I could say to convince you."

"I must admit," Mary replied, looking at the television, "the world is going crazy. There's got to be some reason why millions have disappeared. I do remember, many years ago, someone trying to tell me that the Rapture was going to take place and to be ready. But I don't know, Jake. It seems a little far fetched-I mean, there might be some explanation."

"What could possibly explain this?" Jake responded, "Mary, I've been struggling with this for over a year now ever since my wife accepted Jesus. I know that it does sound weird, but it's the truth. I grew up learning about what the Bible says about the last days, and Tracey would constantly talk to me of end-time prophecy. Looking back at it, I was probably the most well-informed non-Christian on that topic I ever knew. I realized today that I believed in God all along, I just didn't want to submit to the Lordship of Jesus, and I was rebellious. But I'm glad now that she had witnessed to me. I know what happened, and the Bible will let us know what else is coming. We're going to need each other from here on out." Jake wasn't feeling good about his progress with Mary, but he had to try. He needed her, and although she didn't know it now, she needed him.

"Jake, I'm still not too sure. Let's talk more about it when Randy gets here."

Jake didn't understand how Mary could not realize what was happening. He knew now how Tracey must have felt when she could not convince him to accept the Lord. Jake hoped that Tracey's parents would be more receptive of what he wanted to say to them. As the two sat there, a news flash appeared on the television.

"This just in-" the CNN news anchor said, "-the Pope is missing. Repeating, Pope Thaddeus is missing. All attempts to find him have failed, and he is feared to be one of the millions that have disappeared today. In an emergency meeting, the Catholic Church has voted to elect Alexander Christos to rule in his place. This is highly unusual since newly elected popes are selected from within the ranks. Never has there been an elected political leader to such a high ranking position in any church. Repeating, Pope Thaddeus is missing and Alexander Christos has been elected to rule the Catholic Church. We will keep you posted with any updated information."

Jake sat there, amazed at what he had just heard. Everything that Tracey had told him over the last year seemed to be coming true. Alexander Christos was the Anti-Christ; he was sure of it, and he knew that Tracey was convinced of it. A very popular leader with the support of millions, now in control of the church, would surely be in the driver's seat to take over the world. He had almost single handedly saved the European economic system from ruin by creating a common European currency, and now he would lead the church. Jake knew that this man would not stop short of total dominance, and his following would only grow and unfortunately so would his wrath.

"Mary-" Jake said, looking her in the eye, "-this man is the

Anti-Christ. We need to prepare for our survival until the Lord's return. What we need to do is learn more about what the Bible predicts will happen from here on out, until the end of the Tribulation when Jesus returns to earth. The more we know the better we will be able to survive it."

"I don't quite understand it all like you do, Jake, and I'm not sure I believe it. But your emotions are on edge with Tracey and John missing, and it might be better to wait until things calm down. I'll be willing to hear you out Jake, but I just want to think it through for myself."

"Thanks, Mary" Jake replied, thinking that at least, maybe, he got her to start wanting to learn more. "That's all I can ask for. Regardless, were all going to have to help each other in the coming months and years. I hope that you will become as convinced of God's existence as I am."

The two sat there, each deep in their own thoughts, neither speaking. The first day after the Rapture had been a long one for both of them and each just wanted it to be over. Sirens could still be heard through the crystal night air as Jake stepped out onto the balcony. The full moon shone its light over Boston, and it saddened Jake to think that before it was all over the same moon would turn blood red. He thought of his wife and son and how he missed them. He had finally accepted the Lord Jesus as his Savior, and he knew he would see Tracey and John again, but he would have to endure some rough times ahead before he could.

Chapter 4

❧——❧

A light breeze blew inland along the coast, making its way eastward from the Tyrrhenian Sea over the grape orchards of central Italy and cooling the air as it made its way towards Rome. The grape orchards stretched as far as the eye could see, blanketing the rolling hills and coloring them green and purple with its leaves and fruit. The capital city was easily visible upon the seven hills, and the newly remodeled Roman Coliseum stood out, seemed now an eerie reminder of what it once was. Rome, as in ancient days, was again the focal point of the world. Sequestered behind her closed doors, the leaders of Europe were meeting to vote on making all of Europe one country. The strides made over the last few years for a New World Order and unity in Europe had finally culminated in this vote, a vote that, if approved, would change the course of history forever. The vote had almost been postponed twenty-four hours earlier due to the strange disappearance of the Pope and millions of others around the world. But the new head of the church, Alexander Christos, had convinced leaders to proceed, telling them that the people needed the single leadership of a united Europe now more than ever to get life back to normal after the events of the day before. The news media, represented by every country in the world, surrounded the Vatican, where the vote was taking place, anticipating the news that they all had been expecting.

"This is Charles Goodson live in Rome, just outside the Vatican," the CNN correspondent reported, placing his hand on his earphone. "This just in. The leaders of Europe have, moments ago, overwhelmingly voted to merge their countries to form what has been touted to be the most powerful country since the Roman Empire. The leaders have also agreed to abdicate their powers to Alexander Christos, a man who, until recently, was a virtual unknown to most of the world. He is, however, a very popular figure in Europe and the catalyst in the movement to form the new United States of Europe, or U.S.E., having set events in motion with the creation of a European currency and more recently with the formation of a unified European Army. He is also the head of the Catholic Church, taking over the leadership after the disappearance yesterday of the Pope. He is now in negotiations to merge all the churches of the world, and if successful, would become the most powerful man ever in history, both on the political and religious spectrums."

Jake was in awe of what he was hearing as he watched the CNN report from halfway around the world on the television. It had been just a little more than twenty-four hours since the Rapture, and he was amazed at how rapidly the events were unfolding. This man had taken over all of the Europe without shedding a single drop of blood or losing one soldier on the battlefields of war. The Bible predicted that the world leader would emerge as a man of peace, but Jake knew that peace wouldn't last; war was inevitable, and the man responsible for it would be Alexander Christos.

Jake had been unable to sleep the night before and had watched his first sunrise without Tracey or John earlier in the morning. Mary was sleeping on the floor in front of the television next to her husband Randy, a big man with broad, muscular shoulders. His size was intimidating. He was handsome, and his hazel eyes were striking against his brown mustache and neatly trimmed goatee. He had arrived late last night and, like Mary, was unsure whether the Rapture was something that could be attributed to God or to some other event. He didn't seem as open-minded of that possibility as Mary was, and it worried Jake. Another news flash on the television caught Jake's attention.

"This is Charles Goodson in Rome. I have with me Cardinal Francisco Gallo, one of the Catholic Cardinals that voted for Alexander Christos to become the new Pope." the CNN reporter said, turning to face the Cardinal. "Sir, you have voted for Alexander Christos to become Pope. This conflicts with the traditional way that Popes are selected. He was not a cardinal or even a priest, yet he is now the Pope. What made your group of officials vote for him and change the way that you usually elect a new pope?"

"For me the decision was easy," replied Cardinal Gallo in broken English. The short gray-haired man paused, carefully selecting the words he was to say next. He wore a purple robe with gold fringes and held his hands in front of him as he continued. "Alexander Christos has been well known by the Catholic Church for a very long time, not only because he was a personal friend to Pope Thaddeus, who disappeared yesterday, but also because of the miracles and healings that he has performed. Because of his healing touch, we have confirmed that at least three people have been cured of cancer, four paralytics can now walk, and one person has been brought back to life after being dead for more than three days."

"Sir-" interrupted the reporter sarcastically, "-do you mean to tell me that Alexander Christos has brought back to life someone who has been dead? Why is this the first time that we are hearing about this?"

"We like to keep such matters as these a secret until we can conclude that these healing powers came from God. We believe that God is working through Alexander Christos and we also believe God has put him here to unite the churches of the world to create a one-world church. Pope Thaddeus' disappearance was a divine intervention by God because of his opposition to the idea of a one-world church. We also believe that millions of other people have disappeared because of their desire to hold on to traditional views of Christianity. These views were holding back the Church from becoming what God intended it to be. The world is changing, and God has finally taken a drastic step to ensure that a new way of thinking will move the Church forward. God is with

Alexander Christos, and he will move the Church forward in a way that the Lord wants. That is why we voted for Alexander Christos."

"Let me try to understand you," Goodson furrowed his brow, "Are you telling me that Pope Thaddeus and the millions of others that have disappeared have fallen victims to God's wrath?"

Cardinal Gallo smiled, showing no hint of frustration in the reporter's questioning "That is not what I'm saying," the cardinal responded. "I knew Pope Thaddeus well, and he loved God with all his heart, but he was holding on to the traditional ways. Pope Thaddeus' idea of where the Church should proceed in the future was that it should stay the same-with intolerance and the idea that there was only one way to God, and that was through Jesus Christ. But the world is a different place than it was two thousand years ago; the church must meet the needs of a world that is constantly changing. Pope Thaddeus' way was causing the Church to become stale and stagnant. It was God that removed him and the other of millions of people so that the Church could move forward, with Alexander Christos heading the effort. I believe that God has another purpose for Pope Thaddeus now. It's just not here on earth."

"Alexander Christos has also been voted president of the new United States of Europe, how will this affect the vision that he has for the Church?"

"I can only think that it will further the cause of the Church. That is my only concern."

"Thank you, Cardinal Gallo," the reporter concluded then faced the camera, "For CNN ... this is Charles Goodson reporting live from Rome."

Jake sat on the sofa with anger building inside him. "It's just a web of lies," he said out loud, waking Mary. "It's no wonder they can deceive people."

"Jake, is everything okay?" Mary asked, clearing her throat and sounding half-asleep.

"No, everything is not okay," Jake snapped back. "Mary, he's gaining control very quickly and will soon influence the whole world with his power."

"Who?-What are you talking about?"

"The Anti-Christ, Alexander Christos," Jake reached for the Bible that was sitting on the coffee table. "He has been performing miracles, even raising the dead."

"Raising the dead?" Mary sat up from the floor, her hair in disarray.

"I just saw a CNN report of why he was elected as the new Pope. He has been performing life-saving miracles and has raised a person from the dead. It's exactly what the Bible predicted about him." Jake held up the Bible to emphasize what he had just said. "And the Rapture? This new Church says it's a cleansing of the ways of the old Church and that it was a divine intervention to move the Church in a new direction to meet the changing world."

"Jake, are you sure that you're not overreacting to all that's been happening? I mean ... who knows, maybe he's just a man that was in the right place at the right time and-"

"Who just happens to be raising the dead?" Jake was angry. "Come on, Mary, don't be so blind. It's exactly what the Bible predicts. I don't know what else will have to happen before you believe."

"Ok, Jake-" Mary replied concedingly, not wanting to anger Jake any further, "-we'll start reading the Bible today. But don't get your hopes up to much. I'm still going to need some time. I'm not sure Randy will buy much of it either. But like I said earlier, we'll leave the option open."

Jake shook his head, "I hope you two don't wait too long, things are going to happen fast. Look Mary, I need to get to the airport to pick Tracey's parents up; you and Randy stay here and monitor CNN and see for yourselves. They have been constantly giving updates on the whole thing and I think that you and Randy will find it very interesting. If I can't convince you, then I hope the reports will."

"Okay, Jake. I'll get Randy up. We'll see you in a little while."

Jake kept thinking of the CNN report that he had heard earlier as he drove to the airport. He thought of the miracles and signs that were being performed and knew that those who didn't know God would be fooled and would fall into the deceptive trap of the Anti-Christ. He remembered what Tracey had told him, *"The Anti-Christ will come performing miracles, Jake, and he will deceive many, even the elect. But that won't be possible."* And that is what was happening. Millions of people around the globe were being deceived by the lies spun by the Anti-Christ and Church leaders. He wanted Mary and Randy to listen to him and not fall for the lies that were being fed to them by the news media. He also hoped the seeds of faith that Tracey planted with her parents were strong enough to allow them to know the difference between the lies that were being reported as the truth and what the Bible had to say.

Jake arrived at the Pan World terminal and waited for Sam and Joyce's flight to land. Looking out at the airstrip and what remained of the flight 237, he could see, who he thought were inspectors from the Federal Aviation Administration sifting through the wreckage, undoubtedly looking for evidence that might give them clues to the cause of the crash.

"I could tell you what happened," Jake said to himself shaking his head, "But you wouldn't believe me anyway."

He noticed the airport was unusually less crowded then normal; the drastic decrease in air traffic into Boston, and most of the country for that matter, surely was to blame for that. Flight 732 taxied up to the terminal and he waited anxiously for Sam and Joyce to deplane, not really knowing what to expect at the moment he would see them. He thought of the first time that he had met Tracey's parents. It was Thanksgiving Day, three years before he and Tracey were married. He remembered Joyce's radiant smile, the one that Tracey had undoubtedly inherited, and the glow in her brown eyes. Her skin and hair belied her age; her skin was as smooth as a newborn and her brown, shoulder-length hair without a hint of gray. She was a short woman but that only added to her youthful appearance. Tracey's father had met him at the front door with his hand offered in a gesture of true welcome. Sam was also youthful in his appearance, although looking older than Joyce. His hair was thinning and partially gray but it still had some of its original black color. He had quickly become a father figure to Jake, and their bond had grown very close.

After a few moments they stepped off the plane and walked up the corridor towards him. Joyce, upon seeing Jake, was overcome with emotion and ran to him. Jake was heartbroken as he gazed at Joyce. How she had changed since he had first met her. Her hair was now gray and her once glowing brown eyes now blood shot and puffy from almost nonstop crying since the Rapture. Sam had aged in the short time since Jake had seen him last. What little hair that remained atop Sam's head was totally white. His face had thinned and the sunspots on his skin more pronounced, compliments from the years in the Florida sun. His eyes, like Joyce's, were swollen and blood shot but hidden by the thick, dark-rimmed glasses that he wore.

"Oh, Jake-" Joyce hugged Jake and broke into tears, "-I'm so glad to see you. Are you okay?"

"I'm fine." Jake replied, and for the first time in the last twenty-four hours, he was able to hold back tears. "How are you holding up?"

Sam followed closely behind and put his arms around both of them. The three stood in each other's embrace, bound by their common loss of Tracey and John and the fear of what lay ahead.

"Let's go," Jake said, breaking the silence. "I want to go home where we can talk. Is this all the luggage you have?"

"Yeah, we just brought enough to fit in our carryon bags," Sam looked down at the bags on the floor. He paused for a moment then lifted his head, staring at Jake over his glasses. "Joyce and I have been talking, and we've given a lot of thought to what you told us about the Rapture. That, coupled with what Tracey has told us over the last year, well, I can't say that we understand it too much, but we both think that there could be no other explanation for the disappearance of millions of people than the existence of God. If Tracey and John are with God, then that's where we want to be as well. Joyce and I should have done it a long time ago, but we accepted the Lord last night. I don't know if we did it correctly, but we got on our knees and just asked Him to come into our lives."

Jake could not believe it, he had prayed that they would accept the Lord and thought that it might take a while for them to do so. God had answered his prayer, and as he thought about it, He had answered Tracey's prayer as well. Without Tracey's witness of the Gospel, all three would more than likely have not received Jesus as Savior, and Jake was thankful to God for her persistence.

"If you asked Jesus into your heart, then you did it correctly; but Sam, do you realize that your acceptance of the Lord may cause you to die a martyr's death?" Jake asked, wanting them to know that there would be consequences to their decision. He paused for a moment, gauging any response that the two might have, then looked at Joyce. "It's not going to be easy for Christians during the Tribulation, especially the last half, if we live that long. There are going to be wars and famines, executions and persecutions. But if we run the race, and set our sight upon the Lord, then we will be with Him forever, just like Tracey and John, who are with Him now."

"Well, even if we didn't accept the Lord, we're going to die anyway, right?" Joyce replied rhetorically. "So if we don't survive the Tribulation then so be it. I'd rather die in the hope of the Lord Jesus than die with nothing."

"That's true, Joyce, but let's try to survive it. I think that if we learn more of what the Bible says about the Tribulation, the better chance we have to survive until the Lord returns. I have some ideas of what we can do, but I'm not sure if anything will work. Regardless of what we plan, if we all put our heads together, then who knows what will happen."

"Look, we've been standing here long enough; let's get going, we can talk along the way," Sam grew impatient. "I'll be interested in hearing anything that will allow us to survive and to see Tracey and John again, but let's get to your house where we can try to relax a bit."

Tracey's witness had paid off, Jake thought, for the people that she cherished most in life, even after her Rapture. He hoped that the dividends could now prove worthy to Mary and Randy, making them realize the stakes of not accepting the Lord as Savior.

"I have some friends at the house-" Jake opened the trunk to the car and place the bags inside, "-who aren't too convinced that the Rapture is what actually happened yesterday. Unfortunately, they didn't have someone like Tracey who witnessed to them like we had.

They have little, if any, background or knowledge of what the Scripture has to say. Together, with the Lord's help, we can try and encourage them to get into His Word and realize that Jesus is the only way to salvation."

"We'll do what we can, Jake-" Joyce replied getting into the back seat, "-but we don't understand all that Scripture is telling us either."

"That's okay. I don't expect us to learn everything overnight, but we need to study and learn as much as we can as quickly as we can; that will give us the best chance for survival. I think that getting Mary and Randy to believe what the Bible has to tell us will only increase the likelihood of all of us surviving."

Mary and Randy were sitting on the sofa when the trio walked into the front door. Mary had made a pot of coffee, cooked some bacon and scrambled eggs, and was keeping them warm in a casserole dish in the oven. Jake had not eaten in almost two days, and the smell of food and the aroma of coffee made him realize how hungry he was. Jake introduced Tracey's parents to Mary and Randy as they all sat down to eat. Jake said a prayer of thanks for the meal, realizing that famine was predicted for the future. No one spoke as they started to eat; the only voice heard was that of the CNN anchor on the television in the background.

"We need to talk about what we're going to do to survive until the Lord's return." Jake said. No one replied. Randy looked at Mary and rolled his eyes. Sam and Joyce stared at Jake, waiting for what he had to say next. "The Bible is specific about certain things that will happen in the near future. If we all know what those things are and have an idea when they will happen, then we can be prepared to handle the challenges when they arise."

"Well, what do you have in mind, Jake?" Sam held a strip of bacon in his hand using it as an instrument to play with his eggs.

"Randy, do you remember the cave that we found when we were hunting last year near Denver?"

"Yeah, the one that was hidden at the base of the water fall," Randy chuckled and shook his head. "We found it when we were trying to cross a small river by walking over a downed tree. I slipped and grabbed on to Jake and we both fell about thirty feet into a deep pool. When we got our heads above water we noticed a cave hidden behind the falls. I don't think anyone knows it's there."

"That's right. I don't think anyone knows it's there either," Jake replied. "That would be the perfect place to hide out if we had to. The inside of the cave is very large; we could store all kinds of necessities if we had to-food and water and even weapons for hunting."

"What are you talking about?" Randy sat back into his chair. "Something strange did happen yesterday, Jake, I'll admit that, but just listen to yourself for a minute. The world didn't come to an end."

"Look Randy, I know you don't believe this yet, but there is a time coming when you won't be able to buy food, work or have any status in society unless you worship the Anti-Christ and have his mark. That won't be right away, but we need to start preparing now."

"Oh, come on, Jake-" Randy interrupted, his voice getting louder, "-I know you're going through a difficult time with Tracey and John missing, but do you really believe what you're saying?"

"I believe it with all my heart, Randy. Tracey had been witnessing to me for over a year now, and I never listened to her, that is until it was too late. She told me that the Rapture was going to happen and asked me, even begged me, to accept Christ before it did. She warned me that there would be no second chances afterward, that if I missed it then I would have to endure seven years of what the Bible calls the Tribulation. Well the Rapture did happen, Randy, yesterday, and now I'm here telling you what we should do in order to survive."

"And your Bible says that yesterday's disappearances is the beginning of the last seven years of the world?"

"Yesterday's Rapture is just the first of predicted events to happen. The tribulation won't actually start until the Anti-Christ signs a seven-year peace treaty with Israel."

Randy gave a cynical smile and shook his head. Jake sighed, "I don't expect you to believe just because I do, but take a look around and compare what's happening with what the Bible says will happen. You'll find that they will be exactly the same. You can trust that I will be there to point out any fulfillment of prophecy as it happens. The first was the Rapture, and now what I heard today just this morning, the new leader in Europe."

"Ok, Jake-" Mary broke in, "-what if all this is fulfillment of Biblical prophecy. What do you think we should do?"

"I don't think we should do anything drastic right away. The time is not right yet to hide out in the cave. We should live our lives as normally as we can for the time being. Let's continue to go to work, and shop, and do our basic daily routines. As believers, we are obligated to try and spread the Word of God to all those around us-our friends and family-even strangers. Christ does not want to lose anyone, so we need to be a witness to what's going on. We'll need to be careful, maybe not right away, but there will come a time when Christians will be persecuted. Do not share the location of the cave with anyone you don't trust. That will be our place of safety when the time comes to live in it. What I think we should do as well is to start now on stocking the cave with non-perishable foods, like canned goods and freeze-dried items. When it is finally time to go to the cave permanently, then we're going to need all the necessities that we can store. We'll also need to stock up on all the materials we're going to need for hunting and fishing."

"Jake," Randy said sarcastically, shaking his head, "you sound like a leader of a cult survivalist group that's going to barricade themselves away from civilization and wait for some spaceship to arrive to pick him up."

"No, Randy, I'm just going to wait for the Lord to pick me up."

The Roman Coliseum was full to capacity, and the spectators cheered their approval, chanting his name repeatedly as he rode out of the darkness of the tunnel on his white Arabian horse. He wore a white military-type uniform with golden fringes and golden tassels on his broad shoulders and sat tall in the saddle. On his large chest, likened to the breast plate worn by Roman gladiators prepared to fight, hung military medals awarded to him from self-proclaimed achievements. His high cheekbones were enhanced by his thin face and mildly jutting chin, which had a marked dimple at the center. His dark brown hair and penetrating brown eyes stood out against his light brown skin. He was handsome, and his face was that of a man much younger then his forty years; an outsider would be deceived by his boyish appearance. The crowd roared louder as he rode in a counterclockwise direction along the inside perimeter of the coliseum, his right fist raised high, stirring the crowd into a frenzy. The people of Europe loved him, and his influence was rapidly spreading into other parts of the world. This was his day, the official inauguration of Alexander Christos as president of the new United States of Europe.

Jake sat on the rocking chair and Tracey's parents sat on the sofa, watching the news coverage of the events taking place in Rome. Randy was called back to Washington a couple of days earlier to help with the investigation into the disappearance of millions of people around the world, and Mary had gone back to their home in Riverside-both still unconvinced of the prophetic events that have been taking place.

"This is the first time that I've seen him," Jake said, not able to take his eyes away from television. "Despite knowing who he is, I still feel drawn to him. It's no wonder why people who don't know who he is will be deceived by him. His appearance and charisma … it's amazing. The Rapture was only a week ago, but he, somehow, has made it seem like it was years ago. The people appear to have forgotten."

"He's been able to make them forget because he's got the people convinced that the Rapture was a divine plan," Joyce replied. "And with the life-saving miracles that he has been performing, there's going to be no stopping him in his conquest to take over the world."

"I know." Jake sighed and took a deep breath. "I'm worried about Mary and Randy. I'm afraid they're going to be deceived. We're going to have to continue without them if we have to, but I hope and pray that won't be the case."

"Jake, all we can do is be there for them and try to convince them," Sam added, "We'll just have to pray that they will see the light."

"Yeah, you're right. I think we should start stocking the cave and getting everything situated there. Things are going to start happening quickly, and I don't want to be left unprepared."

"Joyce and I have discussed it, Jake, we're going to cash out our retirement funds. We can use the money to buy a place in Denver near the cave. That way we can be there preparing it. You can move there, too, and help us when you're not on duty. I don't know how long you plan on staying at Pan World Airlines, but if you leave, we sure could use your help."

"That's probably not a bad idea, Sam. You won't need your retirement anymore. Money will be worthless in a few years anyway. I can do the same and help pay for the place. I think that the closer we are to the cave, the better off we'll be. I'll stay with the airline for a while longer, but as soon as things get worse, I'll leave and join you in Denver."

They continued to watch the television as the fireworks exploded over the coliseum for the celebration. President Christos stood at the podium, ready to give his speech, and waited for the cheering crowd to be seated. He began to speak and the crowd became silent.

"I am-" President Christos screamed out, purposely pausing after saying these two words, "-I am compelled to respond to those who claim that the Rapture last week was the beginning to the end of the world. The Rapture was not a sign marking the beginning of the end, but a beginning of divine lordship of the earth and its people. I have been given authority to lead the people to the true God. I am-" President Christos could not continue. The crowd stood to their feet again, cheering their approval with a deafening roar. Ten minutes had passed before President Christos could begin again. He seemed to gain strength from the frenzy and held his fist up in acknowledgment. "I am the one given power to lead the people to their destiny, a destiny of a one-world government and a one-world church," President Christos continued. The gesturing with his hands reminded

Jake of the way Adolph Hitler spoke to his people in the late 1930s and 40s.

"The Rapture was needed in order for God's divine plan to set up His kingdom on earth, and I am-" President Christos again purposely pausing after these words and gauging his audience, "-I am the instrument of God that will make it happen. The Rapture was needed to dispose of those that would oppose my kingdom and the kingdom of God that I will set up through the one-world church. As of today, the Catholic Church does not exist any longer; I am renaming it the Unification World Church. I will lead the Unification World Church in its quest to set up God's kingdom on earth-a kingdom that will last forever. I am-" he paused "-I am the one that will make it happen."

The crowd roared, shaking the Coliseum with the vibration of the noise they generated. President Christos stood there, feeding on the frenzy.

"God has also given me a mighty helper," President Christos continued, turning to Francisco Gallo standing just behind him on his right side. "The former Cardinal Gallo, whom God has given to me for divine help, will now be known as Prophet Gallo. He will be the first prophet for the Unification World Church." President Christos paused as the crowd went into another frenzy, screaming a thunderous roar that shook the coliseum again with the noise.

"I have been given the authority to make the United States of Europe the most powerful country the world has ever seen," Alexander Christos shouted out. The mere sound of his voice quieted the crowd instantly. "And with Prophet Gallo's help, we will make that goal a reality. A country separate from the Church will not survive, and I have been given power to unite the two with my leadership. If a country cannot survive without the Church, then the world will not survive without the Church. I will unite the countries of the world and be their spiritual leader. My conquest will be the world and, if God is for me, then who can be against me. Let this be a lesson and a warning to those that will oppose my authority."

It was pure pandemonium in the coliseum when President Christos ended his short speech. Jake just sat there motionless.

He couldn't believe what he had just heard and how the people responded to the Anti-Christ's deception. He looked at Tracey's parents, and they looked back at him in awe at what was happening. They were unable to speak, not knowing what to say even if they could.

Jake finally broke the silence. "My God, I don't know if you realize it, but he set himself up to be God with that speech. He constantly repeated the phrase *I am.* Did you notice how he paused after he said it?"

"But how does that set him up to be God?" Joyce looked at Sam.

"When Moses went to the burning bush on Mount Sinai, he asked God how he should answer his people when they asked what God's name was. God told Moses to answer the people, *I am that I am, that is what you shall tell them.* I don't know how significant it will be to the Gentile world, but in Israel and to the Jewish people, I think its going to be very significant."

"Well, Jake, what do you think we should do?" Sam asked.

Jake paused for a moment, sighing as he looked at the couple. "Let's find a place in Denver."

Chapter 5

⌇——⌇

The Connecticut noon sun was directly overhead when Mary and Randy Johnson walked out of the Unification World Church building located in their hometown of Riverside. Membership registration had been a nightmare with wall-to-wall people waiting in lines that snaked their way throughout the offices and extended out the doors to the parking lot. It had taken them most of the morning to finally finish the paperwork needed to officially join the Church. Mail-in registration was not allowed; all new members were required to register in person. Fingerprints and pictures were taken and would be added to the church file for later reference if necessary. The actual registration form was a simple one, consisting only of a few questions mainly of residence and place of employment. One question, however, asked if they had any knowledge of friends or family that were Christian and asked for their addresses and phone numbers. Mary thought it odd that it would be asked. She did mention Jake Fredricks, but did not know his new address in Denver and had left that portion of the registration form blank. For the first time in their lives, like all of the others that were there, Mary and Randy had something to believe in, something concrete in Alexander Christos, not some invisible God to pray to like the Christians did, but a man who had God's power and who could communicate directly to God.

The three months since the Rapture had brought optimism to the Church for the creation of God's kingdom on earth. Alexander Christos continued to perform miracles, and Prophet Gallo traveled the world to spread the news about the new religious leader's ability to rule and to heal the sick. Word of President Christos' "supernatural" power spread quickly, many believing unconditionally that he was truly sent from God. Prophet Gallo would also perform miracles, doing a "demonstration" of his supernatural powers at each of his speaking engagements. He claimed that Alexander Christos was the "source of his power and that such power was given from above."

"That wasn't as bad as I thought it would be," Randy said. He and Mary walked down the steps of the building leading to the courtyard.

"Are you kidding?" Mary chuckled, "It took us four hours to fill out a one-page document. It was nuts, but I'm glad it's finally over with. Did you answer the question on whether you knew any Christians?"

"Yeah," Randy replied,. "I wrote in Jake Fredricks' name and that he lived in Denver but I didn't know his address so I left that portion blank."

"Me too." Mary opened the passenger door to their red BMW convertible. "The Church doesn't need to know that information anyway."

"This is going to be the best decision we've ever made." Randy smiled at Mary and started the car. "President Christos is going to change the course of history and we're going to be a part of it."

Mary was not as convinced. "We'll see. He's only been in power for three months."

"Don't be so pessimistic, Mary. You sound like Jake Fredricks."

"Oh, Randy, you know he's been through a lot since Tracey and John disappeared. Give him a break."

"I know, but I'm getting tired of him telling you that the end of the world is coming," Randy pulled out of the parking lot and into the flow of traffic. "He believes it so much that he sold his house in Boston and cashed out his retirement just to buy a place close to that cave. I can imagine how tough it would be to lose your wife and son, but that's a little ridiculous. Prophet Gallo himself said that President Christos is performing all kinds of miracles by healing the sick and raising the dead. He's even had fire come down from the sky to show his power. The world is only going to get better; I can't understand why Jake doesn't believe that."

"That's because he's a Christian-" Mary said, the wind whipping her blond hair behind her, "-and most Christians believe that President Christos is the Anti-Christ and that Prophet Gallo is his evil false prophet. They think that those two are going to bring war and destruction to the world. I don't know if President Christos is the Anti-Christ, but I'm not convinced that he is the answer to the world's problems yet, either."

"Oh, come on, Mary," Randy took his eyes off the road and stared at his wife, "In the three months since he took power, President Christos has literally turned the economy of Europe one hundred and eighty degrees. All of Europe has never had an economy like they do now. While our economy here in the States is getting worse. And when have you ever seen peace in the Middle East? Since his peace treaty with Israel there has been nothing but calm in the whole region."

"I admit, Randy, that he has been doing wonderful things in Europe and the Middle East, but that doesn't make him God."

"Well, if he's not God, then he has God's power, and we're going to be witness to it."

"Let's just say that my optimism is a little more subdued than yours."

"General Kemp says that he has a charisma like no other that he has ever met. President Christos' character exudes respect and-"

"When has General Kemp met with President Christos?" Mary stared at Randy.

Randy sighed, disgusted with himself that he let the meeting with General Kemp and President Christos slip out. "I didn't mean for you to know yet," he said, shaking his head, "but General Kemp, President Christos, and other officials at the Pentagon have been meeting secretly." Randy stopped the car at an intersection and waited for the light to turn green. "Look," he continued, pulling his hands from the steering wheel, "let's just end it there; I don't know if I should tell you any more."

"Just wait a minute, Randy." Mary's frustration in Randy's secrecy was evident in her tone. "If you know something more that I should know, then you better tell me. You know that I'm not going to say anything to anybody that might get you into trouble."

"Okay." Randy conceded. The traffic light turned green and Randy looked both ways before proceeding through the intersection. "Mary, you can't tell anyone, all right?"

"I promise-" Mary replied impatiently, "-what's going on?"

"General Kemp has been meeting in Rome with President Christos and a European general by the name of Westheim. They are in negotiations that would merge the military of the U.S.E with the U.S.A. and are hoping that they can remove President Andrews from office. Something like a coup-"

"What?" Mary snapped back. "I don't want you involved in some coup; people get killed that way."

"Now just wait and let me finish," Randy replied. "President Andrews is ruining our country. Our economy has spiraled downward over the last year and a half, and it's not getting any better. We have recognized the success that Europe is having, and we want to be a part of it."

"But a coup? C'mon, Randy?" Mary was angry. She could no longer hide that fact and stared at Randy stone-faced.

"This is the only way that we can get President Christos to be the leader of our country. Don't worry, I'm not involved with the negotiations. I found out because I'm General Kemp's first assistant. Look Mary, this isn't going to happen overnight, it's going to take a while to work out the logistics. The United States is not what she used to be, and we are by far much weaker now than at any time in our entire history. This is our way of making the U.S.A. better then ever."

Randy pulled up into the driveway of their home and stopped the car. The phone was ringing when they entered the front door, and Mary hurried to answer the line in the kitchen.

"Hello," Mary answered.

"Hello," the voice at the other end of the line replied, "May I speak to Mary Johnson?"

"This is she."

"Mrs. Johnson, this is Ed Nathan at the Unification World Church here in Riverside. I've been looking over your member registration form and noticed that you have left some items blank. Do you think you could answer them for me now?"

"I guess that will be fine." Mary responded. She was puzzled that with as many people at the registration today that they would have looked at her registration form so quickly. "What is it that you need to know?"

"You mentioned that you had a friend by the name of Jake Fredricks who is a Christian; you left his phone number and address blank. Do you think that you could give that information to me now?"

Mary was stunned and thrown off by the question. Her stomach was churning and she felt uncomfortable. *Why was this person and the Unification World Church so interested in knowing where Christians were?* She did have Jake Fredricks' address and phone number in her address book, but she decided that she would not give this Ed Nathan the information.

"I don't have that information." Mary replied matter-of-factly, "All I know is that they moved to Denver, and I haven't seen them since."

"Do you think that your husband would know?"

"No." Mary grew impatient by the questioning, "He knows less about it than I do."

"Thank you, Mrs. Johnson. We know he lives in Denver. We'll be able to reach him there. We have your number if we need to contact you. Congratulations on your new life in the Unification World Church. Goodbye and may Father Christos bless you."

"Goodbye." Mary hung up the phone forcefully. It was all she could do to stop herself from screaming.

Father Christos? What nerve! she thought, questioning his title. Mary felt very uncomfortable about the conversation and felt that she had, in some way, let Jake down. She didn't like the way the Church had already invaded their privacy and didn't like them asking questions about their friends; it just didn't feel right with her.

"Randy!" Mary yelled out, trying to get his attention, "Randy, where are you?"

"I'm right here," Randy replied, entering the kitchen, "you don't have to scream."

"Randy, that was a representative from the Unification World Church and he was asking about Jake Fredricks. He wanted to know his address and phone number."

"Yeah, did you give it to him?"

"No. I didn't want to give him any information. It all seems too weird to me."

"Don't worry, honey; they probably want to know so that they can do some more recruiting."

"I don't know, Randy. It didn't sound like that to me. He said that they could get a hold of him in Denver. I should have just told them that I didn't know any Christians."

"Don't make this a bigger issue than it is. Jake will be all right. He can handle himself. He's got a cave to live in, remember?"

Mary was not amused. "That's not funny, Randy. I just don't like the whole thing. And I don't like the fact that you know about the secret negotiations between General Kemp and President Christos."

"Don't worry, Mary. It's just some negotiation. They're trying to do it peacefully, there won't be any blood shed."

"I don't know, Randy, I don't like it."

"Look, Mary, President Andrews' approval rating is down considerably. If the negotiations to merge the militaries of the two countries are successful, it will form the most powerful military that has ever existed. The American people would love it. The economy would be on the right track, and life here will be great. President Andrews would probably resign his office and be given some other office in President Christos' administration. From what I understand, if everything works out the way it should, President Christos will take over peacefully."

"You mean Father Christos, don't you?" Mary couldn't hide her sarcasm.

Randy sighed, "What are you talking about?"

"That's what the man from the Unification World Church called him ... Father Christos."

"Oh Mary, relax; that's just the title the church is giving him."

"I don't like it, Randy. I should probably call Jake and let him know that someone from the Church is going to try and get a hold of him."

"Mary, you're just wasting your time. I don't care if you call Jake or not, but he's a big boy now and he's going to be just fine."

"You don't understand at all, do you?"

"I understand that you're making a bigger deal out of this than necessary. If you want to call him, then call him, but I wish you would hurry because I'm getting hungry."

"I don't need you talking down to me, Randy."

"I'm sorry, Mary. Call Jake. But you'll see; time will prove me right." Randy picked up a church brochure from off the counter.

"Maybe so, but I'll feel better if I call him."

"This pamphlet says that Prophet Gallo is coming to New York in a couple of months." Randy held up a church booklet showing Mary a picture of both President Christos and Prophet Gallo on the cover, "I think that we should try and go and see if all the hype about the man is true. It says that they're going to set up a special area in Central Park."

"I don't know, Randy-"

"Come on, Mary," Randy interrupted, "this will be a good chance to see if this is for real or if it's all just some huge hoax."

Mary hesitated, taking a deep breath. "All right, let's find out for ourselves."

A lone elk grazed quietly on the green grass of the meadow with the sun rising slowly over the Rocky Mountains casting a dark shadow over the marsh where the animal stood. The puff of steam billowing from its nostrils with every breath the animal took was the only indication of the chill in the air. The flaming-orange glow of the rising sun, almost as bright as the star itself, reflected brightly off of the snow at the highest peaks and could be seen for miles. At the base of the mountain, hidden in the pine forest and thick foliage, stood the log cabin that Jake and Tracey's parents had bought a month earlier. The only sign of human life was the white smoke that rose from the red brick chimney and hovered at the tree tops mingling between the branches like a fog descending onto a coastal town.

The two-story cabin was made of pine logs from the same forest where the structure stood. The logs were laid down on top of each other to form the outside of the structure and sealed with grout that was made to resemble the natural sap from the trees. The bottom floor was one large room, except for the bathroom and one bedroom located near the front entrance. The entrance led into the kitchen and dining area, then veered right around the lone inner wall and stair case, which formed the north wall of the down stairs bedroom, exposing the living area. The ivory white walls stood out against the dark hard wood floor, which creaked with every step that was placed on it. The staircase led to the second story, splitting the entire floor into two bedrooms. Jake lay in bed sleeping, the aroma of the coffee bringing him slowly back to consciousness. He had just finished a short stint with Pan World Airlines and had been away for one week and arriving home late the night before.

"Jake?" Joyce called from the bottom of the stairs, "Jake, get up. Breakfast is getting cold."

"Okay," Jake replied, trying to gather his senses, "I'll be right down."

Jake sat on the edge of the bed and paused for a moment, glancing at a framed picture of Tracey and John that was sitting on the night stand. He reached to touch the picture and struggled to hold back his tears. He had missed them so much and still hadn't gotten used to them being gone. He put on some clothes and slowly walked to the bottom of the stairway still thinking of his wife and son. Sam was sitting in the kitchen while Joyce placed a plate of sizzling bacon down on the table. Jake loved the smell of bacon and the salty aroma that filled the room. There were freshly baked biscuits as well and a creamy white gravy made from the grease of the cooked bacon to smother the biscuits. Joyce, even in the worst of times, was always the good mother watching out for the ones that she loved the most. Jake could not help but admire her as she made sure that he and Sam were well fed. He had found same qualities in Tracey, and there was no wonder in why he had fallen in love with her.

"Good morning, Jake." Sam looked up and smiled.

Jake rubbed his eyes and sat at the table opposite Sam. "Good morning. Breakfast smells good."

"I cooked your favorite. How was your trip, Jake?" Joyce asked, "We tried to stay up for you, but we just couldn't keep our eyes open."

"That's okay. I got in late. I couldn't sleep at first but finally managed."

"Sam's been doing a lot with the cave. He can't wait to tell you."

"I've been putting plenty of canned goods in the cave," Sam sipped his coffee. "Mostly beans and canned meats like tuna and chicken."

"Just don't forget the can opener." Jake chuckled. "What have you been doing about non-food items and equipment?"

"I've put a gas-powered generator in there and set up a ventilation system that will allow the fumes to escape. I'm in the process of stocking some gasoline in airtight containers-"

"But we don't have enough room in there-" Jake interrupted, "- to store three or four years of gasoline."

"I'm only going to store enough for emergency situations and for the winters. It can get quite cold in there, and there may be times that we may want to crank it up and use an electric heater that I have set up to get warm. I've have also been collecting car batteries that we can keep charged with the generator. I'm going to string some low voltage bulbs as well so that we won't have to use fire to light the cave."

"We're going to have enough blankets and warm clothing in there too, aren't we, Sam?" Joyce asked.

"Of course we are, but you never know when we'll need a little bit more. I'm not saying that we'll run it all the time, but if we need it, then we'll have it."

"Okay, Sam, what about cooking?" Jake asked. "We're not going to want to light a fire in the cave because the smoke could be dangerous, and it might also give away our location."

Sam poured some gravy over a biscuit. "I thought of that as well. Besides the ventilation system, I've also been stocking the cave with camping cooking fuel. There's no smoke and it burns clean. We'll do all our cooking in the makeshift area near where the generator will be so that ventilation won't be a problem."

"How did you set up the ventilation in there?"

"There was a natural tunnel that led from the inside of cave to the surface. It was just large enough for me to fit a flexible metal pipe down the middle and into the cave. Then I lugged that old wood-burning stove, the one that was in the basement when we bought the cabin, to the cave and attached the pipe to it."

"Is there anything that you didn't think of, Sam?" Jake smiled and sipped his coffee.

"I'll take you up there after breakfast to show you. I need help hauling some more supplies anyway. I'll go get the flashlights; we'll need them."

The trek up the mountain to the cave was only three miles from the cabin, but it was a difficult hike because of the foliage and pine trees and no visible trail to follow. Jake liked the seclusion of the cave, and he felt secure that no one would find it, but they had to be careful and not take any unnecessary chances. The two hiked to the summit of the mountain until they could see the stream and the waterfall that hid the cave. They had to walk down a steep embankment to get to the base of the waterfall. The loose soil and broken granite made the relatively short distance treacherous, and on a few occasions they slipped and almost fell into the deep pool at the bottom of the waterfall.

"How did you ever get the generator and the wood stove down that steep embankment, Sam?"

"It wasn't easy. I had to attach a pulley on the pine tree at the top and let it down very slowly. I almost dropped the stove a couple of times. I won't tell you how long it took me to get them the three miles from the cabin. Let's just say it wasn't easy."

"I can just imagine." Jake shook his head and smiled, "Let's go inside."

There was a four-foot-wide ledge just outside the entrance of the cave; the opening was five feet wide and six feet high and was positioned on the south side of the cave. The flow of water fell just in front of the ledge, allowing the two to stay dry as they entered their future home. The cave was dark, and Jake could not see anything. His flashlight illuminated the cave, and Jake could barely see the back of it as he pointed the light. The cave was approximately forty feet deep and thirty feet wide. Sam had sectioned the cave. On the east side was the wood stove and generator, just in front of what would be the main living area. The north side was stored with canned goods, stacked in uniform order so that they could not fall over. The west side was stored with the gasoline and other fuel products, as well as blankets, sleeping bags and other items that might be needed to keep them warm. Empty plastic containers used to store water were stocked there, and would be filled with the water from the stream until that future day when the water would be made bitter as predicted in Revelation.

"You've done a great job, Sam. Fortunately I don't have to go back to work for a while and I'll be around to help out."

"Yeah, I could use it. Joyce is very helpful with the things she can carry, but the heavy stuff is difficult."

The two men had lost track of time and it was eight P.M. before they started back. The setting sun was glowing bright orange in the west and soon would be below the mountain tops giving way to the darkness of night. It would take a few hours to trek the three miles back to the cabin.

"Thank God." Joyce let out a sigh of relief. "I've been worried sick about you two. It's twelve o'clock, what took you so long?"

"I'm sorry, Honey. We lost track of time. We're okay."

"Don't do that again." Joyce stared at Sam with a look that he knew all too well. "I don't think that my heart can take it."

"We won't let it happen again." Jake attempted to ease the tension.

"Jake, Mary called while you were at the cave."

"What did she say?"

"Well, I don't know how to say this," she said, hedging a little, "but she said that she and Randy have joined the Unification World Church."

Jake was frustrated and let out a long, slow breath. He couldn't believe it. He had thought that if anyone would have joined the church it would have been Randy not Mary. He prayed that both would believe in the Lord but knew that the deceptive powers of the Anti-Christ and his false prophet would convince many to believe in them and not in the true God and Lord.

"Why?" Jake asked, not really expecting an answer. "I can't believe that they have fallen for the Anti-Christ, especially since I have told them many times who he is and that the supernatural powers that he possesses are of Satan."

"I know, Jake, but that's not exactly why she called. She called to let us know that the registration form that she and Randy had to fill out asked for the addresses and phone numbers of any Christians that they might know."

"And?"

"And that she mentioned your name but left the address and phone portion of the question blank. When she got home the phone was ringing and a man from the church was asking her if she could supply your address and phone number."

"Well, did she give him that information?" Sam asked.

"No. She told him that you moved to Denver and that she didn't have that information. She told them that she hadn't seen you since."

Jake shook his head, "I don't like the way that sounds."

"She said that the man will be able to locate us since he knew that we were in Denver. He also addressed Alexander Christos as *Father Christos.*"

"It sounds like the church is going to try and keep track of Christians." Jake replied, "That way when the Anti-Christ reveals himself as God they will be able to find us easier.

"Did she say anything else?"

"Not really. She didn't seem too convinced of the church and actually asked me some questions about end-time prophecy. I still think that we can convince her of Jesus and His salvation. She did say that they're going to try and see Prophet Gallo when he comes to New York in a few weeks. They want to see if he's for real and-"

"He's for real all right," Jake interrupted, "If she's not convinced now then Prophet Gallo will with his supernatural power. Let's just pray that we can convince both of them before they fall too much further into the grip of the Unification World Church."

Chapter 6

❦——❦

Denver's Stapleton Airport was quiet as Jake Fredricks stepped off the plane in the early morning hours and walked to the Pan World Airline terminal. He had just finished a two-week schedule that had taken him to London, Paris, and Rome, and back to New York, and then Denver. He had a lot of news to tell Sam and Joyce about the feel in Europe regarding the new government and the new economy that had been ushered in by President Christos when he took office five months earlier. The economic turnaround and military build-up in Europe over that short period of time was an achievement unmatched in the history of the world, making the country the most stable economically and militarily to have ever existed. Jake had been to Europe many times in his career and had never experienced the confidence that the Europeans felt towards their government and religious leader than he witnessed on this trip. Daily, thousands were joining the Unification World Church, not only in Europe, but in the United States as well, believing that Alexander Christos was God incarnate and the answer to the problems that the planet was facing. *And why not?* Jake thought, *President Christos' ability to miraculously heal the sick and dying, coupled with his ability to rule, would fool anyone who was not aware of the truth.* Prophet Gallo was also performing miracles, giving credit to Father Christos for his supernatural powers.

Pressure had been building in the United States of America from the general public and from the Unification World Church to merge the government with that of President Christos in Europe. The only resistance was coming from America's President Andrews and certain traditional hardliners in Congress. The decline in the economy and the progressive dismantling of the military after the end of the cold war in the late 1980s weakened the country, and the Americans grew weary of not being the power that they once were. Their confidence for an upswing in the economy dwindled as more jobs were being lost, dropping the approval rating for President Andrews to an all-time low. A number of radical groups were formed with the goal of removing the President from office and replacing him with Christos. Top military brass at the Pentagon questioned President Andrews' ability as commander in chief and were deliberating a possible defection by the armed forces to join the military might of the U.S.E. There had been unconfirmed reports of secret negotiations involving President Christos and members of the Pentagon, which further weakened President Andrews' influence in his own country.

Persecution against Christians and other groups that were opposed to Alexander Christos and those that would not join the World Church was on the rise and even encouraged by Church leaders. Most of the persecution came in the form of discrimination and firing from jobs; however, more violent forms were increasing and being reported by the news media on a more frequent basis.

Jake was careful to whom he would witness to about the Lord Jesus telling the Good News mostly to co-workers and friends who he knew were suffering or seeking answers. Most were cordial in their response to him, but a few laughed outright as they indicated their trust in the new religious leader of the world. Jake knew that he would have to be careful. A time was coming when Christian executions would be commonplace and accepted, but he also knew the Lord's command to his followers "to preach to the world," and he would do so for as long as he could.

Walking past the newspaper stand, Jake's attention was drawn to the headline in the *Denver Chronicle*. He trembled at what he read. He reached into his pocket to grab the seventy-five cents required to purchase the paper, dropping the coins onto the floor when he pulled his hand out of his pocket.

"Good morning," Jake said to the clerk, "I'd like to buy the paper."

"Yes, Sir. That will be seventy-five cents, please."

Jake hurriedly picked up the coins, paid the clerk, folded the paper under his arm and walked towards his car. Placing the paper on the front seat he fumbled to get the key into the ignition. The half-hour ride to the cabin seamed like an eternity as he tried to read the paper and drive at the same time. It was 4 A.M. when he arrived at the cabin. He was anxious to read the paper and the headlines that captured his attention. After making a pot of coffee, he sat down at the kitchen table to give the story his full attention. For the next two hours he read the paper and prayed.

"Good morning, Jake. What time did you get in last night?" Joyce, still in her night robe, walked into the kitchen, placing her hand on Jake's shoulder as she walked past to get herself a cup of coffee.

Jake looked up from the paper. "Good morning, Joyce. I got home just about two hours ago and have been reading and praying. Is Sam still sleeping?"

"Yeah, he was tired from all the hauling of supplies into the cave yesterday; I think I'll let him sleep in today."

"I'll be able to help him the next few weeks. How is it coming?"

"It's going as well as an old man can work." Joyce chuckled then sat at the table and took a sip of her coffee. "Sam is amazing with all the work that he does. But I think it's starting to tire him out a little. For some strange reason I think he's enjoying it though."

"Joyce, I know you haven't had a chance to read today's paper yet, but I picked up the *Denver Chronicle* at the airport last night. Here ..." Jake handed the paper to Joyce, "... read the headline."

Joyce reached to grab the paper. "What does it say? "My God ... Jake, I can't believe it. It's all happening so fast."

Joyce placed the paper on the table between them face up so that they both could read the headline that was printed in bold letters: ARAB COALITION SURROUNDS ISRAEL-VOWS TO DRIVE THE SMALL JEWISH COUNTRY INTO THE SEA.

"I've been reading it this morning. It's a response from the Arab countries to the seven-year peace treaty that has been made between the U.S.E. and Israel."

"But just six months ago when the treaty was agreed upon everyone was optimistic about the Middle East peace process." Joyce said, "There has to be more than that. What happened?"

"The Temple. President Christos has promised Israel that they can rebuild their Temple."

"Why would the Arab countries care if Israel builds their Temple?"

"That's just it. President Christos has told Israel that they can build the Temple on the same spot where the Dome of the Rock Mosque is located. The Arab nations will never allow that to happen peacefully, and that is why they are surrounding Israel now. But the treaty that Israel has with the U.S.E. promises to protect the Jewish country against all their enemies. You can't blame them for wanting to protect their mosque. But if they try to do it by taking on President Christos, it's going to backfire on them."

"Are all the Arab countries involved?"

"It looks as though Iraq, Iran, and Syria are the main countries that are positioned along Israel's border, but it goes on to say that another seven Arab countries are involved in some way. It has me worried because the United States is beefing up its naval presence in the Persian Gulf, and the United States of Europe is mobilizing ground troops and increasing its naval presence off the western coast of Israel."

"What about the Russians, Jake? I'm sure they're very interested in what's going on. Are they involved in this in some way?"

"That's what's so puzzling. Apparently Christos has convinced President Vladikoff that this operation will only involve expelling the Arab forces from Israel's border, and that the war won't go any further than that. I can't understand how President Vladikoff could believe that. I can't imagine a man like President Christos stopping there; the Bible predicts that the Anti-Christ will be bent on conquest. He will be in prime position to take over the Arab oil fields, and if he does that, then there will be no stopping him in taking over the world and he knows it. But we shouldn't be surprised because that is exactly what the Bible says that he will do ...take over the world."

"Doesn't Randy Johnson work at the Pentagon? I wonder what he knows about all of this."

"Yeah, he does. He's been at the Pentagon for many years now. He is the first assistant to Brigadier General Russell Kemp. I wouldn't be surprised if he was in Europe now with all that's been going on in the Middle East."

"Haven't you talked to him or Mary lately?"

"I've talked to Mary plenty of times, but Randy has been very distant since I've accepted the Lord. I mean he's been cordial, but nothing more. I'm worried about both of them. Randy has really fallen for the Unification World Church, and Mary tells me that he has really put his trust in President Christos."

"What about Mary? How does she feel about the Church and President Christos?"

"Well, let's say that she is not as convinced about President Christos as Randy is. She's still a member of the Church, but I'm hoping that she'll realize that the Lord Jesus is the Savior and that she is just waiting, for some reason, to accept His grace. She actually seems more receptive than ever when I talk to her, but she may be afraid of what Randy may do if she accepts the Lord."

"Let's just pray about it and wait and see." Joyce picked up the newspaper from the table, shaking her head as she stared at the headline. "It's going to be interesting to see what develops in the Middle East. I hope it won't last long."

"The order has come down from President Christos," Supreme Commander General Joseph Westheim of the U.S.E stated during a secret briefing of his staff. "We will attack first by bombarding the Arab Coalition troops at Israel's border with air strikes using American B-52 and Stealth bombers. We will deploy our cruise missiles and send American Apache helicopters and British Tornados to knock out key areas in the countries of the coalition and shut down any supply lanes and any possible reinforcements.

"Once we start our offensive, we expect Israel and particularly Jerusalem will receive enemy fire. The Arab coalition troops have mobile missile launchers and we expect them to use them as soon as our attack begins. Once we accomplish our goal along Israel's border, our ground troops, backed by air support, will advance into the capitals and capture, alive if possible, the leaders of these countries. The goal that President Christos has is not to overthrow these governments, but to force them into accepting a peace treaty with Israel that will result in a secure peace in the Middle East and the free flow of oil to Europe and the rest of the world." Westheim gestured to a uniformed gentleman standing to his right side.

"General Russell Kemp, commander of the U.S.A military forces, will be in charge of this portion of the operation, and they will work simultaneously and in concert with our maneuvers." Westheim bit his lip, remained standing at the podium, and contemplated his next order. He was a man of action, a no-nonsense personality. His hard-line demeanor demanded nothing less than total respect. His blue eyes stared at the officers who were seated in front of him. His men had seen that stare before. His mere presence in his camouflage uniform demanded their total loyalty and respect. Tension in the room was not only because of the impending war but due in part to the fear of his strong character. He had served in the army for forty-one years, since the age of eighteen, but the order to launch a surprise attack on an old ally would be the most difficult one that he would ever have to give. His allegiance was with his country and to President Christos, and, as difficult as it would be, he would give the order.

"After we take control of the countries of the Arab Coalition and their oil fields-" he continued, "-we are going to launch a surprise attack on the United States Naval Fleet in the Persian Gulf." The General paused, waiting for the commotion of his staff to quiet down. "Don't let the word 'surprise' fool you," he said. "The Pentagon and General Kemp are fully aware of what is to take place.

They have been in secret negotiations with President Christos and myself in this matter, and we have agreed that this is the only way to weaken President Andrews' stance on the merger of our two countries. I will now turn it over to General Kemp who will explain what is to happen."

General Kemp stepped up to the podium and stared down at the staff before him. He was a tall, thin man with gray hair and a crew-cut style. The thin wire-rim glasses that he wore on his long thin face reflected the ceiling lights from above, hiding his dark brown eyes behind the lenses.

General Kemp showed no emotion about what he was prepared to say. He was as cold as the plan that he had personally schemed-it was he who came to General Westheim with the idea to destroy his own fleet. But it wasn't totally for the cause of President Christos as much as it was a way to further his own agenda-to rule a country of his own. He thought by conceiving a plan to help President Christos obtain more power, he would be offered a position in the government. "We will accomplish this mission-" he began, "-by using two, possibly three neutron bomb warheads to be deployed by guided missiles aimed at our fleet in the Persian Gulf. We have most of our fleet there by design so that they can be destroyed with relative ease by these bombs. After we have secured the takeover of Iraq, these missiles will be launched from Baghdad by a team of U.S.E. special troops. We will blame a group of renegade loyalists that we were not able to detect until after they have launched the missiles.

"As you all know, the neutron bomb is a bomb that will kill with the same potential as a hydrogen bomb, but leaves structures intact. Our hope is that the American fleet in the Persian Gulf will sustain minimal damage allowing, us to hand over the ships to the U.S.E. forces helping us to merge the military of the U.S.E and of the U.S.A."

General Kemp's description of the neutron bomb was partially accurate. The bomb does cause massive destruction at the point of impact, but the destruction is confined to a small area. Most of the deaths that occur from a neutron explosion are due to the large number of neutrons being released, inducing radioactivity in materials, especially earth and water. The neutrons can penetrate, not only structures such as buildings, but tanks and other armored vehicles, in addition to large vessels such as aircraft carriers and battleships, killing all occupants and leaving the structures or vessels in place. The radioactivity is short lived, allowing structures and vessels to be inhabited in a short period of time.

The general paused for a moment. Although the best chance for him to obtain his goals was conspiring to destroy his own fleet, he doubted whether they could pull it off. But he remained stern faced in order not to reveal that thought. "The blame for the attack would fall on the shoulders of the Iraqi government, shifting the blame away from President Christos. This would allow the U.S.E. to avoid an all-out war with the United States. A drastic step, I know, but a step that is needed to weaken the U.S.A. military power. This, coupled with the U.S.E. control over the oil fields, will give President Andrews no choice but to concede his power over to Alexander Christos. Thank you, that's all I have for now."

General Westheim returned to the podium and stared at his officers. Taking a deep breath, he added, "As you are all aware, President Christos, in order to make peace with Israel, agreed to a treaty six months ago that would allow the Jewish state to rebuild their Holy Temple. In order for this to take place, the Dome of the Rock Mosque needs to be removed. As I said earlier, when we begin our offensive I expect a counter attack. During this counter offensive the Dome of the Rock Mosque will be destroyed. I have ordered the destruction as soon as the counter offensive begins so that it appears to be destroyed by incoming Arab missiles from their mobile missile launchers. This will allow President Christos to keep his word to Israel." The general glanced at his watch, "Prepare your men. We begin our work at twenty-four hundred hours."

The news media was everywhere along the streets and in the desert as each network tried to get the latest, most compelling pictures of the impending war. The entire Middle Eastern events that were unfolding resembled more of a Hollywood production than possible introduction to World War III. Cameras and lights were positioned at every possible vantage point for the best view and continually broadcast live throughout the world. Jake and Sam sat on the sofa in the living room of the cabin, watching the events on the television as Joyce made lunch, poking her head in periodically to catch a glimpse of the events as they happened. The ground troops and artillery that were positioned against Israel were massive; the entire armies of each of the three Middle Eastern countries were poised, ready to die for their cause, of utterly destroying Israel.

"Will you take a look at that?" Sam positioned himself on the sofa. "Those tanks are just blanketing the desert and all pointing towards Israel."

"And the mobile missile launchers," Jake pointed to the images on the television, "they're all over. If they're armed with any nuclear, chemical, or biological warheads then it's going to kill a lot of people."

"Come on, guys; I've had enough of this for today," Joyce's concern clearly in her voice. "Turn off the television and come have some lunch."

Jake said a prayer of thanks and the three sat eating and not saying much-the impending war on their minds. Jake wasn't hungry and left half the sandwich on his plate. Joyce got up from the table to do the dishes, picking up Jake's plate as she made her way to the kitchen sink.

"Jake, I need to get some more supplies," Sam said, putting the last bite of his sandwich in his mouth. "Would you like to take a ride with me into town?"

"Sure. What is it that you need to get?"

"Just need a few things … thought you'd like to come along." Sam leaned in toward Jake. He whispered, "I want to talk to you about something."

"Okay." Jake took a quick glance at Joyce washing the dishes, "I understand."

"Joyce-" Sam said as they got up from the table, "-we're going into town for a while. I need to pick up a few things."

"Okay." Joyce picked up a towel and started to dry the dishes. "Don't be too long."

"Okay ... see you in a while."

"Okay, Sam-" Jake hopped into the passenger side of Sam's truck, "-what's on your mind?"

"Well-" Sam hedged a little, "-you got a call while you were away. It was from the Unification World Church."

"What? How'd they get our number?"

"They must have got it from Mary and Randy Johnson. Remember that they mentioned your name on the registration form when they joined the Church. Look, Jake, Joyce doesn't know that they called. I thought it might cause her more anxiety than she already has. That's why I asked you to come into town with me. I really don't need anything."

"Yeah, I figured that out already." Jake replied, "Don't worry, I won't tell Joyce. What did the Church want?"

"They were just doing some recruiting. They tried to convince me of Father Christos' power and that he was the only way to God. I just told them that I wasn't interested."

"And that was it?"

"Yeah, they haven't called back since."

"Let's just be careful, Sam. If they can get our unlisted phone number, then they'll be able to find out where we live, if they don't know already."

"That's what has me worried, Jake. If they come calling, I'll just send them on their way, but I don't know how long that will work. There will come a time where I think that they may become aggressive, maybe even violent."

"By that time we'll be living in the cave. They won't be bothering us."

"I hope you're right, Jake. Anyway let's get to the hardware store."

"I thought you didn't need to get anything." Jake replied, "Why do we need to go to the hardware store?"

"I can't go home empty handed. Joyce thinks we're going to get some supplies."

"I guess you're right," Jake chuckled, "let's buy a screwdriver or something."

Joyce was standing in the front door way when Jake and Sam pulled into the driveway, waving her hands anxiously for the two men to hurry in.

"What is it, Joyce?" Sam stepped out of the truck and hurried to the front door.

"Hurry up and get inside. It's started." Joyce replied.

"Give me a second, I'm hurrying. What's started?"

"The war." Joyce replied, "The U.S.E. has attacked first."

The midnight silence over Israel was broken as the ally planes flew over in waves of sorties. One after another they continued to their selected targets, dropping death and destruction out of the darkness above. Glowing streaks of light produced by the launching of surface-to-air missiles lit the night sky, attempting to destroy the war planes that flew above them. As the bombs exploded, the ground shook with the sound of thunder and a flash of bright light, revealing its destruction for an instant before retreating back to darkness as quickly as it came. Air raid sirens sounded in Jerusalem and other cities in Israel as Arab missiles flew overhead, most being destroyed in mid-air by Patriot anti-missile missiles, but the system was not foolproof, and many of the missiles landed randomly, killing with terror. From the Temple Mount, a huge ball of flame rose high into the night accompanied by the sound of thunder. The concussion of the blast shattered windows and set off car alarms for blocks in every direction. The Dome of the Rock Mosque had been destroyed by the forces of the Anti-Christ, giving Israel the opportunity to rebuild their Temple.

The sorties continued killing soldiers and destroying the tanks along Israel's border with swift, unmerciful judgment. Apache helicopters flew low to the ground, destroying everything in their path as they made their way into the countries of the Arab coalition. Once there, they sought and destroyed electrical generators and communication networks along with radar detection facilities. British Tornados and Eagles targeted air and missile bases, destroying the air strips, limiting the amount of enemy airplanes that could land and take off, rendering them virtually useless.

The Arab Coalition was caught off guard, not expecting that the allied forces would strike first, but strike first they did, delivering destructive blows at every turn. Daybreak revealed the destruction: dead bodies and twisted metal blanketed the desert, and craters from the bombs contoured the land with pockmarks. The allied air strikes did not stop their onslaught and continued a systematic invasion into the allied countries of the Arab Coalition. President Christos had ordered the total destruction of every stronghold that remained, turning them into rubble with the bombs and missiles that continued to pour into them. The decisive victory at Israel's border took just over twenty-four hours, but the onslaught of the countries would last for seven more days, ensuring that all resistance would be eliminated and allowing U.S.E. ground troops to secure the takeover of the countries with relative ease. Any Arab coalition soldiers that were captured were to be given the choice of joining the U.S.E. forces or of execution-most chose to live. Civilians were to be executed only if they resisted the U.S.E. Army in the takeover. It took the U.S.E. forces just over a week to complete its mission of over-throwing the three countries and protecting the country of Israel by driving the Arab Coalition from her borders. Seven days of constant bombing took its toll. The Arab Coalition conceded defeat.

The feeling in the war room was one of jubilation as CNN prepared to televise the announcement from General Westheim regarding the end of the war. The room became silent as the general walked in and stepped up to the podium. His staff, including General Kemp and Captain Randy Johnson, was seated behind him.

"I can't believe it," Jake pointed to the images on the television, "that's Randy Johnson sitting there in the background."

"It sure is." Joyce replied, "He is in the Middle East. Mary must be worried sick about him." It was just like Joyce to think of another even in circumstances like this.

"All right." Sam interrupted, "Everyone hush up. I want to hear what this guy has to say."

"I am proud to report-" General Westheim said as he looked into the television camera, "-that the military threat by the Arab Coalition against Israel is over. The Allied Forces have systematically neutralized the armies of the coalition with devastating air strikes aimed at their positions along Israel's border. We have also rendered their military structure virtually non-existent with our unending air strikes and the mobilization of our ground troops, and have also overthrown the governments of Syria, Iran, and Iraq. Their military leaders and subordinates have been given a choice to join our forces in an attempt to unite their countries with ours, or to be executed. I am happy to report that most have agreed to join our forces. We have sustained some casualties, mostly from our ground troops who are receiving sporadic sniper fire in the Arab countries that we have overthrown. Israel has had some civilian casualties and deaths. The major damage has been to the Dome of the Rock Mosque, which has been completely destroyed. I will now answer questions from the media."

"We keep hearing talk that the Soviets were going to enter the war. What has President Christos said, if anything, to President Vladikoff to convince him not to enter this war?" asked a British correspondent working for the BBC.

"We were concerned with the Soviet response to our action here in the Middle East. President Christos has been in contact with President Vladikoff. At this time I do not know the exact details of their discussions. However, I do know and have been cleared to tell you that President Christos has assured President Vladikoff that the forceful takeover will stop with the three Arab countries that are now in our control. And, in time, we will withdraw our troops from those areas."

"There were some indications from the Soviets that they would in fact enter the war when the U.S.E. and U.S.A. forces overthrew the governments of these countries. Why do you think that they stopped short of entering the war when it was clear that the allied forces would soon take over the three countries and the oil fields that are so vital to the Russians?"

"As I stated earlier-" General Westheim replied after taking a deep breath pondering his answer to the question, "-President

Christos and President Vladikoff have been in discussions. I do know that President Vladikoff has been satisfied that the takeover of the three countries in question, Syria, Iran, and Iraq, is only a temporary measure until President Christos is satisfied that their threat against Israel is no longer a viable option for them. However, we were prepared and had a contingency plan for the possible entrance into the war by the Soviets. President Christos has satisfied the Russian government as to the plans he has for the Middle East. He has also satisfied President Vladikoff that the supply of oil that the Soviets need from the Middle East will not be stopped. That is the best that I can explain it from a diplomatic standpoint. As for a military standpoint, I would also say that I believe that the Soviets thought better of entering the war. I personally would not want to enter a war where I knew that the combined military might of the two most powerful countries in the world, namely the U.S.E and the U.S.A, were strategically positioned and armed with everything in their arsenal. That, combined with the fact that the Soviet military has been stretched to the limit with their involvement with the Chechen rebels and civil unrest in some of their other territories, the Soviets had no choice but to sit back and watch what was going on and hope that they could trust President Christos. They just don't have the manpower to get involved in a large war at this time."

"General Westheim?" asked Charles Goodson of CNN, "Why has President Christos decided to overthrow the countries that he has, killing at random innocent citizens in the process, when all he needed to do was to remove the leaders? Why kill the innocent citizens of these countries?"

"Kill innocent people?" General Westheim was angry. "We eliminate anyone or anything that we feel will endanger the chance of peace in the world for us or our allies. These people wanted nothing more than to drive Israel into the sea including the "innocent" citizens as you put it and-"

"But General-" the CNN reporter interrupted, "-the killing of innocent babies, women and children is not an act of bravery or protection, but seems more of a cowardly act."

General Westheim stood motionless, red faced with anger. He

did not like to be second guessed or have his character questioned, especially by anyone without military experience. It took all his strength to keep from lunging out after the reporter. "It should be clear to you that President Christos has shown great restraint. Instead of executing thousands of enemy soldiers, he has offered them a choice to join us ... to be part of the greatest military might in history. These people, the same ones that President Christos has mercifully allowed to live, would have killed innocent babies, women and children in Israel, but I don't see you questioning that. We have done what we need to do to protect Israel." The General stared at the reporter for what seemed like an eternity. His hatred for the questioning and the reporter could be seen in his eyes as he stepped from the podium. "I have nothing further to add."

Jake, Sam and Joyce were surprised at how quickly the war had ended. Seven days was all that was needed for the forces of the Anti-Christ to force the Arab Coalition to their knees and elicit an unconditional surrender. Israel was saved, and President Christos' power now extended into the entire Middle East. The world would be next.

"The prophecies of the Bible are falling into place," Jake said as he stood and reached to switch the television off. "The Dome of the Rock Mosque has been destroyed, giving the Jewish people their long awaited opportunity to rebuild their temple."

"But it doesn't make sense to me," Sam shook his head. "It sounds like the U.S.E. is going to avoid war with the Soviets, maybe even make a peace treaty with them. Doesn't the Bible predict that the Soviets will invade Israel and be a major power against the Anti-Christ at Armageddon?"

"It sure does," Joyce replied, "and if the Bible predicts that the Soviets will play a major role in the end, then they will."

"President Christos will deceive them as well. You can bank on it. But it won't be the Anti-Christ that will destroy them, it will be God Himself who will bring fire from Heaven and destroy them." Jake yawned and headed toward the stairs, "It's getting late, I think I'll call it a night. See you two in the morning. Goodnight."

"Goodnight, Jake."

Jake tossed and turned most of the night, the memory of Tracey and John did not permit him to sleep. He missed them both and at times his mind would play tricks on him. He could hear John calling him in the night. *"Dada, Dada."* He would hear him in his sleep, and it tugged at his heart. He lay there looking at the ceiling, tears streaming down his face. Oh, how he wished that he could be with the Lord and his family. He prayed to the Lord to give him strength to carry on, and the strength to die a martyr's death if he had to. He knew that the odds were good that he would meet that type of death, and he knew that the sooner it happened the sooner that he would be with the Lord. Somewhere in his tormented thoughts, the Lord comforted his pain and sleep found him.

The high-pitched scream jolted Jake from his sleep causing his heart to race and making it difficult to catch his breath. The scream came from the living room as Jake and Sam raced down the stairway to find out what had happened. Joyce sat on the sofa watching the television, her hand covering her mouth. She had a look of terror on her face as she reached to grab Sam's hand.

"What is it, Joyce?" Sam sat next to her and put his arms around her shoulders.

"They're gone." Joyce cried out, her voice cracking, "The U.S.A fleet in the Persian Gulf has been destroyed."

"What?-" Jake replied, "-How?"

"Listen, they're going to repeat the announcement."

The trio watched in horror as the news anchorman reported the story. The aerial pictures of the fleet floating in the Gulf was eerie. The bodies of sailors lay on the decks of the ships. There was no movement or sound, no sign of survivors or life of any kind.

"Repeating this breaking story-" the CNN reporter said, "-we have confirmed reports that a number of missiles, possibly three, have been launched from Baghdad and have targeted the American fleet in the Persian Gulf. They are believed to have been armed with nuclear warheads. All indications are that these warheads were armed with neutron bombs. As the aerial photos show, there appears to be no sign of life in the bodies of sailors strewn on the decks of all the ships in the region. Aircraft carriers and battleships, among others, are drifting with the current with no one manning the controls." The anchorman placed his hand on his ear piece appearing to be listening to someone. "We are now going to the war room where General Westheim will give an announcement."

"Joyce, do they know who launched the missiles?" Sam asked.

"I didn't hear them say; I was too shocked when I first found out."

"Do you think that the Russians are behind this?" Jake suggested; "Who else could do it?"

"Who knows. It could have been anyone." Sam reached to the television to raise the volume, "But I don't know who else would have that type of weapon."

"Here's the general." Joyce sat nervously on the sofa, crossing her arms and placing her hand on her mouth."

The general stood at the podium in his camouflage uniform, for a brief moment looking solemn and fatigued. Not a word was said and an eerie silence was in the room except for the sound of cameras flashing to record the images of this unforgettable turn of events.

"It is with great regret and profound sorrow-," the general began, "-that I have to announce that the American Naval Fleet in the Persian Gulf has, in fact, been destroyed by nuclear weapons. Three missiles carrying neutron bomb warheads were launched from Baghdad which hit their targets with pinpoint accuracy, resulting in the deaths of all sailors aboard the ships positioned in the Gulf. We are unable, at this time, to board any of those ships for fear of the radiation fallout that is still present." His voice cracking, General Westheim stood there trying to regain his composure. The decision to launch this attack was an emotional one for him. He had attacked an ally and placed the blame on Iraq, but he knew the truth and it haunted him. "A group of rene-gade Iraqi fundamentalists-" he continued, "-are responsible for the attack. Their whereabouts have been discovered and they have been destroyed. My heartfelt sympathy goes out to the fami-lies of these brave men and women who have lost their lives so that others may live in peace."

"Can you expand on who it was, exactly, that launched these missiles?" Charles Goodman shouted over the other reporters, "And where exactly were they found?"

"As far as I know the group was a militant group that was not associated in any way with the government of Iraq. How they got the nuclear warheads and the ability to launch them is unknown at this time but will be investigated. They were able to launch from a bunker located deep under ground and undetectable from the air. This bunker was located just south of Baghdad. We were only able to locate them after the launch of missiles when radar picked up the movement from the site. That is all the information I have at this time regarding the rebels."

The trio sat there watching the television, unable to look away from it. Thousands of men and women killed in an instant by an insane group of fanatics bent on revenge. Jake was sickened by the whole event but he could not get himself to look away as the general continued his announcement.

"We will continue to monitor the ships in the Gulf. Right now they are still drifting with the current and when it is safe to do so, we will get some of our people on the ships and bring them to port. These were neutron-type warheads that do little physical damage but kills anything in the vicinity. President Christos is aware of the events that have taken place and he has been in contact with President Andrews on this matter. I have nothing further at this time. I will continue to update you when new information is available and as the situation warrants. Thank you."

Jake got up and turned off the television. He did not want to see any more. The Anti-Christ was now in prime position to take over the world.

"Well it looks like the extent of President Christos' power is increasing, and it won't stop there." Jake looked at Sam and Joyce. "It's going to get worse from here on out. I think it's time to reduce my flight schedule so that I can help out with the cave more."

"That's fine, Jake," Joyce replied, "but consider it long and hard. Times will get worse but not for a while yet. Staying with Pan World Airlines for a while longer may be better for you at this time, and you don't want to leave Mary without hope. She needs you even though she doesn't know it. You'll just get bored here anyway. When we need more of your help, we'll let you know. But right now we're fine."

"I'll think about it a little more. But you're probably right. If I leave now I might never be able to get Mary to accept the Lord. She just isn't responding to the urging of the Holy Spirit."

"You've done all you can, Jake," Sam said consolingly. "But I think Joyce is right. If you leave the airline now, then you may never get her, and Randy for that matter, to accept Christ. And if they never accept Christ as their Savior, then you know you've done your best. We'll just have to live in the cave without them."

"I know." Jake replied, "I'm scheduled for a flight in three weeks that will take me to Tel-Aviv. I'll make my decision when I get back."

———————

President Mikial Vladikoff was an intelligent man, a man with incredible insight who had been fascinated since an early age with religion. He was not a spiritual man, nor did he believe in a creator, but he was very knowledgeable about what the Old Testament had to say. He passed off the New Testament as being just a myth, with no basis of truth and propagated by lunatics. But in the Old Testament were strategies of warfare that he could use even in today's world. So it was with this insight of the Old Testament, and namely the book of Ezekiel, that he had convinced the Arab Coalition leaders to surrender and accept the truce that President Christos had forced them to make with Israel. He had been proud of how he deceived President Christos. During their meeting he had promised to help with a quick end to the war by convincing the Arab coalition to accept the truce and, over the next two years, find a way to merge the government of the Soviet Union and the U.S.E. In return, his government was promised that they would continue to receive oil from the Middle East and an easing of trade restrictions, with an increase in imported food and crops. He knew he would never allow his government to be ruled by President Christos. His plan hinged on the deception that the Soviet Union was seeking a peaceful existence with the U.S.E. The U.S.E. would let its guard down, and that is when he would seize the opportunity to destroy President Christos.

President Vladikoff had invited the remaining leaders of the Arab Coalition to Moscow to discuss the end of the war and the plan that he had devised. He sat at the end of the long conference table waiting for the servants to finish giving refreshments to the leaders seated at the table with him. After the servants left he stood up and turned his back to the men, holding his hands behind his back.

President Vladikoff was a tall man with broad shoulders, and when he stood he towered over them. His mere size was intimidating and no one dared speak without permission. The skin of his bald head shone, reflecting the lights from above. He was no stranger to war and was proud of his service. He had fought in the war for Armenia and had received a severe, almost fatal wound to the face. The disfiguring scar remained and extended from the bottom inside corner of his right eye through his nose and left cheek to the left side of his neck just behind his ear. He was proud of the scar and wore it as a badge of honor. The eye itself had no color. A fibroid, solid, white-gray scar tissue had grown over the eye's entire surface leaving it unable to see. His left eye was of the deepest blue and sparkled in the light with the stare of a man possessed by something evil. He was ruthless and willing to kill without question anyone suspected of opposing his authority. His rise to power was proof. He had gained the office in a coup and was the one who gave the subsequent orders to have all former government officials executed and their bodies to be hung on the gallows as an example.

"I have called all of you here-" The Soviet president turned to face the men at the table, "-to explain to you why I have asked you to accept the truce that was offered to you last week. President Christos has assured me that if I could convince you to accept the offer of peace, he would not destroy you completely but would hold out his hand to you in friendship. When I advised you to accept the truce, I also told you to be patient. And I am asking you again to be patient for a little while longer."

"Yes and we have been patient-" interrupted King Hassan, the Egyptian, "-but you also ask us to do nothing while our brothers in Syria, Iran, and Iraq are murdered and forced to live under the illegal occupation of the United States of Europe. You ask to wait when we want to avenge the destruction of our Holy Mosque."

"Yes, I asked you all to wait. But what other choice did you have? It was either that or the complete destruction of all your brothers. But I have a plan. Soon we will overpower Israel and the U.S.E., and all the Middle East will be ours."

"How?" King Hassan asked. The short, dark-skinned man sat up in his seat.

"The Bible gives us the plan." President Vladikoff smiled, "Ezekiel thirty-eight gives us a plan that is fool proof."

"The Bible? It's nothing but a book of lies."

"Let me explain." Vladikoff continued, "When you accepted the peace treaty with Israel, you promised that you will no longer show aggression toward her. We must honor that agreement. You must open free trade with Israel and not allow terrorist attacks against her. Also, and without hesitation, you must put to death anyone who would try and launch such attacks on her. Become Israel's friend so that they would never expect that you would do her harm. Once this happens, she will ease security and remove any barriers that might be in place to hinder anyone from crossing her borders. When this happens, we will act; when they least expect aggression, we will attack."

"But how will we attack them?" the men at the table spoke almost as one.

"We will do it with horses." Premier Vladikoff could sense the confusion at the table. The men began to talk among themselves, shaking their heads. "Silence!" Vladikoff grew impatient. "We have had, since before our revolution, a cavalry with horses and men, brave men who know how to use them. We have hundreds of thousands of horses. We will gallop into Israel and destroy her, driving her people into the sea. They will not know what hit them.

The U.S.E. will not be able to counter attack unless they want to destroy the country with their bombs and weapons. And if they do? Then we still win, for the destruction of Israel is our goal. It doesn't matter if we do it or if the U.S.E. does it. In the end, the victory will be ours. The Bible gives us this, but the one fallacy that has always been the weakness of the Jewish people is the writer's notion of a God that will protect them. There is no God, and the prediction that such an attacking army could be destroyed by Him is nothing but a lie. When the time is right, we will attack them. Be patient. When that time comes you can rebuild your sacred mosque."

Chapter 7

Security was heightened. Secret Service Agents dressed in street clothes were scattered inconspicuously in the massive crowd that blanketed Central Park. Sharpshooters were positioned atop the buildings that surrounded the makeshift stage where Prophet Gallo was going to speak and getting the best vantage point possible to quell any attempt to harm the right-hand man of President Christos. New York City had anxiously waited two months for his arrival, planning meticulously the agenda for this event that promised to show miraculous signs and healings. Huge speakers, ten feet high and five feet across, were placed on either end of the stage to guarantee that the spectators at the farthest end of the park could hear the speech that Prophet Gallo was going to give. At the center of the stage stood the lectern, made of dark oak with the microphone sticking straight up and a clear bulletproof shield placed along its edges, surrounding anyone that would be positioned there. Directly behind the lectern were five chairs, reserved for the invited dignitaries that were going to be present.

The weather could not have been better as a slight, mildly cool breeze rattled the leaves of the trees that encompassed the park, causing a rustling sound that seemed to sooth Mary as she lay face up on the picnic blanket that she had placed just in front of the stage. The smell of the freshly cut grass filled her nostrils with every breath she took, and the sun's rays warmed her, almost lulling her to sleep. She stared up at the high wispy clouds that moved slowly eastward under the dark blue sky, her thoughts turning towards Randy and the Middle East war that had taken him away from home for the last month. He had so badly wanted to come to this event, but the war had made it impossible for him to attend, and Mary made the trip with Nancy Peterson, a new friend that she had made from going to the Unification World Church in Riverside. Randy would be home soon enough, and she looked forward to seeing him again.

The dignitaries filed onto the stage and took their seats. The Mayor of New York City was first in line followed by the two New York State senators and Vice President Samuelson. Prophet Gallo was last in line and dressed in a white satin robe highlighted by dark red fringes. Something about him caught Mary's attention, and she felt drawn to this man who was said to have supernatural powers. His eyes met hers as he sat into his chair. He was nothing like she had remembered him from television in the early days after the Rapture. He was no longer that meek-looking gentleman that she saw on the CNN reports. The short gray-haired man that she remembered seemed to have a higher level of confidence, and he actually looked younger and stronger. If there ever was a fountain of youth, then Prophet Gallo had found it. Mary could not stop staring at him and looked away only when he would glance at her. She didn't know what it was about him, but he had a magnetism, a presence of confidence that could be seen in his outward appearance, and he had an aura of power in his stride. She had come in doubt with a "seeing is believing" attitude, not trusting in all that she was hearing about Prophet Gallo or of President Christos. But the mere presence of this man and the power that seemed to radiate from him had changed her mind, and the miracles that she had come to see to further convince her were no longer necessary. This man was of God.

"I wish Randy could be here to see this." Mary turned to Nancy. "He was right … things are going to get better from here on out."

"I can just feel the strength that comes from him." Nancy smiled. "He's a handsome man."

"I wouldn't go that far. But you're right; you can tell by just looking at him that he has a strength ... a strength that is unexplainable."

Nancy Peterson was a young and attractive twenty-five-year-old. Her shoulder-length, sandy blonde hair had a silky shine and curled inward towards her face touching the corners of her pink lips. Her green eyes seemed to have a sparkle to them and were enhanced by her light complexion and high rosy cheeks. She was an educated woman, graduating from Notre Dame with a Bachelor of Science degree in Humanities and Social Behavior. Like Mary, she was skeptical of the Unification World Church at first but had been convinced of the godliness of Father Christos by what she had been told and had read in the newspapers. She was here now to see firsthand the power that she had been hearing about.

Mary and Nancy could feel the energy that radiated within the massive audience as everyone sensed that something miraculous was about to happen. A low roar seemed to permeate the entire park as the people in the crowd were speaking to each other. Mary and Nancy could hardly hear themselves. The patience of the spectators had started to wane by the time Mayor Jackson stepped to the podium to start the event. He was a tall, thin man of African-American descent. His white hair betrayed his age, looking much older than his fifty-three years.

"May I have your attention?" Mayor Jackson said, speaking into the microphone, "I would like to start by saying 'welcome,' and I would also like to welcome our honorable State Senators Joe Hatcher and Cynthia Finegold. I would also like to welcome our vice president, William Samuelson, who has come here despite his very busy schedule to join us on this special occasion." The roar of a passing airliner overhead drowned out the mayor's voice, and he paused to take a sip of water and to wait until the plane had flown past. "We are honored," he continued, "to have with us Prophet Gallo who has graciously agreed to demonstrate to us his supernatural powers, powers that have been given to him from God under the authority of President Christos. Prophet Gallo-" the Mayor turned to face the man in the white satin robe and bowed, "-the City of New York welcomes you."

The audience cheered and Prophet Gallo gave a smile, raising his right hand and waving in acknowledgment of the friendly welcome. He had won New York City over to his side without as much as uttering a word, and he would play on the emotions that he was observing.

"Without further delay," the mayor said as he once again spoke into the microphone, "I would now like to invite our vice president to say a few words, and then we will invite Prophet Gallo to give his presentation. Vice President Samuelson," the mayor looked towards the vice president, "the podium is yours."

Vice President Samuelson stepped up to the podium and greeted Mayor Jackson, shaking his hand, and the two smiled at each other. Mayor Jackson leaned into the vice president and mouthed some words to him that were not audible to the crowd. The mayor sat down and the vice president faced the large audience.

Vice President Samuelson was a well-liked political figure in the United States of America because he bucked the tide of political thinking, a rebel *with* a cause as some called him. He was known to publicly speak out against President Andrews and the president's stance on foreign affairs. He was a veteran of the Marines, having served in the Gulf war against Iraq in the early 'nineties and receiving the Purple Heart for wounds suffered as the ground troops launched their invasion after the air campaign had ended. Americans had long been fickle about the importance of military experience of their leaders. They hated soldiers during war, discriminating against them upon returning home and blaming them as if it was they who started the war. But it was war experience that the public used as a measuring rod for any one who would seek public office and so it was for the vice president. Vice President Samuelson's experience added to his credibility, and he was riding high on the wave of the political movement to join the government of the U.S.E. His popularity was increasing, not so much for his achievements in his political career, which were many, but because of the courage to speak out against a president that most Americans felt was ruining the country. And he would use this opportunity to speak out again, bringing more discontent with the president and more respect and honor to President Christos, with whom he hoped to find favor.

Vice President Samuelson was relatively young for a man with such political backing. His appearance did not reflect his forty-nine years but was a mirage of a youthful hunger and ambition striking out at each opportunity to enhance his stature. He had a full head of dark brown hair, which hid any gray that might be found there, and his large light brown eyes seemed to be able to penetrate any who would fall into his line of vision. His large frame was intimidating and his character demanded respect.

"I have been invited," he began his discourse, "not just because I am a member of the Unification World Church, but because, like you, I represent what this country wants for our future. We need to achieve harmony and peace and assurance that we, our children, and our children's children will enjoy a life without war, without hunger, and that we will live in a world where there is no sorrow." He stood there at the podium staring at the crowd, knowing that what he was saying was evoking a heated response in the emotions of everyone in the park. He played with their minds and easily manipulated them like a puppeteer would a puppet show. His hands could easily pluck the strings of the dolls that were now under his control. He used this opportunity, as well, to speak out against President Andrews, further diminishing the power of his office and turning the people against him. "We need President Christos and we need the Unification World Church in order to make that dream a reality. President Andrews, although a man who loves his country, has failed to achieve any stability in this country. He has weakened our military, putting our fighting men and women in harm's way-so much so that thousands were killed last week in a futile attempt by the Iraqi government to defend itself. Prophet Gallo is here today, my fellow Americans, to show us what kind of power that a man who puts his trust in God will have. Believe me when I say this, but the power that Prophet Gallo will demonstrate here today is three-fold in President Christos, the President of the U.S.E. and future ruler of the world." He paused for a moment to let the cheering crowd settle down, then added, "Thank you and let's make our country better.

We can make it happen with the help of the Unification World Church and its leaders."

The crowd roared its approval as the vice president took his seat. Mary was standing as well, giving an ovation with tears rolling down her cheeks. For the first time since joining the Church, she knew that it was worth it. She no longer doubted, believing as Randy did that President Christos with the help of Prophet Gallo was going to make the world a much better place, and they were going to do it by setting up God's kingdom on earth. She knew it now-without even hearing a word uttered from Prophet Gallo.

The mayor got up and stepped to the podium, clapping his approval as well. He stood there waiting for the crowd to settle down before introducing Prophet Gallo. "Without further delay, I introduce Prophet Gallo."

Prophet Gallo stood and slowly made his way to the podium with the audience screaming louder than ever. He stood there looking at the audience that had anticipated his speech, raising his hands to quiet the crowd. He seemed to look right at Mary as he started to speak.

"Why have you come here?" he began, "to see a man give an inspirational speech? Or-" he continued, "-did you come to see me perform miracles?" Prophet Gallo stood there silently, for a moment gauging his audience. "I have come to do neither of these but have come to give glory to God and his son Alexander Christos. It is Alexander Christos that has been given authority to give power to those that trust in him. That power comes from the Almighty God, who has given it to His son and your lord, Alexander Christos. It is he that you need to trust. Follow him and the World will live in peace, without hunger, and without sorrow, just as Vice President Samuelson described it." Prophet Gallo again paused and appeared to glow. His appearance, as one being transfigured, gave the audience the illusion of holiness and many fell to their knees, worshipping the figure on the stage. "I am not here to perform miracles but to reveal the power of our god. For the power of our god is not a miracle, but a supernatural power that has been given to me through his son Alexander Christos so that the son may be glorified.

If you have seen the son, then you have seen the father, for the two of them are one. Therefore worship the son, Alexander Christos, as you would the father."

There was an eerie silence in the crowd, like the calm before the storm or the awkward silence in the court room just before the foreman of the jury renders their verdict. Something tremendous was about to happen and Mary, like all the others, sensed it. The electricity in the air was igniting all the senses in the human body and everyone there knew that the power of God was going to be revealed. The brightness of the midday sun turned dark as the clouds rolled in, and the rumblings of thunder could be heard in the distance. Prophet Gallo looked skyward, and all knew that it was he that was causing the change in the sky. The clouds now seemed to be billowing and taking on a life of their own and getting closer with each passing moment. He reached his arms to the sky and, in a loud voice like the blast of a trumpet, he screamed out, "Behold the power of our god!" And at that moment lightning streaked across the darkened sky, snaking its way through the clouds, causing a thunderous noise and resembling arteries branching out above the entire park, and causing a tingling static to all who were there. Some stood, praising the god of Prophet Gallo and of Alexander Christos. Others fell to the ground, no longer strong enough to stand. But there was no one present that remained unconvinced of the power that was shown to them or from where the power came. God was alive and well in Alexander Christos, and nothing was going to stop God's kingdom on Earth from becoming a reality.

Prophet Gallo took his seat and leaned into Vice President Samuelson. "I would like to have a word with you in my temporary office after this is over."

"Ye ... yes, Sir Prophet Gallo," Samuelson stuttered, seemingly in shock himself, "a ... as soon as we get backstage I'll be at your disposal."

"Good. What I have to say to you is very important and cannot wait. President Christos will want to hear from me tonight when we are finished talking. We both hope that we can count on your help."

"You can count on me, sir. I'll help you in any way that I can."

"I hope so." Gallo replied, "For the sake of the world, I hope so."

It didn't take long for Vice President Samuelson to arrive at the temporary office of Prophet Gallo located inside the U.N. building. He had been nervous about the meeting and could not think of why the world depended on his help. But he wouldn't question Prophet Gallo on that point, especially after what he saw at Central Park. Was this his chance to find favor with Alexander Christos? The world was going in the direction that he hoped the Unites States of America would, but President Andrews insisted on still doing things his way which only had resulted in a poor economy and a country populace that felt it had no leadership to guide them. He stood outside the door and took a deep breath before entering.

"Ah ... Vice President Samuelson." Prophet Gallo held his arms out and embraced him by the shoulders, "Please be seated. Can I get you anything to eat or drink?"

"No thank you, Sir." Samuelson sat on a chair next to Prophet Gallo's desk, "I'm fine."

Prophet Gallo sat in his chair, placing his arms on the top of the desk, and interlaced his fingers.

"Let me be direct, shall I?" Prophet Gallo took a deep breath then sat back into his chair. "As you know President Andrews has been resisting our attempts to 'merge,' if you'll allow me to use that term, our two great countries. He resists even after President Christos has promised not to remove him from office. He would still be the leader of America, although the title would be changed from president to governor, and still have all the benefits of being the leader."

"Yes, Sir." Samuelson replied, "I am aware of his resistance. But he is of the old school. National sovereignty and survival are his main concerns."

"I admire his loyalty. But this is a new world. President Christos is not concerned with national sovereignty but of world sovereignty and survival. We thought that with the tragedy in the Gulf last week with the destruction of the American fleet that he would see how weak he had become and come running to join our government."

"He was very saddened by the tragedy-"

"As we all were." Prophet Gallo interrupted, "But he is holding us back. As you know we have been meeting with your people from the Pentagon. We were hoping that the military would join us without President Andrews' permission, but there are some who, like President Andrews, remain loyal to a national survival way of thinking. What we need is a man, who if he were president and commander in chief, would order his nation's government and military to join ours."

"But it would take more than just the president to force such an order. There are some in Congress who think the same way as our president."

"But they are only a few."

"But it takes only a few to tip the scales one way or the other."

"Yes. But if those few were gone and replaced by others who, let's say...were more sympathetic to our goal, then you would agree that it would be possible."

Samuelson stared at Prophet Gallo ever so briefly, "What are you suggesting, Sir?"

"What I'm suggesting-" leaning forward on his desk, "-is that if we can arrange for you to become president of the United States of America, would you order the military to merge with ours?"

"But like I said, Congress-"

"That will be arranged as well. You will have no obstacles with the order, not from Congress or the Pentagon."

Samuelson took a deep breath and leaned his head on the back of the chair. This is what he'd always wanted and now it was in his grasp. Should he ask how? Would he want to know? It didn't matter; he wanted the job at all costs.

"Okay," he said, "if you can arrange for me to take office, I'll give the order."

"Good. And you will remain in office even after the merger of our two countries. But you will answer to President Christos."

"But how? How will it take place?"

"Shall we say ... that President Andrews and those few in Congress who oppose us will not live to see the sun rise tomorrow? You will be sworn into office and then you will give the order. Congress will not deny you your order, and our countries will be one."

———————

The Jerusalem sun was setting in the westward sky over the Great Sea, the Mediterranean, as Randy Johnson and General Kemp traveled in their jeep to the headquarters of General Westheim. It had been a week since the end of the war and already there was talk of rebuilding the Jewish Temple on the site of the destroyed Dome of the Rock Islamic Holy Place. The Jewish people and all of Israel celebrated the victory that would now allow peace in the Middle East and the rebuilding of a long-lost temple to worship as they should. Randy Johnson was driving and General Kemp was his passenger, both relieved that the war was over and pleased to know that soon they both would be allowed to return to the States.

"These people sure are fanatical about their temple aren't they, General?" asked Randy, "They're already talking about rebuilding it and it's only been a week."

"I've never seen a people so happy about something being destroyed," General Kemp responded. "They've been waiting for this a long time. Rumor has it that Israel will reestablish animal sacrifices for their sins. A strange lot of people they are."

"This country will celebrate for a long time to come. They no longer have to worry about being driven into the sea by their long-time enemies."

"The war was a total success, and they know it," the general quickly added. "President Christos has taken over Syria, Iraq, and Iran." The general chuckled a bit, "He's got the Middle East so scared that another seven countries of the Arab coalition want to join the U.S.E They're afraid that he will take them over by force if they don't join, so they'd rather join."

"Yeah-" Randy responded, "-the war was a success except for the destruction of our fleet in the Gulf."

"Don't be so naive Randy-" the general said, shaking his head, "-that was all planned. It was part of the price we were willing to pay for victory."

"What?" Randy looked at the general and had almost driven off the road. "What do you mean the attack was planned?"

"Just keep your eyes on the road. Do you honestly think that a renegade group of Iraqi terrorists could obtain one, let alone three, nuclear weapons and the missiles required to deliver them? We launched those missiles at our fleet. I devised the plan and President Christos and General Westheim ate it up."

"How could you do that?" Randy's voice got louder. "How can you live with yourself, Russ?"

"You better watch how you talk to me, Randy. Friends or not, I am still your superior."

"Yes Sir, General, but why? Couldn't there have been a better way? I still can't believe that you could help plan such a thing."

"Look Randy, if there was a better way, don't you think we would have tried it? I didn't want to lose those men and women, but something had to be done to get President Christos to take over the United States. The American people wanted it and we at the Pentagon wanted it. You knew that our goal was to merge the two countries."

"Merge the two countries? Yes, that's what I wanted too. But to murder your own is not the way I would have done it."

"Randy, in order to become great, sacrifices, sometimes costly sacrifices, have to be made. Yes, thousands of lives were taken, but it is going to merge the two most powerful countries in the world. That sacrifice was a necessity for it to happen."

"But, General, how could a man like President Christos, who claims to have the power of God, do such a thing? If he has God's power, then he could have done it in a different way. He is no religious leader of mine." Randy was disgusted. Could he have really fallen for this man? It was all fake-the church and all the false promises.

"I'm going to forget you said that, Randy," Kemp was angry and stared at Randy. "President Christos is not only my president but he is also my spiritual leader as well. It will go better with you to not question his leadership."

"Is that a threat ... General?" Randy said condescendingly, "Well, I still don't buy into it. He's not the president of America yet."

"He will be and soon. It's all but a done deal. If things go as we have planned, then President Christos will be taking over the leadership of the U.S.A. this week, and America will have me to thank for it. I came up with the plan to launch a strike on the fleet in the Gulf and as a result the two countries will join together. President Christos is going to take over; I have no doubt. That's why I am being called to meet with General Westheim today. They're probably going to give me a medal for this." The general sat there with a smile on his face. He had longed, ever since his childhood, to be a military hero and to be awarded handsomely for it. This was going to be his day, and he looked forward to the accolades that he knew he deserved.

A medal? Maybe the medal of shame is what Randy wanted to say but dared not. They reached the outskirts of the temporary headquarters of General Westheim, neither of the two men speaking. Kemp seemed to be basking in a daydream, probably of himself being pinned with a medal. For the first time in his career Randy was ashamed to be in uniform. He had wanted the merger of the U.S.E and U.S.A. as much as anyone, but not this way-with the murder of thousands of men and women-but in a peaceful way. It sickened him that a high-ranking official such as General Kemp could conspire to destroy his own. He no longer looked at President Christos as one that was going to save the world, for one would not have to do it by destroying human lives. He started to doubt all that the Unification World Church stood for. President Christos' hypocrisy and evil nature was revealed by the ruthless action conceived from the heart of a so-called man of God. Maybe Jake was right, he thought, for only a man possessed by Satan could follow through on such an evil act. The American people would have never wanted a man like that to rule them if they knew who was behind the attack and then blame the ingenious plan, and the murder of thousands, on the people of Iraq. His mind still racing with the thought, he pulled up in front of General Westheim's headquarters and turned off the ignition.

"I want you to come in with me," General Kemp said as he got out of the jeep.

"I'd rather stay here if you don't mind, General." Randy responded still overcome with anger and guilt.

"I do mind." the general responded, "I want you to come in."

"Yes, Sir." Randy sheepishly stepped out of the jeep mocking a salute.

The two entered into the outer office where the secretary was sitting behind her desk.

General Kemp and Randy walked up to the desk as the short blonde-haired secretary looked up at them.

"General Kemp to see General Westheim," Randy said to the secretary.

"Just a moment," the woman responded, then called General Westheim through the intercom. "General Westheim? General Kemp is here to see you."

"Send him in," the voice on the other end said.

The two walked towards the door of General Westheim's office. There were two chairs just outside the door positioned on either side of the opening.

"You have a seat here, Randy; this probably won't take too long."

"Yes, Sir, General."

General Kemp entered the door but failed to close it fully, leaving it ajar a few inches. Randy could see a soldier in the room with his back towards the door. He was a large man with broad shoulders, but he moved out of Randy's view before he could get a better look. Randy could hear every word said through the narrow opening; the conversation was as clear as if it were in front of him.

"General Kemp," Westheim said, "have a seat."

"Thank you, Sir"

"This is Sergeant Miller and Sergeant Reed," General Westheim introduced the two soldiers that were present. Randy sat there looking down at the floor and fidgeted uncomfortably-the conversation with General Kemp about the American fleet still on his mind and piquing his anger.

"You're probably wondering why I called you here, Russ. I wanted to congratulate you in person on a job well done for your effort in the war."

"Thank you, Sir."

"As you know, we have been able to take over the three countries that we did battle with-also there are a number of other Arab countries that will join the U.S.E next week."

"Yes, Sir." General Kemp responded. "I have heard that."

"President Christos is very pleased with the outcome, that goes without saying. This action will force the Arab countries to accept a peace pact with Israel. He is especially pleased about Iraq, taking a special liking to its territory. He is even talking about rebuilding the ancient city of Babylon and making it a great city again. He wanted me to give you, personally, his thanks for a job well done on the matter of the U.S. fleet in the Gulf; it will help him in his goal of taking over the leadership of the United States. Again, a job well done." General Westheim paused for a moment as he stared at General Kemp. Turning to Sergeant Miller, "Sergeant?"

"Yes, Sir." the sergeant replied.

"Take General Kemp to the courtyard and have him shot for treason."

"What!" General Kemp shouted out, his heart racing. "What do you mean?"

"You turned your back on your country and your men-" General Westheim responded, "-you can't be trusted."

"No-" screamed General Kemp and ran towards the door, "-you can't do this to me. You and I planned this together with President Christos."

Sergeant Miller and Sergeant Reed blocked his path to the door, each grabbing General Kemp's arms, hand-shackling him and restraining him from reaching the entrance.

"You're going to do this to me without even a trial?" Kemp

shouted out in a vain attempt to buy time.

"Trial?" General Westheim replied, walking up to the prisoner and staring him in the eye. "President Christos is judge and jury ... and you've been convicted. After you shoot this traitor-" he said, looking at the two soldiers, "-round up all his assistants, secretaries and anyone who might know the truth about the missile strike against the fleet and have them executed as well. This secret can't get out."

Randy stood, his heart pounding, not wanting to believe what he had just heard. He had to get out of there-but to where? They would find him if he went back to his headquarters. *Just get out of here.* Making sure no one was looking, he ran out of the door that he had entered and jumped into the jeep. Night had settled on Jerusalem as he drove off into the darkness with his headlights off. His headquarters were out of the question if he wanted to survive. Desertion was his only option, but it would come with a price on his head. He had found out the hard way about the falsehood of President Christos and of the Unification World Church. Jake was right, he thought, as he drove on, not paying attention to where he was going; President Christos did not have the power of the true God but of Satan, and he would use that power to take over the world. Where he was going he did not know. All he knew was that he had to get away from there.

The headlines the following morning surprised an already mourning country and world. President Andrews, along with eight senators and two representatives, were dead. The cause of the deaths was unknown, but all had died in their sleep. An investigation had begun. The newly sworn President Samuelson mourned the death of his friend and ordered that flags were to be flown at half-mast in honor of the fallen leaders.

Chapter 8

*J*ake felt nauseous sitting in the darkness of the holding cell as he recited Psalm 23 to himself. The only light that entered were the rays of sunlight that filtered through the small cracks that permeated in from the outer walls. The light was barely able to illuminate the inside of the small chamber, but there was nothing inside that was worth seeing anyway. He could see the blade of the guillotine through one such opening, raised to the highest point of the device and supported there by a thick rope. It would remain there until it was time to be released again to slice through the neck of its next victim, severing the head with a sound resembling a meat cleaver striking a butcher block. Jake watched the blade fall again, getting louder as it picked up speed and approached its victim. He could hear the crowd scream their approval as the severed head fell into the large straw basket positioned below the table where the victim was strapped. Jake was going to be next and was powerless to do anything about it. He could hear footsteps just outside and the clanging of the key entering the keyhole. The executioner opened the door to the holding cell and looked in at Jake.

"It's time," the executioner said.

Jake paused for a moment looking up towards the doorway. He could see only the black silhouette of the large man against the *bright aura of sun light that streamed in around him. Jake's plan to survive the Tribulation had failed, but he would not resist his fate for soon he would be with the Lord and with Tracey and John. Jake emerged from the cell and stepped up onto the platform where the guillotine was place. Two guards tied his hands behind his back and led him towards the killing device. He could see the blade being lifted again with blood still dripping from its edge. Blood remained on the table where the victims lay, the executioner not wasting time to clean the crimson fluid from the table's cold surface. The guards placed Jake on the table and put his neck in the restraining apparatus and closed it tightly. There was no escaping its grasp. Jake looked into the basket below and saw the head of the previous martyr with its eyes wide open and staring back. The executioner stood alongside, wearing a black hood over his head and waited for the order from Alexander Christos to drop the blade. Jake closed his eyes and awaited his fate.*

The ringing of the phone aroused Jake from this nightmare. His heart was racing, and he sat straight up in bed with beads of sweat trickling down his face. He could see the phone clearly, illuminated by the light blue glow of the full moon that streamed through the window and into his room. Jake looked at the clock and rubbed his eyes. *Four in the morning?* Jake sat up in bed, trying to catch his breath, as the phone repeated its ring and begged to be answered. His hands were wet with perspiration and still trembling when he reached to answer the phone, wondering who could be calling this early in the morning. Jake was anxious and inhaled deeply before picking up the phone.

"Hello."

"Hello Jake?" the voice on the other end said, "Is that you?"

"Yeah. Who is this?"

"It's Randy."

"What?" Jake reached to turn on a light, "My God … Randy, where are you?"

"I'm in Jerusalem. I've been hiding out here for the last month."

"What the hell is going on?" Jake asked. "Everyone is looking for you. Your picture is posted everywhere. You've even made the

FBI's Ten Most Wanted list. They're saying that you and General Kemp helped plan the attack on the American fleet in the Gulf with the help of the Iraqi government. Randy, General Kemp has been executed." There was an awkward silence, and Jake tried to make sense of it all. Could he really be talking to Randy? A close friend now wanted by the government for treason?

"I know they have," Randy said dejectedly breaking the silence, "Don't believe everything that you've been hearing. It's not true. They would have executed me too if I didn't run. Jake, I didn't know anything about the attack on the fleet. It was a plan by President Christos and his generals to merge the United States of Europe and America. I had nothing to do with it and neither did the Iraqi government."

"What do you mean the Iraqis didn't have anything to do with it?"

"The whole thing was a secret plan by President Christos and Generals Westheim and Kemp. They schemed the plan to blame the Iraqis. The missiles were launched from Baghdad by the U.S.E. military. Afterwards President Christos ordered General Kemp and his staff to be executed so that the secret wouldn't leak out. But I overheard the plot and escaped."

"My God, Randy, what are you going to do now?"

"I don't know. I was hoping that maybe you could help me."

"I'm flying to Tel Aviv next Wednesday. I had planned on going to Jerusalem for a couple of days to take in some of the sights. Do you think that you could meet me?"

"Yeah, I'll meet you." Randy answered, "In the meantime maybe we can figure out a way to get me home."

"Maybe we can slip you onto the plane when we depart. I'm not sure what we can do … I need to think this through. Don't worry, we'll figure out something. Do you think you can hang on until then?"

"I think so. I've been hiding out with a Christian family in the Christian Quarter of the city. I'm safe here for now."

"Have you called Mary?"

"No." Randy replied. "I'm worried that they may have her phone bugged. I've missed her. How is she holding up?"

"She's holding up as well as can be expected. She's worried sick about you." Jake hedged a little, "Randy, she's convinced more than ever about Alexander Christos and his powers-"

"What?"

"She saw Prophet Gallo at Central Park about a month ago and he put on a display of power for the audience. I'm worried about her."

"I got to get home," Randy replied, sounding desperate, "You have to help me."

"I will Randy ... just hang tight. Do you want me to tell her that you called?"

"No. I don't want her to know anything yet."

"But she's worried about you and-"

"No, Jake." Randy interrupted, "That will only increase the chance of the government finding me. I'd rather wait until I get back to the States. It will be safer that way."

"Okay," Jake replied, "I won't say anything."

"Jake?" Randy's voice cracked and he sounded as if he was crying. "I've accepted the Lord as my Savior. It took some drastic measures, but I know now that you were right. You've got to get me home so that we can help Mary."

"We'll get you home and help Mary," Jake replied consolingly. "Just don't worry."

"Living with this Christian family over the last month has taught me a lot. I understand more now of what you tried to tell me. I just wanted you to know."

"Thanks, Randy, you don't know how much that means. In the meantime, keep the faith. I have an idea that might get you back in the States and here in Denver. The cave would be the perfect hide-out for you."

"How are we going to do that?"

"What do you think about sneaking you on the plane as a pilot for Pan World Airlines and you can fly back with us in the cockpit. I can get a pilot's uniform for you."

"But what about your copilot?"

"Steve's a Christian," Jake replied. "He's been my copilot for a few months now. He accepted the Lord shortly after the Rapture like I did. When I tell him the story, I know that he'll do anything to help."

"Are you sure that he can be trusted?"

"I'm very sure. But we don't have much of a choice. We're just going to have to take a chance."

Randy hesitated. "Okay. But if we're caught together, that means that you'll probably get executed along with me."

"I know." Jake replied, "But it's a chance that I'm willing to take. Let's meet in Jerusalem on Friday next week. Is there a place that I can meet you?"

"In the heart of the Christian Quarter there's a produce market. You can't miss it. It's the biggest one in that section. I'll be at the north side at noon. Just be there, and I'll find you."

"Okay, then it's settled. I'll see noon next Friday."

"Remember, I don't want Mary to know about this yet. I'll see her soon enough."

"Okay, Randy. Hang on another week and we'll get you home."

Jake hung up the phone and sat on the bed, not believing what had just occurred. Randy was alive, and now he was going to try and get him back to the States. He lay back down on the pillow and looked up at the ceiling. What had he gotten himself into? But he had no choice except to help his friend and fellow Christian. Would his plan work? He wasn't sure but he had to try. His copilot to Tel Aviv was a Christian and zealous about his new faith, but would he lay his life on the line for a friend of a friend?

"Jake, is everything okay?" Joyce poked her head through the bedroom door. "The phone woke me up."

"What?" Jake was startled and let out a long breath. "Oh, Joyce. Come in … You won't believe it. That was Randy Johnson."

"Randy Johnson?" Joyce responded, "Where is he? Is he okay?"

"He's fine … a little anxious, but fine. He's in Jerusalem hiding out in the Christian Quarter." Jake got out of bed and put on his robe. "Let's go downstairs and get some coffee. I'll tell you more about it then."

The two went down the stairs quietly so as not to wake Sam. Joyce turned on the kitchen light and sat impatiently at the table, curiosity building inside her. Jake made a pot of coffee, which to Joyce seemed to take forever, then came to the table and sat down.

"Well, what's going on?" Joyce was no longer able to contain her curiosity.

"He was set up. He had nothing to do with the attack on the fleet. It was a conspiracy by President Christos and his general. The reason Randy fled was because they were going to execute him along with General Kemp."

"But why would President Christos want to attack the American fleet and execute General Kemp and Randy?"

"So he could take over the United States. And the plan worked, but it backfired on General Kemp. General Kemp was the one who came up with the plan to launch a strike against the fleet. He was executed because President Christos wanted to make sure that the secret didn't get out. He also ordered the execution of his staff, but Randy escaped and he's been hiding in Jerusalem ever since."

"So it was a plan all along to gain control of the United States?" Joyce shook her head in disbelief. "And now Randy is being made a scapegoat. What is he going to do now?"

"You mean what are we going to do now?" Jake replied. "I'm going to try to get him home next week when I fly to Israel."

"How are you going to do that? Jake, I don't know. That's going to be dangerous."

"I know, but I have to try. I think that I can get him on the plane if he wears a pilot's uniform and disguises himself as my copilot."

"But what about Steve? Have you asked him if it is okay with him? He may not want to take that risk."

"I know. I'll have to talk to him. I think that he will want to help, but I won't know for sure until I ask. He's been really zealous with his faith, and I think that anything that could be considered a Christian victory will spur him to do it."

"I hope so," Joyce stood and went to pour herself and Jake a cup of coffee, "it would be nice to get Randy home. Are you going to tell Mary?"

"Randy doesn't want her to know yet. He doesn't think that it will be safe."

"Do you plan on Randy living here?"

"I think that it would be too dangerous for him to stay at the cabin. But the cave would be perfect for him. He's had survivor training with the commando elite force, and he would adjust well."

"But that's a long time to stay there-"

"He has no choice if he wants to survive," Jake interrupted. "We'll be with him soon enough once we have to go there permanently."

"What about Mary?" Joyce placed a cup in front of Jake then sat in the seat next to his.

Jake sighed. "I don't know. I'm hoping that when she hears what happened to Randy that she'll have second thoughts about President Christos and the Church. But let's take one thing at a time. Let's get Randy home."

The plane sat on the tarmac at JFK International Airport, waiting to depart for Rome. The storm had kept planes grounded for more than four hours but now had shown signs of easing, with the sun making a periodic appearance through the holes in the dissipating dark clouds. Ground crews worked feverously to clear the runway of snow and ice in the hope to relieve the long line of planes that had been mounting for the last few hours. Jake sat fidgeting in the cockpit, waiting for permission from the control tower to take off. He hated long delays, but this one stretched his patience to the limit. His plane would be the first to take off, but that was no consolation to him. He had yet to discuss his plan to rescue Randy with his copilot, and that added to his anxiety. He would talk to him during the flight to Rome and hoped that Steve would agree with the plot.

Steve Anderson was a short, muscular man with a deeply receding hairline. He had dark brown hair, and although clean shaven, his thick beard gave him a constant five o'clock shadow. He was an intelligent man, and he knew by the nervous habits that Jake was expressing that something was not right. Jake's constant tugging of his mustache and the tapping of his feet against the floor board was getting under Steve's skin until he couldn't take it any longer.

"Are you okay?" Steve asked.

Jake looked over at Steve and gave a slight chuckle, "Is it that obvious?"

"Yeah." Steve responded, "You've been pulling at your mustache ever since we sat down. I'm surprised that you have any hair on your lip. And you've been doing a tap dance that would put Gene Kelley to shame. I know it's been a long delay, but relax, we'll get to Rome."

"I know. But that's not all that's bothering me."

"What is it then?"

Jake wiped his mouth and took a deep breath and started to speak.

"Flight 642, you are clear to take off." The voice on the other end of the radio interrupted.

"Roger," Jake spoke into the microphone then looked at Steve. "We'll continue our conversation when we get in the air, Steve."

The plane taxied to the beginning of the runway and remained there for a moment. The vibration of the jet engines shook the plane and increased in intensity as the power was increased. The plane moved forward; slowly at first before picking up speed then lifting off the runway and ascending high above New York City and into the clouds. It took only a few moments to pierce the dark cloud cover revealing the bright sunshine and dark blue sky that was hidden by the storm below. This is what Jake loved most about flying-the endless space and openness that surrounded him at cruising altitude. It was there, high in the sky, that he found freedom from the cares of the world. He was at home in the cockpit and felt safe there, especially in the months since the Rapture. There was always sunshine and blue sky during the day or bright moon light and stars at night, regardless of the weather that raged on earth below. Jake took a slow, deep breath as though the peace that he found at such a high altitude could remain deep within his soul if only he could inhale as much of the air as he could. It reminded him of the day he brought Tracey and John home from the hospital. He remembered that day clearly. There was a crisp chill in the air that day, and the sun shone brightly. It was so peaceful and he couldn't remember when he had been so happy. That was the happiest day of his life, and he hadn't felt that kind of peace since then, that is until now. And as he sat in the pilot's seat, the Lord eased his anxiety. He no longer worried about revealing to Steve his plan to save Randy.

"All right," Steve said, "What's on your mind?"

"I should have asked you sooner." Jake responded, "But until just a few moments ago I didn't know how to ask. I have a friend who needs my-," Jake searched for the right words, "-I should say our help."

"Okay, that's all you need to say. What do you need me to do?"

"Let me explain the situation before you give me your answer. The friend that needs our help is Randy Johnson."

"Mary's husband?" Steve responded quickly, "The same Randy Johnson that's wanted by the government?"

"Yeah-" Jake replied slowly, "-the same Randy Johnson."

"I don't know, Jake. You do realize what he did, don't you? He conspired with the Iraqis to destroy the fleet in the Gulf."

"No, he didn't. He was framed by the U.S.E. government. It was President Christos that gave the order to launch those missiles from Baghdad-"

"What?"

"It was done as a way for Christos to gain control of the United States and the western hemisphere."

"Are you sure of that? ... How would you know?"

"I talked to Randy a few days ago, and he explained everything that happened. He's been living with a Christian family in Jerusalem for the last month. He ran because he overheard orders from General Westheim to execute General Kemp and all his staff. Randy knew nothing of the attack on the fleet until after it happened."

"And you believe him? What if he's lying?"

"Steve, I know Randy well ... he's not lying. He told me that he has accepted the Lord as his Savior. He believes that Alexander Christos is the Anti-Christ just as we do. It was this whole mess that finally convinced him."

"Okay-" Steve wiped his hand across his mouth. "-how do I help?"

"Think about this first. If you get caught with us we'll probably all get executed. Are you sure you want to help?"

"I'm single and have no children," Steve answered, "It doesn't matter what happens to me. If I can help a fellow Christian, then that's what I'll do."

"Thanks, Steve. I think that we can get him back if we disguise him in a pilot's uniform and have him fly with us back to New York in the cockpit. That's why I needed to tell you. There was no way that I would have been able to do that unless I told you about it first. That's why I need your help."

"I'm not sure we can do it even with my help. But if I have to die, then it might as well be in an effort to save a Christian brother."

Chapter 9

⚜

T he control tower at Ben-Gurion International Airport had
cleared the plane for landing. The relatively short flight
from Rome had passed quickly and Jake prepared the approach
into Tel-Aviv. The city had been established in the early 1900's
by Jewish settlers just north of the ancient site of Joppa, located
on a small promontory jutting into the Mediterranean and almost
completely fronted by white sand beaches. The view from above
is striking with the dark blue water of the Mediterranean Sea
streaked with the white color of breaking waves that line up one
after another, awaiting their turn to crash to the shore. Modern
high-rise hotels contrasted in the background with the old buildings and ruins of Joppa, seemingly uniting the new age with the
old. The early morning sun, rising over the eastern horizon and
glowing golden, reflected off the eastward side of the hotels and
cast shadows that stretched westward over the Mediterranean.
The black silhouette of the plane's approach to the airstrip against
the bright sunrise just above the purple mountains hid the intricate
details and writings on the outer walls of the fuselage, the shadows hiding its identity and only revealing it slowly as the plane
taxied closer to the terminal.

The plan had been agreed upon. Jake and Steve would try to get
Randy on the plane by passing him off as another pilot. Jake knew

that the most difficult part would be getting Randy past the guards. Surely, he thought, they would check passports. Did Randy even have a passport? And if he did? His name and picture would be on it and the guards would most certainly recognize him as being a wanted fugitive. They would have to discuss the options later when they met Randy at the produce market. Randy said the market was located in the Christian Quarter of Jerusalem.

Steve and Jake stepped off the plane and walked up the terminal. Jake was surprised to see wanted posters of Randy hanging on almost every wall of the building. It reminded him of the pictures that saturated the bulletin board at the local post office of the FBI's Ten Most Wanted. But this did not have the ten most wanted fugitives, just one-Randy Johnson. Police officers and security were checking the identifications of everyone. The only identifications that were not checked were those of the pilots that departed or boarded planes.

"What's the matter?" Steve asked.

"We're going to need a better plan." Jake replied, "Randy's picture is everywhere and the guards are checking everyone."

"Yeah." Steve looked around, surveying the airport, "I think you're right."

"Let's get to the hotel. I want to get changed and go into Jerusalem to see if I can find that produce market where Randy wanted to meet me."

"I'd like to go with you if you don't mind. We can take the afternoon bus."

"You're putting your life on the line, too," Jake replied, "I think you should come. I'll probably need your help in finding the market anyway. Let's go."

The forty-five minute bus ride from Tel-Aviv to Jerusalem passed quickly. The whole time Jake prayed and thought of the Lord knowing that he was now witnessing the very landscape that Jesus saw thousands of years earlier. His mind wandered; if only the Jews had accepted the Lord when He was here two thousand years ago. He surely would have set up His kingdom then, and the victory would have been won. But that wasn't the Father's will, and so it was that he was now in this period of the Tribulation, afraid and with a risky plan to rescue a Christian friend that may lead to the death of all involved.

The bus pulled up in front of the Western Wall, the only remnant of the second Jewish Temple built under the reign of Herod the Great. It had come to be known as the Wailing Wall, so named for the cries and lamentations of the worshippers that come to visit. It was made of huge lime stones, chiseled to fit perfectly and placed on top of one another and layered to sixty-five feet high. Two thousand feet and more in length, it dwarfed the worshippers that stood at its base and was a dim suggestion of what it once was, a retaining wall to the Temple Mount built thousands of years earlier. The pinkish-white stones, changing hue with the reflection of the rising and setting sun, were contrasted with the sporadic green growth of the hyssop plant that grew from within the cracks and chinks in the stones and which hung precariously above the worshipers below. And now it would, once again, be a vital part of a Temple to God, the retaining wall to the new Jewish Temple being constructed above on the site of the destroyed Dome of the Rock. Jake was in awe of the enormous structure and, walking up the steps leading to its base, he was overcome with emotion by the significance of it all. Jesus had walked these very steps and had gazed upon this wall when He entered the Temple. Jake felt humbled as he walked closer. He placed his trembling hand on the wall and leaned his cheek against a stone, wetting it with his tears. But he wasn't sure if the tears were the product of the joy of knowing the Lord, or of sorrow for not accepting Him sooner. Whatever the emotion, Jake felt His presence, and he was overcome. The Holy Spirit was springing up from within his soul and overflowing into his consciousness. The Lord was with him, and he was no longer afraid.

"He's still here." The deep voice startled Jake, and he looked up to see who it was that seemed to know what he was thinking. Standing next to him was a Jewish man; his long beard with streaks of white flowed over his chest, and his blue eyes, standing out against his brown skin, gazed unwavering at Jake. "Two thousand years ago-" he continued, looking towards the steps that led to the wall then turning his attention back to Jake, "-the Son of God walked those very steps and witnessed these very stones that make this wall. But He is still here in Spirit. My people rejected Him and now it has resulted in the worship of the false Christ, the one who will lead the Promised Land to its destruction."

"Not just the Promised Land but the entire world." Jake replied, looking at the stranger. "But He who your people rejected will come back and set up His kingdom."

"The Lord, I pray, will give my family and me the strength to continue on until that time." The stranger again looked at Jake and smiled, "I can see that you are troubled. I pray that the Lord gives you strength as well, my friend."

"I have no family, as you do, to be concerned with. They were Raptured." The pain of Tracey's and John's absence was etched on Jake's face. "My troubles are nothing compared to yours. Yet you seem at peace. I will pray for you and your family as well."

"The Lord has given us peace of Spirit, my friend." The stranger turned and walked slowly toward the steps. Looking back at Jake, he added, "May the God of my fathers and His son Jesus our Savior keep you from harm's way and give you strength and peace."

Jake stood watching the stranger walk down the steps that led to the wall and onto the walkway and then disappear into the crowd. He hadn't asked his name but he would pray for the stranger and his family.

"Who was that?" Steve asked, walking up from behind.

"I don't know." Jake looked at Steve and shook his head. "He was just there talking to me."

"Let's get going and find this produce market. It shouldn't be too far."

"Randy said the market was in the Christian Quarter. That should be north-east of here. It shouldn't take too long to walk it."

The produce market was a twenty-minute walk from the Western Wall. The outdoor market, composed of hundreds of booths containing fruits ranging from oranges to Arabian dates, was separated by the street that extended through it and stretched the entire length of the city block. The crowded market left little room to roam, the crowd pressed in on the two men as they made their way to the other end.

"Steve, this must be it."

"What's that?" Steve replied, leaning towards Jake to hear better.

"This is it." Jake raised his voice over the low rumble of the crowd.

"Yeah, I think so. What time are we to meet Randy here tomorrow?"

"I told him that I'd be here at noon."

"How are you going to find him?"

"I'm not sure." Jake glanced around the market then turned his attention back to Steve, "He told me to be here and he'd find me."

"Well I hope that he can find you with all these people here."

"Me too. Let's get back to the hotel."

It was five o'clock when the men entered the room, exhausted from the activities of the day. They hadn't had a chance to rest from the morning flight from Rome, and the chance to be able to relax was welcome by both of them. Entering the rectangular hotel room, one would notice two queen-size beds against the wall on the left. Just past the farthest bed, against the wall sat a roll top desk made of the finest oak and painted in cherry red. The sliding glass door at the far end, just past the desk, opened out to the balcony that overlooked the blue Mediterranean Sea and the beaches of Tel-Aviv. Located opposite the beds and against the wall was the television cabinet, painted in cherry red to match the desk, with the television placed within its cubicle. A large oak table, again cherry red, was placed just in front of the sliding door, the sun's glare reflecting brightly off its polished surface. The restroom was located to the immediate right of the entrance of the large room, and a coat closet was located just past the restroom's door. The plush, champagne-pink carpet highlighted the dark cherry red furniture, and the light walls added brightness to the entire room.

"What time do you want to leave here tomorrow?" Steve sat at the table and leaned back into the chair.

"I'd like to leave here on the early bus. I don't want to leave anything to chance." Jake pulled a chair from the table and sat down. Leaning back, he placed his feet on the table and gazed out through the glass door taking in the view. "That would give us plenty of time to make it into Jerusalem and to the market. It would be safer that way, even if we have to wait there for an hour or two."

"We don't have a clear plan on what we're going to do after we meet him. Any ideas, Jake?"

Jake sighed and looked down at the floor. Running his hand across his face, he shook his head. "I haven't a clue of what we're to do. I don't know if he's expecting us to take him back here with us or if he has a plan of his own. I think it will be too risky to take him back here. Suspicion may arise when three men are seen in a room where only two are supposed to be registered."

"Not only that, but I also don't like the idea that three pilots will be reporting for duty on Saturday's flight when only the two of us are scheduled."

"There are certainly a lot of holes in our plan." Jake stood up and stepped toward the glass door and looked out over the Mediterranean Sea. The white sand beaches and the blue ocean were now fading with the setting sun. The sail boats and ships on the surface of the water were just dark shadows against the horizontal orange glow in the west, but Jake hadn't noticed the spectacular view. How were they going to help Randy? They would need help-Divine help. *For with the Lord all things are possible.*

"Thy will be done." Jake uttered under his breath.

"What's that?" Steve asked.

"Oh … nothing," Jake shook his head. "I'm just thinking out loud. We haven't eaten all day. Let's go get something to eat; I think that will help us feel better and think more clearly."

They made the morning bus ride back to Jerusalem in silence, both preoccupied with the events that were going to unfold later in the day. Neither knew exactly what those events might be, but both knew that the risks were high. As the bus pulled up in front of the Wailing Wall, the two men stared at each other momentarily, and, as if reading each other's mind, stood up together and exited the bus.

"You can still change you mind if you want to, Steve. It's not too late."

"I've already made up my mind, and I have nothing to lose." Steve replied. "Remember what John 15:13 says, *'Greater love has no one than this, that he lay down his life for his friends.'* If that's what I have to do, then so be it."

"You're a true friend, Steve. I hope that we won't have to lay down our lives. Sometimes, though, I'm not sure that would be the worst thing to happen."

The walk to the market passed quickly. Jake, in a daze, was unconscious of the surroundings between the Wailing Wall and the market. His thoughts were racing with many scenarios of Randy's rescue that may play out. It was eleven thirty in the morning, and soon Jake would find out whether Randy would show up. Time passed slowly. The market now was becoming more crowded with shoppers, and it was getting more difficult to move about. Despite the mass of people, Jake noticed a young boy, no more than sixteen years of age, that had seemed to be shadowing every move that Jake made.

"Steve." Jake leaned into his partner. "See that boy near the end booth? He's been mirroring every move we make."

Steve stared in the direction of the boy then looked back at Jake, "What do you make of it?"

"I'm not sure. Let's move over to the north end of the market and see if he follows us."

The two men forced their way through the crowd to the farthest, north end of the market. They turned south in the direction of the boy, but he was gone.

"Did you see where he went?" Steve asked.

"No. I lost him in the crowd. But he's been tailing us; I'm sure of it."

Steve slowly turned back to the north end of the market, closely surveying the shoppers.

"Jake?" Steve pointed in the direction of his line of sight. "There's your boy."

Jake turned quickly and started towards the boy. The boy was a handsome young man with dark blue eyes and with skin the color of a light coffee bean. His dark brown hair was cut short, exposing his ears that stood out away from his scalp. His high cheek bones narrowed to his chin, thinning his hairless face.

"You've been following us," Jake said standing in front of the boy. "Do you have business with us?"

"I have come to meet a friend of a friend of mine," the boy responded. "His name is Jake Fredricks. Would you happen to know him?"

"I'm Jake Fredricks."

"Who is this man with you?" The boy gave Steve an inquisitive glare.

"A friend willing to lay down his life to help," Jake responded.

"I have been instructed to bring you only." The boy turned his attention back to Jake.

"I have brought a Christian friend to help. He has put his life on the line to do so, and I trust him with my life. Where I go, he goes."

The boy stared at Steve, gauging him. He looked at Jake quickly then back at Steve.

"Very well," the boy said. "Follow me."

The boy led the two men down a narrow stone walkway that had been worn smooth from the years of foot traffic. The walkway had been bordered on either side with buildings of stone, mostly private residences and businesses, constructed hundreds, even thousands of years earlier. They were built close to one another, and seemed attached with little if any space between them, giving it the appearance of one long structure. The windows were square openings with no glass. Wooden shutters were attached to the jambs of the windows, allowing the occupant to close the opening if wanted and iron rods crisscrossed within the opening, creating a barrier to any would-be thieves. The doors were the same in each unit, arching at the apex, and were constructed of two-by-four cypress wood and sealed with sap. Archways overhead connected the long structure of one side of the walk-way to the structure on the other side, providing a passage without having to cross on the street below. The constant shadow cast by the buildings provided a cool dampness within the corridor, allowing moss to grow between the chinks in the walls and the cracks of the walkway. The appearance of the walkway never changed, the next building looking the same as the last. The boy quickened his pace ahead of the two men, periodically turning his head to see if the visitors were still following.

The boy stopped in front of a bookstore then knocked on its large wooden door. The door made a creaking sound as someone inside opened the door just enough to allow a narrow opening.

"It's Ze'ev. I have him with me. He has a friend." The boy said quietly. The two men could only hear a muffled sound coming from within the doorway.

"He says he has a Christian friend," the boy responded to the voice from within. "He wouldn't come without him." The door closed and the boy looked expressionless at the two men and gave no clue of what was happening.

"I heard you say that your name is Ze'ev. Is that right?" Jake asked.

"Yes," the boy responded.

The door opened again. The boy spoke to the voice from within then looked up at the men. "Come this way."

The door opened to a narrow stairway leading down to the basement. It was illuminated from above by a lone hanging light swinging back and forth. A door at the bottom was open, light shining through, and a shadow of a man cast on the wall opposite the opening. In the doorway, at the base of the stairway, the Jewish man that Jake had met at the Wailing Wall the day before was looking up at the two men.

"Come this way." The man's deep voice was unmistakable.

The door opened into a bookstore. Shelves along the walls and freestanding within the room carried books to be sold. At the near end of the room was a counter where books could be bought. The Jewish man continued to the far end of the room, entering another doorway. The two men and the boy followed him into the room; the Jewish man closed the door behind them and sat at a table located at the center of the room.

"We meet again, my friend." The Jewish man looked up at Jake and gestured to a seat at the table, "Sit down and make yourself comfortable."

Jake and Steve took a seat at the table. The room was bare except for the table and a sofa along the far wall. The walls were made of concrete marked with cracks. The near wall had yet another wooden door that was closed.

"My name is Yitzhak Benziman," the Jewish man said. Gesturing to the boy, "You have met my son Ze'ev."

"We've come to help a friend." Jake leaned closer to Yitzhak, "Is my friend here?"

The door behind Yitzhak opened and a man stood in the doorway, silhouetted by the bright light illuminating from behind him. His features were hidden in the darkness but Jake knew instantly, by the man's stature and size, that it was Randy. Randy walked closer, revealing himself in the light that hung above the table. He had thinned and his face looked drawn. The gray in his hair was more pronounced and his sunken eyes made him look tired and worn. The worry and anxiety that he had experienced the past month had taken its toll and had manifested itself upon the outward appearance of this once-healthy, vibrant man.

"Hello, Jake. Thanks for coming." Randy hung his head and started to cry.

Jake got up from the table and placed his arm around Randy. "It's okay. We'll get you out of here, but you have to collect yourself."

Jake and Randy sat at the table with Steve and Yitzhak. The four men sat in silence for a moment. Yitzhak motioned to Ze'ev, who was now sitting on the sofa, to exit the room. Ze'ev got up and exited through the door that Randy entered and closed the door behind him.

"Have you given any thought to how we might be able to get you home?" Jake leaned forward and looked at Randy.

"I have given some thought to what you said to me on the phone last week." Randy composed himself. "I think that if I can get on as one of the pilots or even one of the service personnel, then maybe there won't be many questions asked."

"It would have to be as one of the pilots." Steve moved his seat closer to the table. "The service personnel won't necessarily know the pilots on any given flight, but they will know if you are one of them or not. I think you have to get on as a pilot."

"I would have to agree." Jake added, "But I think that there being more than two pilots might raise some questions as well. Another problem may be the guards checking passports and identifications. They don't seem to be checking the identifications of the pilots, but that was yesterday. Do you even have a passport, Randy?"

"Yeah, I have a passport. But what good is it if all it will do is cause me to be recognized as a wanted fugitive?"

"We can doctor it up a little. Even change the picture just enough so that it won't look exactly like you. Do you have access to a computer and scanner? It would make altering the picture much easier."

"We have both a computer and scanner upstairs."

"Good. You may want to shave your beard Randy. The guards may be looking for someone that looks like your wanted posters. With sunglasses and the pilot's uniform, we just might get past the guards and onto the plane."

"But what about there being three pilots?" Randy asked.

"What if Steve stays here with us?" Yitzhak joined the discussion, "We will take good care of him. He could fly back on another flight at a later time."

"I don't know," Jake replied. "I think that-"

"I'll do it." Steve interrupted. "I've always wanted to visit Israel anyway. This would allow me to do so."

"Steve, you don't have to do this."

"I know, Jake, but I want to. I don't really have anything to go back to, so there's no hurry in getting there."

"Then it's settled." Yitzhak stood up from the table, "Let's go upstairs. My wife Hannah has fixed us something to eat. So come. We shall celebrate our decision."

The men followed Yitzhak through the door from which Randy had emerged earlier. On the other side was a stairway that led up to the home of the family. Just at the top, to the left, was the main living area, approximately ten feet wide and twenty feet long, the room was rectangular and contained dilapidated furniture. Located along the near wall, which bordered the stairwell, was a dark brown sofa, which had seen years of use; it slanted toward the left and had worn seat cushions and arm rests. Located on the opposite wall, just in front of a large window, was the television on a small table. The entrance to the quarters was to the right of the television, and it opened to a different walkway than the one they had originally taken to enter the bookstore at the opposite side of the building. Located against the left wall was a wooden rocking chair and end table, which had a lamp placed on it. Along the right-hand wall, which separated the kitchen from the living area, was yet another sofa, newer in appearance than the latter, but still showed signs of wear in the light blue fabric. Paintings and portraits hung on all four walls, mostly family of generations past, and of biblical saints and prophets. Straight ahead of the stairway was the entrance to the kitchen and dining area containing a large wooden table with bench seats. To the right of the stairway was a hallway that led to the two bedrooms. The windows that were located in the bedrooms were those that opened to the original walkway just prior to the large wooden door that led down to the bookstore.

"Welcome." Hannah Benziman stood in the entrance way of the dining area. She was a short woman with gray, shoulder-length hair. She had light brown skin, and the small circles under her hazel eyes and the slight wrinkling on her face could not conceal the many hard years of work that had been her experience. Jake sensed an innate kindness and gentleness from her. Her soft voice and meek appearance reminded him of his grandmother; a woman who had raised him after his parents' death and who was the epitome of unconditional love, until her death when he was twenty years old. "Come and eat." she added, "I will serve you."

"You are a good woman." Yitzhak held his hands out to his wife and smiled. Turning toward the men, he gestured to the table and said, "Sit and refresh yourselves."

The men sat at the table with Yitzhak at the head. Hannah served a meat soup with bread and a vegetable similar to a squash. The soup had been tasty and Jake wondered what the meat was but didn't want to ask, he assumed it to be lamb. After lunch, Hannah cleared the table, leaving the men to further discuss the plan to get Randy on the plane.

"I think that Steve should come back with me to the hotel tonight." Jake suggested, "that way there will be no questions if anyone notices that someone other than Steve is seen with me."

"How do you want to meet tomorrow then?" Randy asked.

"Yitzhak, do you have a car?" Jake looked at the Jewish man.

"Yes." Yitzhak responded, "I have a red Chevrolet-it's a little beat up, but it works. It is yours to do what you will."

"Can you pick Steve and me up tomorrow in front of the hotel?"

"Yes, but what are you getting at?"

"When you pick us up, Randy will be hiding in the back seat. Steve can change into civilian clothes on the way to the airport and Randy into the pilot's uniform that I have brought. That way you won't bring undue attention to you and Steve when both of you return here."

"When we arrive at the airport," Steve added, "there will only be Jake and Randy in pilot's uniforms."

"I see." Yitzhak said, "Where do you want me to drop you off?"

"Drop us off at the Pan World Airline terminal," Jake responded. "We'll try and get on the plane as soon as we can."

"We can park the car and go inside to see you off." Yitzhak said, "Hannah and I want to wait inside to make sure that you get on the plane."

"Then it's a plan," Randy said. "Yitzhak and I will work on the passport tonight and on other loose ends here. We have some photo paper that will make a good picture for my identification card."

"Okay then; Steve and I should go and prepare as well. Meet us in front of the hotel at nine A.M."

"I'll get Ze'ev to see you out." Yitzhak said, "We'll see you at nine A.M."

Jake was up early in the morning, before the rising of the sun. He had prayed for guidance and deliverance from the possible risks that they were going to take. But he was prepared, if necessary, to pay the consequences of imprisonment or even death. The sun rose quickly and soon he and Steve would be meeting Randy and his friends. The two men put on their pilot uniforms in silence. They both knew what they were to do and nothing needed to be discussed. It was 8:55 A.M. when the two men started down the hallway, skipping the elevator in favor of the stairway, not wanting to leave anything to chance such as a mechanical breakdown. The automatic doors opened to the street and a large four-door Chevrolet was parked along the curb. Yitzhak was in the driver's seat and Hannah was sitting in the back. The men walked to the car as Jake held the spare pilot's uniform for Randy. Jake got into the front passenger seat and Steve in the back. Randy was huddled on the bench seat in the back.

"Ok, Randy," Jake said, "put this uniform on. It's a large one and should fit you. Steve, you start putting on your civilian clothes."

The ride to the airport passed quickly and everything went as planned. Yitzhak dropped Jake and Randy off at the Pan World Airline entrance to the airport.

"We'll meet you at the terminal before boarding," Jake said.

"Yes." Yitzhak responded, "I'll park the car and see you in a few moments."

The two men walked into the airport and proceeded toward the airline's terminal. They passed through the metal detectors without problems, and all seemed to be going as planned. Wanted posters of Randy were still located at all terminals, and guards were positioned in front of all walkways leading to the planes.

"Let's just stop for a moment," Randy said looking at the guards. "I just need to think for a minute."

"Okay." Jake replied. "But don't take too long. We need to get going." Looking just behind Randy, Jake noticed that Steve, Yitzhak and Hannah had come. "Take a look Randy; they've come to say goodbye."

Randy turned to look at the three. He stared with tears in his eyes and mouthed *thank you* to them. He turned back to Jake. "Let's go."

The men approached the guard and tried passing without giving their passports.

"Hold on," the guard said, "I need to check you passports."

"Look, Mac-" Jake said, "-we're in a hurry to get on the plane."

"Your passport, please." The guard interrupted holding out his hand.

Jake took out his passport from his breast pocket and handed it to the guard. The guard looked at it and waved his hand indicating that Jake could pass.

"Your passport, please." The guard held his hand out to Randy.

Randy handed his passport to the guard. The guard looked at

the passport then at Randy. He stared at Randy for what seemed ages. The guard looked at the passport again-studying it. In the background Steve could sense something going wrong.

"I don't like this." Steve said.

"He's not going to make it." Yitzhak responded.

Hannah also knew that the guard was taking too long. She grabbed Yitzhak and turned him to face her.

"You pig!" she screamed out and slapped Yitzhak. "You're a pig!"

"What are you doing, Hannah?" Yitzhak held his hand to his face.

"Play along," Hannah whispered and started pushing Yitzhak. "You pig!" She screamed out again.

The screaming caught the attention of the guard. He quickly handed the passport back to Randy and ran to the commotion.

"Hurry," Jake said. "Let's get on the plane."

The plan had worked with the help of a small woman. Jake and Randy were now on the plane to Rome. They would be refueling at the Rome airport and taking off again. They would not need to switch planes. But Jake would not be comfortable until they were in the air.

"We did it," Randy sat in the copilot's chair.

"Yeah. But let's get in the air first."

The passengers had boarded and the control tower had given permission to take off. It was a feeling of relief and exhilaration when the plane finally left the ground. They were on their way home-back to safety, if only temporary, and back to the ones they loved.

"Once we get to New York we should rent a car to travel to Denver. I don't want to take any more chances with flying back."

"Okay. At this point, I'll crawl back to Denver."

"I didn't tell you this sooner Randy, but we have invited Mary to the cabin to be there when we arrive."

"I didn't want her to know anything about this."

"She doesn't," Jake responded, "She thinks she's coming to get away from everything.

"She's been having a tough time of it. She doesn't know that she will be meeting you."

"Thanks, Jake. I'm glad you invited her. It will be a relief for both of us."

The flight to Rome and then to New York went smoothly. The security at JFK International Airport was not as tight as in Tel-Aviv, and the two men were able to get to the car without concern. The two-day, non-stop drive from New York to Denver seemed a lifetime, but both men were relieved to get to the cabin in the early morning hours. The lights to the cabin were on, and Jake could see Joyce looking out the window when the car pulled up into the driveway. The two men got out of the car and entered the front door. Mary was sitting at the kitchen table when the men walked into the room. Randy stood staring at his wife whom he hadn't seen in months. Mary sat in disbelief and put her hand over her mouth. She got up, trembling and barely able to stand. Randy walked to her and without a word they embraced each other, both crying and thankful to be in each others arms. Randy was finally home and with the woman he loved.

Chapter 10

—⚏——⚏—

The early morning chill awoke Randy, and he pulled the sleeping bag closer to his chin in an attempt to keep warm. He lay there unable to sleep and stared into the darkness of the cave as his thoughts wandered back to his rescue from Israel. *Had it really been almost three years already?* He had lived through two full winters and this, his third in the cave, had been the harshest yet with record-breaking snow fall and consistently sub-zero temperatures. The thick rock insulated the cave from the weather outside and kept the air temperature within at a constant, but Randy thought it chilly nonetheless. Jake and Randy had constructed a door of plywood at the entrance to keep the mist and water from the falls from entering the living area. The cave had been supplied with everything that Randy needed to survive and even luxuries that citizens of some third world countries did not have, but still he longed for a warm home and a warm comfortable bed to sleep on. Life had not been easy since his escape from Israel. The wilderness had been a curse as much as it had been a blessing. It was a lonely place, especially at night when his thoughts of Mary and her non-belief were relentless and, at times, not allowing him to sleep. But the time alone was also a blessing. It had been time that he spent with the Lord, and it had allowed him to grow in spirit. He often joked about his similarity to the Apostle Paul who had exiled himself to his hometown of Tarsus after his conversion to study the Word of God and to prepare himself for the ministry. Lately, he had felt guilty for not being in the "front lines" of the spiritual warfare that was taking place in the world. He often thought about leaving the cave to witness to unbelievers and to spread the Gospel of the Lord Jesus. The Apostle Paul would not have remained idle, even in the face of death. Randy knew that hiding in the cave was going to be temporary. But he feared that if he left now, Mary would not follow him. She still had not accepted Christ-even after over two and one-half years of being witnessed to by Randy and the others. So he stayed, praying constantly that she would accept the Lord into her heart.

Randy longed to be with Mary, and he found that the most difficult part of the whole ordeal was not being with her more often. His time with her was determined by the weather. The summers allowed her to come to him and even stay with him in the cave. But the winters were long and cold, and just occasionally when the weather was favorable, she would outfit herself with snow shoes and brave the three-mile trek to the cave. Winters, without Mary, was the most unbearable season of the year for Randy. He worried about her reluctance to accept the Lord as Savior, even after all that had happened, she still did not believe. The miraculous signs that Prophet Gallo had shown to her at Central Park had left an unwavering belief in the power of Alexander Christos. Although she did not understand why he blamed Randy for the attack on the American fleet in the Persian Gulf, she did believe that he was the one who was going to lead the world to an everlasting peace. Other than the witness of Randy and Jake, there was no reason to think differently.

The past two and one-half years had shown a remarkable time of peace, a peace that the world had never known. The truce that Alexander Christos had forced the Arab nations and Israel to accept had produced a region of stability that had not been witnessed in thousands of years. The Jewish people were allowed to rebuild their temple and to worship the God of Abraham with the reinstitution of the practice of sacrificing animals for the forgiveness of their sins. The Arab Confederation was allowed to build a new mosque, replacing the destroyed Dome of the Rock Mosque, to be constructed in Babylon. Although forced upon, the truce allowed Israel to finally live in a land without the fear of being attacked by other countries. Many Jews from around the world came to live in Israel and had gathered to resettle among the ruins, rebuilding them without walls and without gates or bars for protection. The Israelis had become a peaceful and unsuspecting people. The seven-year covenant with President Christos and the U.S.E. was the major reason for their confidence. All was happening as the prophets of scripture had predicted. One only had to look to them to know what lay ahead.

Randy got up and slid the door to the cave aside. The thundering roar of the falls was deafening and the light of the morning sun filtered in through the water and poorly illuminated the cave. It was springtime, and the snow receded with every new day, slowly revealing the budding aspens and other trees native to the area. The flow of the river was high but still poured past the lip of the cave's entrance, allowing easy access to the opening. Randy stepped out and climbed up the embankment to the top of the falls. He looked downstream shading his eyes against the bright light of the sun that reflected off the melting snow. The rustling of the brush from behind startled him, and he turned quickly to see what was causing the noise.

"Jake!-" he said with a sigh of relief, "-you scared me."

"Sorry," Jake replied. "I wanted to see you before my next trip. I'm going back to Israel."

"Israel?"

"Yeah. It was a spur-of-the-moment decision. The pilot scheduled to do the flight had a family emergency and they asked me if I wanted to take the flight."

"When do you leave?"

"Tonight at nine." Jake placed his left foot up on a stone and surveyed the area, "I've already called Yitzhak and we are going to meet when I get there. I haven't seen him and his family since we left with you."

"He's a good man, he saved my life. I wish I could go with you."

"I've brought some food. Joyce fried some chicken and wanted me to bring it to you."

"That sounds good," Randy looked downstream then back at Jake. Sounding more serious, "Have you talked to Mary?"

"I have. She's going to come this Monday to see you."

"I'm concerned about her." Randy stared at the ground then looked back at Jake. "She hasn't accepted the Lord as her Savior, and I'm not sure that I'll be able to get her to."

"She'll come around. Continue to pray and God will be faithful. It's getting close to the time that all of us will be here permanently in the cave. Have you asked Mary if she will stay in the cave with us when the time comes?"

"Yeah, but she doesn't sound too thrilled about it. I'm not so sure she'll be willing to stay."

"In a few months, it will be the mid-point of the tribulation. We have that much time to try and get her to think differently. I'll give up flying, and Sam and Joyce will probably be spending more time here with you."

"Jake … if Mary doesn't move into the cave, then I'm going to have to take my chances living on the outside. I know it will be dangerous, but I can't leave Mary lost and alone with no one to turn to."

Jake nodded in agreement. "I know, Randy. I would do the same. Look … I don't have much time and I should be going." The men embraced each other. "I'll see you when I get back. I'll tell Yitzhak and Hannah hello for you."

"Give them my love."

"I will, Randy … I will."

Monday had finally come and Randy could not wait to see Mary. She usually came in the morning, and Randy anticipated her arrival by waiting at the top of the water fall. Mary was still in the meadow when he spotted her, and in his excitement he ran to her. Embracing her tightly, he gazed into her eyes without speaking. When he was with her, nothing else mattered. The hardships that he had endured, the self-imposed exile from civilization, and the doubts that would invade his mind were shattered by the love for his wife. With her, the world was lifted off his shoulders and the loneliness that the wilderness could bring was no more.

She gazed back at Randy and softly kissed him on the lips. He was her rock, the driving force that kept her going. Coming to the cave to be with the man she loved was an escape for her from the ridicule of peers for being married to a war criminal and a wanted fugitive. But that was going to change. She had a plan of her own, and it would allow them to be together forever.

"I'm not going back without you," Mary said releasing her grip. "Where you are is where I want to be."

"Mary, are you sure? It's not easy here and there are still a few months left before things in the world will get worse." Randy let his hopes rise. "Have you thought about what we've discussed about Jesus and His salvation?"

"Randy, I know what I saw at Central Park," Mary replied straightforwardly, "I haven't seen anything yet from your God. If he really existed, why has He made you a fugitive?"

Randy was hurt and stood staring, offering no answer. In a way, he understood why Mary felt the way she did. President Christos did have supernatural powers that were both tangible and visible-signs that were required as proof of deity by a wicked generation. Mary glanced away. She knew that she had hurt Randy. "I don't want to leave you, Randy. We'll be together now, forever." Randy remained silent. "This world has gotten strange. I know ... I've seen some powerful things with my own two eyes." Mary stared at the ground. "Randy, the only thing I know for sure is that the love that I have for you is more powerful than what I saw from Prophet Gallo. I don't fully understand what's going on, but where you are, I want to be there. If you are to die, then I want to die with you. Besides, I wouldn't want your child to be without a father."

Randy was in shock. "My child?"

"Yes, Randy. I'm pregnant."

"But when?-" Randy stuttered in his surprise. "How?"

"How?" Mary smiled shyly, "We both know how. But as for when ... well, I'm four and one-half months along."

"Four and one-half months." Randy smiled, "It must have been when Jake was in Europe and Sam and Joyce were in Florida."

"We had the cabin to ourselves." Mary grabbed Randy's hand. "That night made me realize how much I missed you, and I have made the arrangements for us, all of us, to be together."

Randy assumed that Mary had made arrangements to stay in Denver. He had been overcome with emotion about finding out about becoming a father. If things worked out, Mary could stay in the cabin when the baby was born. She could stay there another year or two in seclusion allowing the baby to grow strong before coming to the cave permanently.

"I want you to stay." Tears ran down Randy's face. "We have all you and the baby will need, both here at the cave and in the cabin." Today, he thought, was a new beginning, and if he could convince Mary of Christ's salvation, then it would also be the first day of eternity for them and for the baby.

The following day Randy and Mary lay on a blanket in the meadow and watched the clouds slowly pass by overhead. Randy was still on cloud nine about the news of the baby. That was all that he and Mary could talk about since yesterday. The days were becoming warmer, and the roar of the waterfall in the background seemed to relax both of them. The two started to doze off when something in the trees startled Randy.

"Mary? Did you hear that?"

"I didn't hear anything." Mary looked up over the tall grass. "What is it?"

"I don't know. Maybe nothing." Randy surveyed the entire area. "Just my imagination I guess. Let's get back to the cave."

The two stood and walked toward the cave. They could hear rustling in the trees and brush-more pronounced now.

"Stop right there. We have you surrounded." A voice from the brush yelled out. "We got them, men. Let's go."

About twenty-five men came out of the brush wearing the standard blue and white military uniforms of the U.S.E. security forces. All carried Uzi-type firearms that were locked and loaded and pointing at the couple.

"Well…Well-" the commander of the group said, "-if it isn't Randy Johnson. Did you think you could run forever? I was ordered to bring you back alive, otherwise I would shoot you right here. We would have never found you if it weren't for your wife."

"What?" Randy glanced at Mary.

"That's right. She led us to you."

"They promised me a deal if I told them where you were," Mary quickly spoke up. "They would pardon you if you admitted your involvement in the attack on the fleet."

"But I had nothing to do with it," Randy said, looking at his wife. "Mary, you have no idea what you've done. They've fooled you."

"I did it for us, Randy, and our baby. That's why I did it." Tears cascaded down her cheeks. "We'll be able to be together now."

"We followed her here yesterday, and when we confirmed that it was you, we came back today to get you," the commander added. "I'm sure the reward money will come in handy for her. We have also arrested the old couple in the cabin. We're still looking for Jake Fredricks, but we'll find him."

Randy stared at his wife as the men shackled his arms and legs. "Mary, I know you thought you were doing the right thing. Call Yitzhak in Jerusalem. You have his number. I want you to stay with him. He will offer you protection." The soldiers yanked Randy away, leading him back to the trail. Mary stood watching the men get farther away. "Randy!" she screamed, before falling to her knees and sobbing uncontrollably.

The flight to Israel passed quickly, and Jake could see Yitzhak and Hannah through the window of the airport as the plane taxied to the terminal. They both had looked the way that he remembered them. Jake chuckled to himself, recalling the last memory of them as Hannah struck Yitzhak to avert the guard's attention from Randy. Jake couldn't help to think that Hannah had gotten pleasure from her actions, and it made him laugh when he thought about it. Yitzhak greeted Jake with a tight embrace, a hug similar to a father meeting a prodigal son after many years. Releasing him, Jake turned to Hannah and she grabbed Jake's cheek and kissed them on each side.

"Welcome, my brother," Yitzhak said with a smile.

"We have longed for this day," Hannah added. "I have prepared a feast for you. We have slaughtered the fatted lamb in honor of your return. Come, Ze'ev is waiting for us in the car. He has a new wife, Anna. She has become like a daughter to Yitzhak and me."

Ze'ev and Anna were standing outside of the car when the three approached. Ze'ev had grown tall and had become very handsome. The hair on his cheeks had thickened, and although his beard was sporadic upon his face, it had made him look like a man in his twenties rather than a teenager. But he had become a man with an attractive wife. At first glance, she appeared even younger then Ze'ev, but she was actually two years his senior. She had long blond hair held back tightly in a ponytail with a red bow. Quiet and shy, she held her head low, hiding her dark blue eyes. As they approached, Ze'ev went to the back passenger seat and opened the door for his mother. Anna quickly followed behind her without saying a word. Ze'ev walked around to the driver's side and got in.

"There have been many changes since you were here last," Yitzhak said, getting into the car. "The Jewish Temple has been rebuilt and the ancient city of Babylon is nearly restored to its former days of glory."

"Does that surprise you?" Jake sat into the front passenger seat with Yitzhak sitting directly behind Ze'ev. "The Bible predicts that all this will happen."

"It does not surprise me," Yitzhak replied. "It has been three years since the Rapture and all that the Bible predicts is happening quickly. We are approaching the second half of this seven-year period; it is only going to get worse from here on out."

"Do you and your family have passports?" Jake asked. "I'll take you back to America when I go, and all of you can live with us in the cave."

"Is there room-" Yitzhak attempted to say.

"We have passports." Hannah replied, quickly interrupting Yitzhak.

"Hannah, don't interrupt," Yitzhak scowled at his wife. "Is there room in the cave for four more?"

"Plenty of room. There will be a better chance to survive until the Lord comes if there are more of us. But you'll have to come soon. In six months the last three and a half years of the tribulation will be here, and I want to be in the cave permanently by then."

"What should we bring?"

"Just bring clothes and essential personal items. Valuables such as jewelry won't be worth much in a year's time, so just leave them. We already have everything in the cave that we need so you won't have to bring much. No sense in taking up space in the cave with things that we don't need."

"We'll talk about it, Hannah and I. In the meantime let's get going; the food is waiting."

Jake felt good to be in Israel again. The ride to Jerusalem passed quickly, and he could barely get a word in as Yitzhak spoke continually of the rebuilding of the Temple and of the ancient city of Babylon. Jake could sense the excitement that exuded from Yitzhak as he spoke of the Temple in the minutest of detail. Yitzhak's speech quickened as he described the Temple, and it was as if he was describing it from a photograph that was placed in front of him.

The Temple, as Yitzhak explained, had taken just over two and a half years to complete and was considered the jewel of the entire country; it was a huge building and almost identical to the first temple built by Solomon. It was ninety feet long, thirty feet wide, and forty-five feet high and built with blocks from a quarry in Jerusalem. The portico, as wide as the temple, extended another fifteen feet from the front entrance. The roof of the portico was supported by four large columns, chiseled from the stones of the quarry with images of cherubim, or winged angels, carved at the top. Vertical grooves extended the entire length of the column, from the feet of the cherubim to its base. The base of each column was carved in the image of giant lion paws with the claws extending two feet in length. Narrow clerestory windows allowed sunlight to enter the sanctuary illuminating it through stain glass. But Yitzhak saved the best for last. His voice rose with excitement, and the tempo of his speech quickened. He could hardly contain himself as he spoke of the inner sanctuary. The room was thirty feet long, thirty feet wide, and as high as it was long. The entire room had been overlaid inside with pure gold; the altar within had also been overlaid with pure gold. Gold chains extended across the front of the inner sanctuary. Against the back wall of the innermost room, stood two cherubim made of olive wood, each fifteen feet high and each with a wing span of fifteen feet. The wing of one cherub touched one wall, while the wing of the other touched the other wall, and their wings touched each other in the middle of the room. Both cherubim were overlaid with pure gold.

"We are almost there," Hannah interrupted Yitzhak. "Give Jake some silence. You have been speaking all the way home."

"Hannah is right." Yitzhak looked at Jake. "I ask your forgiveness for being so rude. We shall eat first, then I shall tell you more. Better yet we shall walk to the Holy Mount and I will show you. We won't be allowed into the inner sanctuary, but I have photographs that I can show you."

"That sounds fine," Jake answered. "I would love to see it. We shall eat first, then we will talk more."

The meal had been finished, and Jake hadn't realized how hungry he had become. The lamb had been roasted and seasoned to perfection. The bread freshly baked in the stone oven was set out to cool, filling the entire room with the mouth-watering aroma. Dried fruit and dates had been served for dessert with wine for drink to wash it all down. Hannah and Anna had cleared the table and were washing the dishes.

"A feast fit for a king," Yitzhak smiled at Jake, "Or for a brother. Come ... I can wait no longer. I want to show you the Temple. We can walk off some of this meal at the same time."

"I look forward to seeing it," Jake replied. "Ze'ev can come too."

"Ze'ev has become a man." Yitzhak looked proudly at his son, "He has honored me with a beautiful daughter. Come with us, Ze'ev."

The Temple was as Yitzhak described it, almost to the exact detail. But something was not right. Jake could feel it. He could hear a strange distant thunder. But unlike the deafening rumble after lightning strikes, which comes quickly and is then silenced, this was a continuous roar that seemed to get louder with every passing moment. Yitzhak said something and pointed northward. In the distance, a wall of dust billowing skyward and stretching the entire horizon approached Jerusalem. They could feel the vibration under their feet, a weak trembling at first, then getting stronger in intensity with each passing moment.

"An earthquake!" Ze'ev shouted.

"No!" Jake pointed to the horizon. "Horses-thousands of them-coming this way." Jake stood motionless with his mouth open, staring to the north. He could do nothing but watch.

Chapter 11

The size of the horses in the army advancing toward Israel were massive. The Russian army had, for many years, been proud of their cavalry and of the soldiers that had bravely gone into battle riding on the backs of these animals. But these horses were not the same as the horses used in past conflicts; these horses were an anomaly and a product of genetic manipulation. Years of Russian research and experimentation had produced a horse that was almost twice as large as their natural counterpart with an endurance level that was five times as long. They were nearly eight feet high, from hoof to shoulder, and weighed up to a ton or more. The girth of the animal, made almost of entire muscle, measured ten to twelve feet around the torso, and their length was nearly ten feet. Modified saddles were made just so the riders could stay mounted on the large animal. Their speed was measured at sixty miles an hour in quick bursts and forty-five miles an hour for long distances. Their numbers were staggering; hundreds of thousands of them were galloping southward towards Israel with their riders pushing the horses' stamina to the breaking point. Those that could not keep pace would stumble, and both horse and rider were trampled underfoot from behind by the speeding animals, killing them instantly with the crushing blows from the hooves that pounded down with each stride.

The riders were comprised from each nation that was involved in the attack. Iraqi, Iranian, and Egyptian soldiers were riding side by side with their Syrian, Armenian and Russian counterparts and united by their common goal-the destruction of Israel. So confident that the attack would be successful, the invaders were armed only with bows and arrows, clubs, and swords. Their plan was to take over Israel without a bullet being fired. The battle would be won on the streets by trampling any one who would get in the way. Those unlucky enough to escape the charging horses would be beaten to death or killed by the sword or flying arrows. The dust that rose above the earth by the charging horde was as a cloud that covered the horizon, and it quickly advanced nearer to its target. Israel had long since disposed of her military might and could do nothing but let her defense fall solely in the hands of Alexander Christos. News of the advancing army spread quickly throughout the Holy Land, but all anyone could do was to find a hiding place and hope not to be found. Jake felt helpless as he watched with Yitzhak and Ze'ev the advancing army approach the northern mountains of Israel. The sand and dust that was thrown into the air had reached Jerusalem far in advance of the invading hoard. Jake and his friends covered their mouths protecting themselves from the choking dust and debris. In a daze, and not knowing what to do, the men stood motionless looking at the incredible sight.

In an instant and without warning, the earth shook with a mighty earthquake, and the ground in front of the invading army opened. The large crack in the earth stretched to Mount Tabor, splitting it in two, and the first three waves of attackers were unable to stop and were swallowed up by the gaping chasm. The riders that followed had difficulty in stopping the huge and speeding horses, causing the horses that were behind to ram into the horse immediately in front, throwing both man and horse to the ground. The northern Mountains of Israel were overturned, tossing giant boulders and sulfur into the sky, and the cliffs that faced the valleys of Israel crumbled to the earth. Thunder cracked the heavens as fire and sulfur dropped from the sky, falling on the soldiers of the invading armies. In the confusion, they had turned on themselves, fighting each other with the weapons that they had carried with them, killing those that had survived the rain of sulfur that had fallen on them. Torrents of hailstones, the size of large boulders, fell onto the army, crushing man and horse, and leaving only corpses and rivers of blood.

In Moscow, President Vladikoff waited with the leaders of the other attacking countries for word from the Middle East. His dream of ruling the entire world was at hand and he waited to hear from his field officers. As they sat at the conference table, they felt the ground shake. A mild trembling at first, it was increasing with intensity. President Vladikoff looked out the window and saw fire and sulfur falling from the sky and hailstones crashing to the earth. The roof above them collapsed from the weight of the hailstones, burying the Russian leader along with his conspirators under tons of rubble. Fire from the sky quickly devoured the building and the man who would be king, and his men with him. From the coastlands to the heart of the country, hailstones and fire had fallen from the sky, destroying the entire country and leaving nothing but rubble. The destruction had been swift and without warning. The invading army, and the countries from which they came, were destroyed. They had aroused the anger of God and had paid the price of God's wrath with their lives.

The earthquake had knocked both Yitzhak and Jake off their feet. Ze'ev somehow remained standing. When the ground had stopped shaking, they stood up and viewed the destruction that lay before them. Looking northward and scanning from west to east, they observed a sea of red blood with the bodies of the men and the larger horses lying across the landscape. There was an eerie silence. There were no birds singing as usual, nor could they hear the sound of motor vehicles that would normally permeate the air this time of day. Still dazed, Yitzhak broke the silence.

"We must go. We must make sure that Hannah and Anna are all right."

Yitzhak turned and walked at a quickened pace as Jake and Ze'ev followed closely behind. Not a word was said along the way. Despite the powerful earthquake, not a single building had been destroyed in Israel. People were gathering in the streets; some panicked, and others, dazed, appeared to be walking aimlessly. When the three men arrived at the front of the living quarters, Hannah opened the door and rushed to Yitzhak with tears in her eyes. Ze'ev followed closely behind, searching for his wife, and embraced her tightly upon finding her.

"We were worried," Hannah wiped the tears from her eyes. "What happened?"

"It was what Ezekiel had prophesied," Yitzhak answered, relieved that Hannah and Anna were all right. He appeared to be deep in thought with a distant look in his eyes. "God's mighty hand has destroyed the invading army. He has destroyed the army of the North. Ezekiel called them Gog and Magog."

"We were standing at the Holy Mount when we saw them," Jake added. "Thousands of horses coming towards Jerusalem and kicking up the dust. Have you ever seen images or footage of the eruption of a volcano? The smoke and debris that is thrown from it overtakes and smothers cities and people in its wake. That's what it looked like to me."

"The earthquake was terrible," Anna said in her soft voice. "I thought that the building was going to come down on us and crush us both."

"Yes." Yitzhak said slowly, nodding his head. "God has protected His people Israel. Let's go inside. I think we should all sit down. We should pray."

They prayed and gave thanks to God. The Lord had been faithful and had delivered them and the land of Israel from annihilation. The prophecy found in Ezekiel thirty-eight had been fulfilled, and Jake had been an eyewitness to it. They turned on the television to get some updated information. The pictures were gruesome as the dead, both of man and animal, could be seen covering the entire landscape. The birds and wild animals had already begun to scavenge the corpses and to devour the flesh that lay motionless in the pools and rivers of blood that had been formed from the slaughter. The news anchor cut away from the images to report another breaking story.

"We will return to this story in a moment," the female anchor said. "This just in. Randy Johnson has been captured in Denver, Colorado. The man who co-planned the attack on the American fleet two and one-half years ago has been arrested along with an elderly couple who have been helping him elude capture since that time. A third suspect, Jake Fredricks, has not been found, and authorities are looking for him. Reports indicate that Randy Johnson's wife, Mary, led the authorities to a cave high in the Rocky Mountains where she said he would be found. We will update you when we receive more information. Let us now return to the top story of the day and the failed Russian attempt to invade Israel."

Silence again filled the room as the five of them sat looking at the television. Hannah started to cry as the realization of the capture sunk in. Jake tried to stand, but his legs were too weak and he fell to his knees.

"Jake," Yitzhak said. "Are you all right?"

"I need to lie down." Jake stared at Hannah and Yitzhak. He wiped a tear from his eye. "I'll be all right. We should all just rest. Maybe get some sleep."

Jake lay in bed and stared at the ceiling. The plan to survive the Tribulation in a cave had failed. His wife and son had been gone for three years and the only family that remained and had been able to help him with the grief of losing his wife and son had been arrested, and he knew that they would probably not survive until the Lord's return. There was no returning to Denver. If he was to survive the Tribulation, then he would have to do it in Israel. He was now a wanted man. He knew that the odds in surviving the Tribulation were slim at best. He lay there, and with his mind racing with the events of the day, he started to cry. A white dove landed on the window sill and Jake sat up to take a better look. It was as white as the virgin snow. *Could it be the same dove that appeared to him just after the Rapture?* He wasn't sure, but it had comforted him as before.

Yitzhak comforted Hannah by holding her and wiping away her tears. They sat on the couch, still in shock from all that had happened. Hannah separated herself from Yitzhak and wiped her face.

"What will we do now?" she asked, trying to compose herself.

"When Jake is feeling better, we will discuss what we shall do. We are in the Lord's hands; let's leave it at that for now. Come, Hannah, go lie down and get some rest. I'll join you in a while." Yitzhak turned to Ze'ev and Anna. "You, too, my son and daughter, go and get some rest."

Yitzhak watched as Hannah went to the bedroom to lay down; Ze'ev and Anna went downstairs to the room at the bottom of the steps that had been converted to a bedroom. Yitzhak lay on the sofa, still not totally believing everything that had happened. The capture of Randy had disturbed him more then the invading Russian army that had been destroyed at Israel's border. Scripture had not left him unaware of the invasion, but he was not prepared to hear of Randy's capture. He had helped nurture Randy's spirit when he was an infant in Christ and had heard of how he had grown into spiritual manhood over the past two and one-half years. He had not seen Randy since the escape at Ben Gurion Airport, but they had spoken to each other regularly. He knew now that they would probably not see each other again until after the Lord's return. The ringing of the phone startled Yitzhak, and he slowly reached over to answer the call.

"Hello." Yitzhak struggled to get the word out.

"Hello Yitzhak? This is Mary Johnson."

"Mary-" Yitzhak sat up quickly, "-Mary we heard the news about Randy."

"Oh, Yitzhak." Mary began to cry, "It's all my fault. I didn't realize what was happening until it was too late. I was told that if I led the authorities to where Randy was, they would not prosecute him. They said that they only wanted to question him about the attack on the fleet."

"Okay, Mary, I want you to compose yourself. Where are you now?"

"I'm in Denver. As they took him away, he told me to call you. He wants me to stay with you."

"I'm glad you called. He is a brother in Christ and you are his wife. You are welcome to stay with us."

I'll be on the next plane to Tel-Aviv. It will arrive at noon tomorrow."

"Hannah and I will meet you there at noon then."

"There's something that you should know Yitzhak ... I'm pregnant."

Tears welled in Yitzhak's eyes, "You come. We will take care of you-both of you when the time comes."

Yitzhak hung up the phone. Had he made a mistake by letting Mary come? It didn't matter. She needed him, and he would be there for her, the wife of a Christian brother. Yitzhak decided to wait to tell Jake until he had some rest. He turned on the television to watch the news coverage.

"This is Elizabeth Osborn," the news anchor said, "President Christos and Prophet Gallo were in Jerusalem today as the invading Russian army was making its charge on the ancient city. Charles Goodson is there to interview Prophet Gallo. I turn it over now to Charles Goodson."

"Thank you, Elizabeth," newsman Goodson said as he turned to the camera. "I have with me Prophet Gallo. As you have reported, he and President Christos were here in Jerusalem when the Russian Army attempted to invade Israel. They have been uninjured in the attack." Turning to Prophet Gallo, "Prophet Gallo, can you tell me where you and President Christos were when you found out that the Russian army was invading Israel?"

"We were on Mount Olivet when the attack occurred." Prophet Gallo was calm. There was no hint of nervousness or of fear following what had happened. He exuded confidence, even a pompous attitude that can only come from someone in his position. "President Christos, in his power-" he continued, "-raised his mighty hands, and the ground began to shake. He caused the earth to split and the fire from the sky to destroy the invading Russian army."

"He caused the rain of fire and the powerful earthquake?" asked the newsman.

"He has the power of God." Prophet Gallo looked to the sky, "For he is the son of God."

Yitzhak had heard enough. The words of Prophet Gallo were nothing but lies, and he knew that they would mislead many. It was God the Father that had protected his people and Israel from the invading army just as had been predicted in Ezekiel. But the Anti-Christ would use the event for his own purpose. Yitzhak took a deep breath then went to the bedroom to lie down.

Yitzhak and Hannah were sitting at the kitchen table when Jake finally awoke. Ze'ev and Anna had taken a walk to get the latest response from the neighbors regarding the failed invasion of the Russian army. Hannah forced a smile as Jake entered the room and kissed him on the cheek before going to make some coffee. She personally did not like the hot drink, but knew that Jake liked it. He sensed something wrong and took a seat across from Yitzhak.

"Is Hannah all right, Yitzhak?" Jake nodded toward Hannah.

"She's fine, my brother." Yitzhak leaned closer, "I got a call from Mary Johnson while you were sleeping."

Jake took a deep breath then exhaled slowly. "What did she want?"

"She said that she was deceived by the authorities, that they told her that all they wanted was to question Randy about the attack on the American fleet. She thought that by turning him in that she and Randy would be allowed to return to a normal life."

"Do you believe her?"

"She sounded sincere ... convincing even."

"Did you tell her I was here?"

"No. Her phone line may have been tapped."

"Why would she call here if she didn't know I was here?"

"She said that Randy wanted her to come here to stay-"

"What?"

"He told her that, as she puts it, when they were leading him away." Yitzhak sat back into his chair while Hannah placed some coffee in front of both of the men. "Jake, she told me that she was pregnant."

"Pregnant?"

"Yes. That's probably why Randy wanted her to stay with us. He knows Hannah would take very good care of her."

"But, Yitzhak, can we trust her?"

"If there is any hope for her becoming a Christian, then we're going to have to."

Yitzhak had never met Mary but knew from pictures who she was as soon as she stepped off the plane.

"That is her," he said pointing.

"Are you sure?" Hannah stretched her neck looking in the direction of Yitzhak's gaze.

"I am sure. Randy has described her to me many times. Come, Hannah, let's meet her."

Yitzhak and Hannah greeted the disheveled woman. Mary had been crying. Mascara streaked her wet cheeks, and her eyes were puffy.

Mary noticed the bearded man staring. "Are you Yitzhak?" she asked.

"Yes. I am Yitzhak Benziman." He answered then gestured to Hannah, "And this is Hannah, my wife."

Mary lowered her head and started to cry again. "I'm sorry. I didn't know a person could cry so much. I haven't been able to stop since they took Randy away."

Tears welled up in the eyes of both Yitzhak and Hannah. Hannah reached over and put her arms around Mary. "It's okay, my child. Everything will be okay. We will take care of you."

"Do you know where they took Randy?" Yitzhak reached to pick up Mary's bag.

"They told me afterwards that they were going to take him to Rome."

"Rome?" Yitzhak shook his head, "Why Rome?"

"That's where they will hold the trial."

Yitzhak took a deep breath, "Let's get back to our home. We can talk more later."

Jake was staring out the front window when Yitzhak, Hannah and Mary arrived. He stood motionless as Mary walked through the door. She stopped in her tracks, surprised to see Jake. Her tears flowed freely once again and she ran to Jake squeezing him tightly. Jake could not hold back his tears as he held Mary. He felt sorry for the lost soul that he now was responsible for. *Could he trust her with their lives?* He didn't know. All he knew is that he now had to nurture her and the coming baby. With God's help she would realize that Jesus the Savior loved her as much as anyone.

Four months had passed and there had been no word about Randy or of Sam and Joyce. It was as though they had vanished from the earth. Not even CNN had any information released to them. Mary had been in a deep depression since her arrival, eating only when Hannah or Anna had forced her to. Most of the time she would just sit in her room, the room that had been Jake's before Mary's arrival. Jake had since been sleeping on the sofa in the living room. Mary had become irrational. At times she would "snap" out of her depression for a few hours or at the longest, a day or two, and then just as quickly, return to her depressed state. The baby's birth was coming quickly, and Hannah had been preparing for the event. Anna was also preparing, being trained by Hannah what she should do when the time came.

The screaming from Mary's room came early in the morning, awakening everyone in the house. The time had come for Mary to have her baby. Hannah forced everyone but Anna out of the room and asked Yitzhak to boil some water. The labor lasted for hours. Occasionally Anna would enter the kitchen to get some more water and give a progress report. Jake got up and paced the floor as if it was his own baby being born.

"How long have they been in there?" Jake stopped from his pacing momentarily to ask the question.

"Be patient. These things take time. Hannah knows what she is doing."

"She's very good, Jake," Ze'ev added with a chuckle. "Rumor has it she delivered me." Yitzhak and Ze'ev smiled, but Jake didn't see the humor.

"It's a boy." Anna walked into the kitchen. "Mary had a baby boy. Mother and child are doing fine."

Six months had past since the Russian army had been destroyed. Not wanting to chance his own capture, Jake had stayed in Israel with Yitzhak and his family. The plan to live out the remainder of the Tribulation in the cave had been ruined by the apprehension of Randy and Tracey's parents. Jake had heard nothing of the fate of his friends. News broadcasts and newspapers had been silent about the three since the first few days of their imprisonment. Mary had grown more depressed over the capture of Randy. She had blamed herself and stayed mostly in her room, only getting up occasionally to change or feed her son. Randy Jr. was a healthy baby and was growing quickly. Now a month and one-half old, he knew his mother only on the occasional feedings and diaper changes, but it was with both Hannah and Anna that he truly bonded. Mary's mental condition was not getting better, even with the encouragement offered by everyone. Even her son was not motivation enough to snap her out of her condition. Randy Jr. had been a Godsend, all agreed. There is something about young innocence that seems to cross all barriers. Jake had been thankful for Randy Jr.'s birth. Jake often thought of how much of John's life he had missed when his son was the same age. *Was Randy Jr.'s birth a gift from God so that Jake's ever present grief over his wife's and son's absence would be eased?* He did not know, but his grief had been less ever since.

Jake had thinned in the past months, his appetite not being what it once was. Sleepless nights had taken its toll, and he had looked aged and ragged. His eyes had sunken a little into their sockets and the lines in his skin under his lower eyelids deepened. He had more gray than black in his hair, and the beard that he had grown was thick and almost entirely gray with a patch of black extending from his lower lip to under his chin. Despite his appearance, he felt strong in both body and spirit. He had prayed daily with Yitzhak and his family, and with the Lord's help, they remained committed to the faith.

Events had unfolded quickly. Babylon had been restored fully and was now a thriving metropolis. News accounts reported that President Christos was going to make Babylon the new capital, replacing Rome. The Anti-Christ's influence now extended to the whole Middle East and Russia. He had taken over Russia and all her allies after her destruction from the fire and sulfur that had rained on her. A standardized currency was created which was used by all the western hemisphere, Europe, Russia, and parts of northern Africa. The U.S.E.'s influences were also extending to Pakistan and India and, to a smaller extent, into Asia and Australia that had joined the U.S.E a year earlier.

Today was a day that Jake had waited for in anticipation. Today was going to be the official dedication of the rebuilt Jewish temple, and the guests of honor were going to be President Christos and Prophet Gallo. All who wished to attend were welcome, and Jake and Yitzhak wanted to see firsthand the Anti-Christ and the man that Jake knew was the false prophet.

The crowd had gathered at the western wall just in front of the platform from which Alexander Christos would give the dedication. The platform backed to the wall itself and the podium was located at the center. Located just in front of the platform and facing the crowd, security guards formed a human wall to keep people from getting too close. Jake and Yitzhak were able to come near to the platform, within a few feet of the security guards, but Jake did not want to chance getting closer and being recognized. They had never seen Christos in person, only on television and in pictures, and they nervously anticipated seeing him for the first time. There was a low murmur in the crowd as Christos stepped onto the platform followed closely behind by Prophet Gallo. Jake could not take his eyes off President Christos as he took his place at the podium and stared down at the crowd. Prophet Gallo was positioned behind the President and to the right, just as a dutiful servant should, anticipating any need that may be required by the world dictator.

"I am honored-" President Christos began, "-to be invited to dedicate this temple in the name of my equal in heaven, God the Father. God promised to send a king to Israel, a king whose kingdom would have no end. I am pleased to dedicate this temple for I am the king of whom God has spoken. He and I are one. He who believes in me believes in God the Father who has sent me and believes that He and I are one. I have just come from the inner sanctuary and have spoken to the Father. Worship me as your God, for I am your God."

"You are Satan," an angry voice screamed out from behind Jake. A young Jew-no more than eighteen years of age-quickly made his way to the front of the crowd. The boy was tall and slender with dark brown hair and a sparse beard. His skin was the color of a light coffee bean and his brown eyes were angry as he stared unwavering at the president. In his right hand he held a revolver, shining blue as he lifted it up and took aim.

"He's got a gun," shouted one of the guards.

The guards converged on the Jew, but it was too late. The young man had time to fire three shots, all striking President Christos in his forehead. The first two bullets entered above each eye while the third bullet entered at the center of his forehead a little higher than the first two. President Christos dropped instantly to his knees then fell like a rag doll to his back. The bullets had traveled through his brain and exited the back of his head, leaving a gaping wound that splattered Prophet Gallo with blood and gray matter. He lay there, quivering on the verge of death as a pool of blood grew steadily around him. Prophet Gallo kneeled down to touch the fallen leader. There was no doubt in his mind, and the truth was revealed in his eyes-President Christos was dead. At the same instant of President Christos' death, a flaming ball with a tail like that of a comet fell from the sky and appeared to land on the eastern side of the Temple Mount. A plume of smoke and debris filled the air, but it was ignored by Prophet Gallo.

"Bring that man here." Prophet Gallo motioned to the guards holding the Jew. They brought him to the platform and positioned him in front of the corpse. Prophet Gallo approached the killer and stared at him.

"He has murdered the Son of God," Prophet Gallo addressed the crowd.

"He is not the Son of God," the young Jew shouted out. "He is the Anti-Christ."

"Silence." Prophet Gallo struck the young man causing his nose to bleed. His anger now peaked as he turned to face the crowd and spoke. "Witness the wrath of God to all those that will try and defy him."

A pillar of fire streaked from above striking the young man at the top of his head and extended to his feet, devouring him instantly in flames. He screamed out in agony as the odor of burning flesh filled the air. Most of the spectators thought that the fire was just a continuation of the flaming ball that had fallen to the earth just moments earlier.

"We need to get out of here now while the guards are preoccupied with what's going on," Jake said anxiously. "They may want to detain everyone and I can't chance that."

"I agree." Yitzhak responded, "Let's get home."

Back at the house Jake and Yitzhak gathered the group together. "President Christos has been assassinated," Yitzhak said. "But as Revelation tells us we know that he will be indwelt with Satan himself and be raised back to life. The ball of fire that fell from the sky at the time of Christos' death was Satan himself, being thrown from heaven to earth. Satan will indwell the body of Alexander Christos."

"He will also desecrate the Temple," Jake added, "What Daniel calls the 'Abomination that causes desolation.'"

"Yes." Tears welled in Yitzhak's eyes, "We must flee Israel. The Anti-Christ's wrath will come with a fury now against Jews and Christians. Jesus tells us that when the Anti-Christ desecrates the Temple we should flee, and that is what we will do."

News of President Christos' assassination spread quickly. Prophet Gallo denied reports that he would be taking over as the new president and leader of the World Unification Church. He encouraged the citizens of the world to be patient regarding a successor to

Alexander Christos and had scheduled a news conference to explain why he had not moved more quickly filling the newly vacated office. News agencies from around the world had gathered to cover the conference and had settled into their seats as Prophet Gallo took the podium.

"Three days ago." Prophet Gallo started, "President Christos of the United States of Europe and the Son of God was brutally murdered by a fanatical Jew. We all grieve the death of our leader, no one more than I. The wounds to the head of our president were massive, three in all, not counting the large exit wound, and no mere man could have survived it. Therefore, our leader died." Prophet Gallo paused as he stared down at the reporters, "But President Christos is no mere man. He is more than just a man; but he is God. Behold your leader and your God."

A curtain just behind Prophet Gallo rose, and standing behind it was President Christos. He appeared to be glowing, and the massive wounds to his head were completely healed, save for the three entrance wound scars. The scars that remained were distinctive and very visible, even from watching the images on the television screen. The significance of the scar that remained on President Christos' forehead did not escape Jake's attention. It was as clear as if Jake was just two feet away. Each bullet had left a circular scar, one above each eye and the third at the center of Anti-Christ's forehead and just a little higher than the others. Each circular scar had a "tail" that seemed to spin off to the left of the circle, extending to the hairline. The "tail" was actually surgical scars formed by the incision of the surgeon's knife at the time when President Christos was rushed to the hospital on the day of the assassination. Each scar resembled the number six, and, placed in sequence, formed 666.

Jake, Yitzhak and Hannah watched the television broadcast of the news conference and were amazed at what they were seeing. Jake and Yitzhak had seen the devastating wound that had been inflicted on Alexander Christos during the dedication at the Western Wall, and now he was made new-except for the scar 666.

"Behold your God!" Prophet Gallo shouted out, "He has been raised from the dead. The scar on his forehead remains to remind us that he was once a man, then raised to life as God himself to save the world. The mark of a man, an imperfect creation made perfect by worshipping Alexander Christos. Everyone shall worship Alexander Christos, and to prove your loyalty, every man, woman, and child will be required to have the mark 666, either on the forehead or the right hand. You will not be allowed to buy or sell without his mark. If anyone is captured that does not bear his mark, the penalty will be death."

"In honor of his godliness and to set an example for those that will not accept the mark, His Almighty has ordered the execution of Randy Johnson and his two accomplices. The execution will be held next week in Rome at the famous Roman Coliseum. In his mercy, the Almighty Christos has offered to spare their lives if they accept his mark, but they have refused. They have sealed their own fate."

"How can this be?" Hannah asked, "He was dead and now he is alive again? How can he order the death of our friends?"

"Do not be alarmed, Hannah." Yitzhak responded, "This has been predicted in Revelation 13: *One of the heads of the beast out of the sea seemed to have a fatal wound, but the fatal wound will be healed.* The Bible predicts this. Let us be ready then to go forward. Those that don't know the Lord are amazed by this man and they will worship him now as never before. But we know the truth."

Something had stirred in Mary. Hearing her husband's name seemed to awaken her from her deep depression. "I must go to Rome!" she screamed. She stood from the sofa, inadvertently letting Randy Jr. fall to the floor. The baby, uninjured, cried out loudly. Hannah rushed over and picked up the baby.

"He must accept the president's mark if he wants to live." Mary continued, unconcerned with Randy Jr.

"No!" Jake shouted out. "You can't go. There is nothing you can do. You're needed here. Your baby needs you."

Mary sobbed and fell to her knees. Jake reached to keep her from falling completely to the floor.

"Is she all right, Jake?" Anna asked as Hannah handed over the baby.

Jake shook his head. "She's passed out. Ze'ev, help me get her to her room."

The next morning Hannah and Anna had prepared breakfast. The men slowly made their appearances and sat at the kitchen table.

"Anna." Hannah placed bread on the table, "Wake Mary up and have her come and eat."

Moments later Anna rushed back to the kitchen, holding Randy Jr. "She's gone. Mary's not in her room. How can she leave her baby?"

Chapter 12

———

It was unknown from where the two nameless men came. Like the mighty winds that swirl from a raging storm, blowing trees to the ground and houses from their foundations, they came to tear down the evil ways from the foundation within the souls of the lost and to turn the heart of mankind back to God. And, like the wind, they came without warning and unwelcome by those whose souls they intended to uproot with their message of the wrath to come. They wore sackcloth made of dark goat's hair, and each carried a gnarled wooden staff, the length of which was a foot longer then the height of each of them. The men were almost identical in appearance; both having long white hair and thick beards that flowed over their breasts and contrasted against their dark coarse garments. The one with the blue eyes had light brown skin, smooth and without blemish; the one with the brown eyes seemed the elder, with wrinkles on his high cheeks and on his forehead. His skin was slightly darker than his companion's and as tough as leather with slight chaffing at the corners of each eye. They brought with them an air of confidence and resolve, fearing nothing that might try and hinder the message that they were sent to bring. They came with power to shut up the sky so that it would not bring forth rain for the remainder of the Tribulation, and to bring plague and pestilence to those that would not give glory to God the Father. Their authority was given from above to strike the earth with these plagues as often as they wanted. It was no coincidence that they first appeared the same day that President Christos was raised back to life seven days before. Their ministry started at the Wailing Wall, and they had been seen everyday since in the streets of Jerusalem.

Today Jake would hear them at the Garden of Gethsemane on the Mount of Olives. Jake knew who these men were. They were the two witnesses of Revelation eleven, who would prophesy for three and one-half years, the remainder of the Tribulation. Jake's mind wandered as he walked to the garden. He thought of the two witnesses and how they had come to warn the people of the earth of the wrath that God was going to pour out onto those who rejected the Lordship of Jesus Christ and on those who would accept the Anti-Christ as their false god.

Word had spread that one hundred and forty-four thousand Jewish men, twelve thousand from each of the ancient tribes of Israel, had been sent to evangelize the world and to reach out to those who would accept Jesus Christ as Lord and Savior. Again, Jake was not ignorant of who these one hundred and forty-four thousand men were. Revelation held the answer; they were *those that were sealed by God, who had not defiled themselves with women, for they kept themselves pure.* Because of them, multitudes from every nation, tribe, people, and language would find salvation through the Lord Jesus Christ. Jake was overcome by emotion, and he gave thanks to God the Father for His mercy.

Jake journeyed along a narrow path that split an olive grove into two equal parts. The branches of the thick trees that bordered the trail grew parallel to the path and made an impenetrable wall. The top of the trees extended over the path creating a natural canopy that blocked the view of the sky and formed a tunnel that ended at the base of the mountain. Bright light entered in at the end of the pathway and the faint voices of the two witnesses became louder as Jake reached the opening at the end of the grove. At the first of four summits on the mount, Jake saw the two men standing at the center of the crowd that was seated around them. Jake found a patch of grass and sat to listen.

"The wrath of God is at hand!" the elder witness screamed out. "He will send judgment on those who accept the Anti-Christ's mark and will cast him into the lake of fire where there will be pain and suffering, and his suffering will not end."

"Beware the Anti-Christ and his false prophet," the blue-eyed one added. "God's judgment will be poured out from the bowls of His wrath onto the Anti-Christ and those who worship him and his evil prophet, and on those who will not give glory to His Son, the Lord Jesus Christ. Listen to what we tell you. God will turn the sun black and the waters bitter, and no one will be able to escape his judgments."

"What shall we do?" a shout came from within the crowd.

"Accept Jesus Christ as Savior!" the elder responded, "and reject Alexander Christos the Anti-Christ. He will lead you to destruction and to the burning fires of Hell where there will be weeping and gnashing of teeth."

"He who overcomes-" the younger prophet shouted out, "-and accepts Jesus, who was crucified, will eat of the tree of life and drink from the living waters that spring from God the Father. But if you reject Christ, fire and brimstone shall be your reward, and you shall suffer the plagues that will come to the earth in the days to come."

The afternoon passed quickly, and Jake left the garden, passing back through the olive grove. He had listened to the two men for most of the day, and, remembering what they had proclaimed about the wrath to come, Jake was flooded with a feeling of doom. He could not shake the anxiety building within him, something was not right, but he attributed it to the message that he had just heard. Stroking his beard as he walked along the path to Yitzhak's home and contemplating the uneasy feeling that was consuming his thoughts, he was startled by a voice from behind.

"Jake!" Ze'ev ran up from out of the shadow. "Jake, come quickly. It's Randy and your friends."

"What about them?" Jake grabbed Ze'ev' by the arm, restraining him. "Are they here in Jerusalem?"

"No." Ze'ev attempted to race ahead of Jake. "They're reporting it on the television. Papa has sent me to look for you. Hurry." The two raced to the front door and hurriedly pushed it open.

Yitzhak and Hannah were sitting on the edge of the sofa, engrossed in the broadcast. Yitzhak got up quickly to meet Jake in the middle of the room.

"What's going on?" Jake stared at the television.

"I can't believe this is happening." Yitzhak turned to the television.

"What is it?" Jake asked, his voice getting louder with impatience.

"They're going to execute Randy and the parents of your wife. We were warned by Prophet Gallo himself, but I never believed that it would be televised." Yitzhak's voice tapered as he tried to hold back his emotion.

"My God. I prayed for a miracle." Jake's knees buckled as he realized what was happening.

"They're at the Roman Coliseum. Alexander Christos is there to personally witness the event."

"Have they shown Randy yet?" Jake questioned Yitzhak. "Are Sam and Joyce there too?"

"Yes." Yitzhak looked at Jake, "Sam and Joyce are there too."

The Roman Coliseum was full of spectators. Like a sporting event, the excitement of the crowd peaked in anticipation of what was about to take place. Vendors were selling food and other refreshments-executions were going to become a money maker, and they were going to take advantage of every one. Everyone in the stands had paid a premium to witness the first public execution at the Coliseum in more than two thousand years. The president's box was located on the north side of the inside perimeter and arrayed with the flags of the United States of Europe. Within the box, President Christos sat in the front row; Prophet Gallo sat just behind him and to the right. At the south side were three large posts sticking straight up from the ground lined in a row. Randy was tied to the center post. Tied to the post to his right was Joyce, and tied to the post on his left was Sam. At the center of the coliseum sat a large rectangular cage, approximately ten feet wide and twenty feet long, all sides ten feet high and made with black steel bars. There was an opening at the front, or short side, that could be closed with a gate that slid side to side, and another three gates located on the long side of the cage. The three gates could be pulled open by sliding upward, and each led to three separate holding cells with solid walls, hiding anything inside them.

Mary had promised herself that she would not come, but her love for Randy would not allow her to stay away. Standing just inside the wall that formed the inside perimeter of the arena, she stared at her husband with tears rolling down her face. The six months since her betrayal of her husband had been a time of deep depression for her. She blamed herself for what was happening now by believing that Randy would be spared. She had believed a lie, and Randy was paying the price. The crowd closed in on her in an attempt to get closer to the action. A silence fell over the entire Coliseum and then everyone took their seats when President Christos stood to speak.

"Today we have come to witness the execution of Randy Johnson. He has been convicted of planning and causing the attack on the American fleet and of treason." The crowd began to yell insults at Randy and throw objects in his direction. President Christos raised his hands in an attempt to quiet them. "We have also convicted his companions who tried to hide him from justice. All three have admitted to being Christians and-" the roar of the spectators interrupted the speech. Anyone that did not worship Alexander Christos was worthy of death, especially if they were Christians or Jews. Christianity was considered an insult to their God and leader, and they were expressing it with their shouts of hatred. Again President Christos raised his hands, "Patience. Am I not your God? Am I not merciful? I am your God and I am merciful. Witness my mercy." President Christos turned to Randy and spoke. "Randy Johnson, you have been convicted of treason and of being a Christian. But I will show you mercy and will pardon you of your crimes. All you have to do is accept my mark."

"Burn in Hell, Satan!" Randy shouted out. "I will never accept the mark."

The crowd roared again with their insults, once again throwing objects at the prisoners.

"Very well," President Christos responded, calming the people. He turned his attention to the guard located in front of him. "Guard!"

"Yes, Your Holiness," the guard stood in front of Christos.

"Take the woman and put her in the cage. Lock the gate so that she can not escape."

The guard untied Joyce and placed her in the cage and locked the gate then returned to his position in front of the president's box. President Christos looked at Randy and spoke.

"I will give you another chance. Accept the mark and I will pardon not only you but your friends as well."

Randy hung his head and started to cry. He knew what was happening and he knew that the Anti-Christ was playing with him. They were all going to die today regardless of what Randy would say.

"Don't accept the mark." Sam yelled out, "We all knew that this day would come. Don't let him fool you."

"I am ready." Joyce screamed, "Don't accept the mark. Today we will all be in Heaven."

"I have already given you my answer." Randy could barely look at his friends. "I will not accept the mark."

President Christos took a deep breath and paused momentarily. "Let the executioner in."

The door to the tunnel opened and a large man wearing a black hood over his head walked out. He had broad muscular shoulders, which seemed sculpted and cut to perfection. Black hair covered his back and abdomen, hiding the muscles that rippled underneath. He wore black, brief-type shorts that barely covered his loins and buttocks. His muscular thighs were uncovered and narrowed at the knees, then broadened again at the calf giving the entire leg the shape of an hour glass. Leather thongs covered his feet and were tied above his ankles. In his right hand he carried a large two-edged sword, the silver shining brightly against the sun. In his left hand he carried a bow that had been strung tightly, and the arrows were in a sheath strapped over his shoulder. He came to within twenty feet of the cage and faced the president.

"Executioner-" Alexander Christos paused, surveying the spectators, playing them for the fools that they were, "-release the lions."

"No!" Sam screamed out. "My God, no."

Joyce looked at Sam with an expression of fear that he had never seen his wife of forty-five years have before. She reached her arm towards Sam through the steel bars in a vain attempt to grab hold of him. Joyce slumped to her knees and started to cry.

"I love you, Joyce!" Sam screamed out before hanging his head to cry. "I love you."

The executioner took his place atop the second of the three chambers located at the side of the cage. Everyone now knew what was inside the holding cells. The four hundred-pound lions had not been fed for almost a week to ensure that they would attack their victims without hesitation. The executioner attached a bar to each of the gates so that he could open them simultaneously then turned to face the crowd and raised his hands. The crowd roared in anticipation as he slowly rotated in place to stare at each section of the Coliseum. He faced the president to wait for the signal. Alexander Christos stretched out his hand holding a white cloth. The spectators became silent in an instant, waiting for the president to drop the cloth.

"Don't look, Joyce," Randy shouted. "You'll be with Jesus soon."

President Christos released the cloth and it slowly floated to the ground. The executioner pulled up on the bar and lifted the gates that separated the lions from Joyce. The three lions walked out of the holding cells warily. Their large bodies were covered with a short, golden fur. The hair grew longer at the back of their heads forming a dark brown mane, then back to the short golden hair on their faces ending with the black nose at the end of the muzzle. Their heavy panting revealed their large pointed teeth and caused saliva to moisten the edges of their mouths and to froth at the corners, like an animal infected with rabies. They were unaware of Joyce until she let out a loud sob.

Instantly, and as one, the animals pounced. Paws first and claws extended, they tore at her flesh, then taking her in their mouths they shook her like a rag doll, violently biting into her with their razor-sharp teeth. One lion bit into her leg, tearing the limb from her body. Her blood pulsated from the severed arteries of her upper thigh and sprayed the face of the animal. The other two were tugging her in opposite directions, one crushing her skull in its powerful jaws, killing Joyce instantly.

The roar from the coliseum was deafening and the crowd chanted for more blood. Man had always been a race that would kill their own for pleasure, feeding on the torture of others to fulfill some primitive need from within. The frenzied crowd chanted for another gruesome murder. Feeding on itself, the chanting became louder and with more purpose; they wanted more and did not want to wait any longer. Sensing that he would lose control, Alexander Christos began to speak.

"Executioner," he said silencing the coliseum. "Prepare the horses."

The executioner entered the tunnel and returned, leading two black Arabian horses. On the back of each was a saddle, and attached to each saddle was a rope trailing behind and dragging on the ground, leaving a small, snake-like trail in the sand. He led the horses to the front of the presidential box and dutifully stood waiting for the order from Christos.

"I will give you one more chance," President Christos said looking at Randy. "Accept the mark and I will spare your other friend. Don't have his blood on your head as well as the blood of his wife. You have the power to save his life."

"Don't do it, Randy," Sam could barely speak. Watching his wife die had left him weak. Tears flowed from his eyes as he tried to speak again, his voice no louder than a whisper. "They're going to kill us whether you accept the mark or not. Let's just get it over with. I want to be with Joyce."

"No." Randy responded to the Anti-Christ. "We are prepared to die for Christ."

"Very well." President Christos motioned to the executioner. "Kill his friend."

The executioner untied Sam from the post and brought him to the horses. He ordered Sam to lie on the ground and tied his hands to the rope of one horse and his legs to the rope of the other horse. He commanded the horses to slowly walk forward. The tension created on the rope pulled by the horses caused Sam to rise up off the ground until he was almost horizontal. The tension stretched Sam, causing his shoulders and hips to pop out of their sockets with a loud crack that could be heard by even those at the highest balcony of the coliseum. Sam screamed out in pain as the horses maintained the tension on the ropes.

"Accept the mark and I will let him go," Alexander Christos said. "Accept the mark and I will heal his wounds."

"No!" Sam shouted, mustering just enough energy to get the words out. "Don't listen to him."

"Go to hell." Randy hung his head and sobbed.

"Executioner, he has made his decision. Get your sword and finish his friend."

The executioner grabbed his sword and positioned himself so that Sam's head was to the right and his feet to the left. He raised the sword and held it above his head and looked at the president and waited for the signal from the Anti-Christ. Alexander Christos nodded his head and the executioner swung the blade downward with a mighty blow, severing Sam into two parts. The horses edged forward from the sudden release of the tension that was holding Sam in the air. With Sam's entrails exposed, the horses slowly dragged each half of his body along the perimeter of the arena, leaving a trail of blood behind them.

Mary could no longer hold herself back. Wanting to hold Randy one last time, she jumped the wall and ran toward her husband. Reaching Randy, she threw her arms around him and sobbed. She had found her way to Rome after hearing that Randy was scheduled to be executed.

"No!" Randy screamed. "You can't stay here."

The executioner grabbed Mary around the neck from behind and held her in his grip.

"Let go of her, you murderer." Randy struggled to get loose of the ropes that tied him to the post.

"Prophet Gallo, who is that woman?" Christos leaned his ear to the man seated behind him.

"That's the traitor's wife."

"Perfect." The idea to use Randy's wife to get him to accept the mark was better than he had anticipated. "Executioner, let her go to him. Accept the mark and I will let both of you go and live in peace."

The executioner let go of his grip and Mary again wrapped her arms around Randy.

"Accept the mark, Randy," Mary pleaded. "We will be together again with our son."

"No!" Randy responded quickly. "Don't you understand? To accept the mark would mean to reject Christ. I'd rather die."

"And you will die if you don't receive the mark." Mary put her face in her hands and sobbed uncontrollably. "Didn't you hear me? You have a son now and he needs his father. Accept the mark and we will all be together."

Randy sobbed. He would never see his son, at least on this side of Heaven.

"Mary, accept Christ in you heart and you will be with me in Heaven forever. Do you think that if President Christos was the true Son of God he would put Sam and Joyce through the death that they just suffered? Or the one that I am about to suffer? The power that those two have shown you has come from Satan. Whatever you do, don't accept his mark"

"How am I going to live without you?" Mary lifted her head, "Who will show me the way?"

"Accept Jesus Christ as your Savior. He will show you the way."

"Enough." Alexander Christos grew impatient. "Have you made your decision?"

"I will not accept the mark." Randy answered the President and then stared at Mary. Not knowing that she had been staying with Jake and Yitzhak, "Find Jake. He'll help you."

"Guard?" the President spoke to the uniformed man just in front of him.

"Yes, Your Holiness."

"Escort the woman out through the tunnel. But make sure she witnesses the execution."

The guard took Mary to the tunnel and into the shadows. "Take a good look. The President wants you to remember him this way."

Mary turned to see Randy staring back at her. He mouthed *I love you* then turned his attention back to the executioner.

"Executioner, take your bow and show the world what we do to traitors."

The executioner positioned himself twenty feet in front of Randy. Taking an arrow from the sheath, he then placed it in the bow and took aim. He let the arrow fly and it struck Randy just above the right knee, shattering the bone before exiting cleanly out the other side of the leg. The excruciating pain radiated from the point of impact throughout Randy's entire body, causing him to scream out in agony. The executioner raised his hands in victory, igniting the crowd into another frenzy, and they cheered him on to grab another arrow. But the executioner waited. A quick death would be too easy for the victim. Man, generally, does not fear death as much as the process of dying. True torture comes when dying is prolonged and fear adds to the agony of the process, causing the victim to beg for death to come. And so, the executioner would wait before delivering the next arrow, thus prolonging the process for Randy and adding to the agonizing torture that he would have to endure. The waiting ended as another arrow was aimed at Randy. This one shattered Randy's left knee cap, blowing through his leg and embedding itself into the post that Randy had been tied to. The pain nearly drove Randy into unconsciousness. Again the executioner raised his hand in a mock victory taunting his victim.

Mary fell to her knees, too weak to stand. She covered her face with her hands in an attempt to shield herself from her husband's execution. The guard pulled her head up by her long hair and forced her to look.

"Look what happens to traitors," the guard said. "All he had to do was to accept our lord's mark and worship him. But now he will pay with his life."

The executioner took aim again. This arrow stuck Randy above the navel penetrating his abdomen. The executioner had done his job well. Abdominal wounds inflict a tremendous amount of pain and death comes slowly. Randy's mouth was open, and he seemed to be gasping for air. Blood trickled out of his mouth and onto his chest and his face became pale, but he would have to wait to die. The executioner waved the final arrow in his hand, taunting the crowd to scream louder. Finally he turned to face his victim and placed the arrow in the bow. Randy could do nothing, not even scream, as he saw the executioner raise his bow and take aim. The arrow streaked out of the bow and struck Randy in the forehead, penetrating his brain and exploding out of the back of his skull and pinning his head against the post. Randy was dead.

"Remember this day." Alexander Christos stood and surveyed the crowded coliseum. "This will be the fate of any who will not accept my mark and who will not worship me." He turned and walked through a door at the back of the presidential box, followed closely behind by Prophet Gallo. The sun was setting low in the sky, flaming red against the clouds in the horizon. The spectators slowly filed out of the Coliseum, all taking a last look at what was left of the bodies of the three Christian martyrs.

The next morning Mary stared into the mirror and slowly brushed her hair. With trembling hands she dragged the brush over her scalp to the end of her blonde hair and then unconsciously repeated the motion. For two hours she sat there in a daze with her blue eyes glazed over and an empty, far-off expression on her face, remembering in detail the execution of her husband. *What went wrong?* Just three years earlier she and Randy were on top of the world with a new outlook on life. They had joined a new church that promised peace and security. She had even witnessed the power that came from Prophet Gallo, and their lives were going to get better. But why? Mary kept asking herself the question. Why? Why did all of this happen?

Jake, she thought. It was Jake that changed Randy with his talk of Jesus and of the Tribulation. *If it weren't for Jake.* Tears streaked down Mary's face and fell from her chin and landed on her lap. *If it weren't for Jake,* she continued her thought, *Randy would be alive today, and they would be together.* The anger within Mary was building. She quickened the stroking motion and placed increasing pressure on the hair brush causing skin to be rubbed off of her scalp. With her anger peaking, she looked past her reflection in the mirror and did not notice the small trickle of blood on her forehead caused by the self-inflicted wounds on her head. "Find Jake." Mary spoke aloud, remembering Randy's last words to her. *Find Jake. For what? So that I can have the same fate? To be brutally martyred for a false God?* Mary placed the brush down and stared into the mirror. She noticed the blood on her forehead and wiped it away. No, I won't worship Jake's God. Alexander Christos is the Son of the true God. If Jake's God was the true God, then He would have saved Randy. *Find Jake?* Randy's last words to her repeated in her mind until she no longer could take it. She hung her head and clasped her hands over her ears, attempting to silence the voice in her head that kept the words ringing over and over. "Why should I find Jake?" she screamed. Looking up at the mirror, she had an answer: "Revenge." She would not forget what Jake did to Randy, nor would she forgive. "Jake's in Jerusalem," she whispered to herself, "Yes, Randy. I will find him. I'll find him and get sweet revenge."

Chapter 13

⊱——⊰

Y itzhak was worried. Jake had not left his room since yesterday's executions of Randy and Tracey's parents. He had
hoped that the deep depression that had affected Mary Johnson had
not taken its grip on Jake. But time was short and they had to
prepare; Yitzhak could not allow Jake to mourn any longer.
Alexander Christos was soon going to begin his persecution of
Israel, and Yitzhak knew that it would be suicide to stay; they
would have to leave Jerusalem and the sooner the better.

"I must get Jake." Yitzhak stood from the table. "We can't wait
any longer."

"Let him be." Hannah reached for Yitzhak's hand, "He needs
time."

"We don't have time," Yitzhak responded, quickly pulling his
hand from Hannah. "Don't you know that we have a place prepared
for us in the desert where we will be taken care of and protected
from the Anti-Christ?"

"What?" Hannah looked puzzled. "Speak to me plainly,
Yitzhak."

"Satan has been cast to the earth in that great fire ball that fell to
the earth at the time of President Christos' assassination and now he
will take his wrath out on us. Alexander Christos has disgraced the
Temple and he has declared himself to be the true God. Daniel called

it the "Abomination that causes desolation." He will now persecute Jews and Christians without discretion or second thought."

"I don't understand." Hannah shook her head in confusion. "You're not making any sense."

"Hannah … Alexander Christos is coming to Jerusalem to proclaim himself as God in our Temple. His assassination only postponed what he had started. In the Gospel of Matthew, Jesus tells us that when we see the "Abomination that causes desolation," we should flee and shouldn't even take the time to look back or to get our belongings. But Revelation tells us that God will protect us in the desert. And to the desert we are going. But we need to leave soon."

"But where will we go?" Jake entered the dining area and stood next to Yitzhak. "I overheard what you said. But where will we go?"

"Are you all right?" Hannah stood and embraced Jake. Her concern for Jake was genuine. She had come to love him as her own son and would lay down her life for him if necessary. "We were worried about you."

"I'm fine." Jake took a deep breath and released his embrace. The events of the day before had taken its toll on him but he knew, as did Yitzhak, that they had to act soon. "I know what Revelation says about a place prepared for Israel. But where should we go?"

"Petra." Yitzhak said with confidence, "It's an ancient city carved into the cliffs of Mount Seir in the land of Edom."

"Edom?" Jake asked, "Where is this … this Edom?"

"It's approximately eighty kilometers southeast of the Dead Sea," Yitzhak answered, "The land of Edom is where the descendants of Esau, the brother of Jacob, lived. The Rocky Ridges of the mountain will allow us protection, and Petra is a city that has been carved from its stones. It's a fortress that will give us shelter. It is large enough to hold many, and I have already spoken to our neighbors who want to go."

"But the area is barren." Hannah sat down at the table, "What will we do for food and water?"

"The Lord tells us that He will supply our needs; 'He shall prepare a place for us and take care of and feed us until the end.'

Revelation chapter twelve gives us this promise." Yitzhak looked at Jake. "But we need to hurry. Alexander Christos has said that he will be here today to finish what he had started the day that he was shot."

"And you suspect that he is going to desecrate the Temple again and order the persecution of Jews and Christians?"

"That's exactly right." Yitzhak sat at the table next to Hannah. "The bullets that entered his head only postponed his plan. But today when he gets here he will again proclaim himself as God the Almighty and force the Jews to worship him or face death."

"But why Petra?" Jake asked, not sure of the plan. "Why not some other place. There are many places that we can hide. Why not Masada or some other place in the desert?"

"Although I know of many who will flee to Masada, I think it best to go to Petra. Masada is in Israel and it would be easier for the army of President Christos to overtake it. No one will question him on why he would persecute us if it's within the borders of Israel, especially the Arab countries who hate us." Yitzhak thought for a moment. "Petra is in Jordan, and it would be more difficult for the President to explain away an invasion into an Arab country."

"But, Yitzhak, God can also protect us if we go to Masada."

"God can protect us anywhere we go. But Petra is already fortified. I think it best to journey there."

"How will we get there?" Hannah asked. "Can we take the car?"

"We can take the car only to the base of the mountain," Yitzhak answered. "We will have to get to the other side and into Jordan by foot. Then to Petra and safety."

"You said that you have some friends that are going to Petra as well." Jake ran his hand across the top of his scalp and took a deep breath, "Will they be coming with us?"

"No. Most are concerned with their own families and will tend to their needs. They will be leaving soon, if they haven't already, and we will meet them in Petra."

"How different my survival plan has become." Jake sat at the table opposite his friends. His thought brought him back to the plan that he had made to live out the Tribulation in a cave in Denver. The painful memories of the last three and one-half years invaded his mind and were manifested outwardly by his empty gaze. Engrossed in the memory, he seemed to stare through Yitzhak and Hannah to a spot on the wall directly behind the couple. Hannah was speaking, but Jake did not hear. He thought of Tracey and John and then of Tracey's parents. They had, what they thought at the time, a fool-proof plan-a plan to spend most of the Tribulation in a cave in Denver until the Lord's return. But that was a distant memory that had been replaced with the sorrow of martyrdom of his in-laws and of a close friend. Where Mary was, he did not know but he could do nothing about it now. Randy Jr. would go with them to live out the remainder of the Tribulation in safety and enter the Millennial Kingdom. Fate had given Jake a strange turn and was now forcing him to flee to a rock fortress in a place that he had never heard of before today.

"Father!" Ze'ev ran to the top of the stairs from the cellar book store and turned the television on. "He's at the Temple. CNN is broadcasting it live."

Jake and Yitzhak stood and hurried to the television with Hannah following close behind. Anna went to get the baby then returned to the living room. The screen showed the podium set in front of the entrance of the inner room with the curtain drawn closed. Prophet Gallo stood silently to the right of the podium, offering nothing to the media that was present. There was silence, not even the sounds of cameras flashing or the lead of a pencil against a note pad. Something was about to happen, but no one knew exactly what it was. It had all seemed rehearsed, as actors in a play giving little or no clues of the surprise ending, or of an orchestra building a melody to a final crescendo. Finally, Alexander Christos emerged from behind the curtain and stepped out of the inner room and to the podium.

"I am the son of God." The Anti-Christ began his speech, "The true god, the god that has given me new life and has raised me back to life from the grips of death, has come to earth and will set up his kingdom through me. In the sanctuary of our most high god, he shows himself to me and gives me direction. He has raised me from the dead because he has found me worthy to be worshiped. Because I am the one to be worshiped, any Jew or Christian that will not worship me or my father shall be put to death. My god is more powerful than the God of the Jews and Christians and is worthy of worship. The Jews will not be allowed to worship their false god, nor will I continue to allow the horrible sacrifice of animals for the forgiveness of their sins. Christians shall meet the same fate if they do not bow down and worship me. I am the son of God who is to be worshiped. My god has given all authority to me and therefore you must worship me as God himself."

"He has desecrated the Temple yet again as I said he would." Yitzhak's eyes moistened with tears. "He is evil."

"It is as was predicted long ago." Jake could not take his eyes off the television. "Daniel predicted that this day would come."

"We need to heed the words of our Savior and leave." Yitzhak turned and put his hand on Hannah's shoulder. "We must leave at once."

"To ensure that I will be worshiped," President Christos continued, "I have deployed one hundred thousand of our finest ground troops to Israel. Their mission is to seek out anyone that will not accept my mark and worship me as God. As an example to the Jews, I have ordered that the high priest and rabbis of local synagogues to be arrested and to prove their loyalty to me. They can do this by accepting the mark. If they refuse, they will be executed immediately. I will give all Jews until six o'clock in the evening tomorrow to accept my mark. After this deadline, I will order house-to-house searches for any that will refuse me. They will be given one last chance to choose between worshipping me or accepting death. The choice will be theirs."

"Ze'ev, Get the car." Yitzhak turned to Hannah, "We are going to leave now. Hannah, get your coat-and hurry. Anna, bring the baby."

"How can he call himself God?" Jake asked, "The wars in Russia and in Central and South America have caused fires that have burned up crops and livestock … and terrible famine as a result of them. If he was God he could end the worldwide drought and put those fires out with a tremendous rain and save the hungry and poor. And now he is hell bent to destroy Israel. How can anyone worship him? How can anyone not see through his lies?"

"The car is ready." Ze'ev said, entering the house through the front door.

The telephone rang. They stood there looking at each other.

"Who could be calling now?" Hannah asked.

"Ze'ev … Help you mother into the car." Yitzhak walked Hannah to the door and gave her a kiss. "I'll be right behind you."

The loud bell of the phone repeated its ring. Jake picked up the receiver.

"Hello."

"Yitzhak-is that you?"

"Who is this?" Jake asked.

"This is Steve. Steve Anderson."

"Steve … This is Jake."

"Thank God we found you."

"Where are you?" Jake asked. "Who's we?"

"Mary and I."

"Mary? Is she all right?"

"She's doing as well as can be expected. Jake, Randy's last words to her were that she should stay with you. When I ran into her at the Rome Airport, I knew that you would be with Yitzhak."

"We are about to leave Jerusalem. The Anti-Christ has desecrated the Temple-we are fleeing to the desert."

"Can you hold off until tomorrow?" Steve asked. "Mary and I are flying to Tel-Aviv at noon."

"We can't wait. Get a car and meet us at the base of Mount Seir. It's about eighty kilometers southeast of the Dead Sea."

"But-"

"Just do it." Jake interrupted, "President Christos has deployed ground troops to round up Jews and Christians. We can't wait in Jerusalem."

"Okay. We'll get a car and meet you. I don't know what time we'll be there."

"If you'll be in Tel-Aviv by noon then you should be able to be at the base of the mountain in the afternoon or early evening. I'll wait there for you."

"What if we can't make it that soon?"

"I'll be there and stay until the morning if I have to. But if you don't meet us just continue on to Petra. Yitzhak says that you can find it. Just follow the trail."

"Okay. We'll see you tomorrow, Lord willing."

Jake hung up the phone. "That was Steve Anderson. He's flying in tomorrow with Mary."

"But we can't wait until tomorrow." Yitzhak replied. "We have to leave now."

"They will meet me tomorrow at the base of Mount Seir. You and your family can go ahead of us, and we'll catch up to you the day after."

The road to Mount Seir was crowded with refugees fleeing from Israel. Cars were packed with the possessions of those fleeing and stretched for miles. Camel caravans traveled the same direction along either side of the highway. The camels had been used for centuries as work animals because of their strength and stamina. Their huge muscular bodies and large humps stored precious water. All these characteristics gave this large yet nimble animal its ability to survive the heat of the desert. Burdened with supplies that draped over either side of the animals hump, they were called upon once again to help their masters. Without hesitation, they dutifully performed their task.

Occasionally a U.S.E. Air force reconnaissance plane would fly over head surveying the area and the progression of the refugees. "They're watching us," Yitzhak said, looking up at the plane overhead. "They know that we are here."

"We're sitting ducks if they want to get us," Jake said, "At this rate the camels are moving faster than we are."

The usually short one and one-half-hour drive to Mount Seir took five hours, but they finally made it. The landscape was barren with rock outcrops and an occasional hyssop plant. The sand and rocky soil, crusted from the baking heat of the desert, could not sustain a plentiful array of plant life. Scorpions and lizards, feeding off the insects that would mistakenly get too close, cooled themselves under the rocks and large boulders.

A large natural valley had been carved out of the mountain and a wide path, which had been used for thousands of years, passed from one side to the other. Rocky ridges and huge boulders bordered either side of the path and extended thousands of feet above. The path extended for miles until it seemed to narrow into a fine point, the scenery unchanging for the entire length.

"At the other end is the land of Edom." Yitzhak looked at the path, "We will continue on, my friend."

"I will camp here tonight and wait for Steve and Mary," Jake replied. "When they get here we will continue on and meet you at Petra."

"When you get to the other side-" Yitzhak said, "-follow the base of the mountain. You will come to another rocky area with cliffs. There will be another entrance similar to the one here. It opens to yet another path. That path is about two miles and leads to the ruins of Petra."

"We will see you then." Jake embraced Yitzhak. "May Jesus be with you."

Jake watched the family walk down the path, Anna holding Randy Jr., until he could not see them any longer. Little did he know that it would be the last time that they would see each other. Streams of refugees continued to come to the mountain and enter the path and then disappear into the distance. The sun was lowering in the sky and the night chill was setting in. Jake pulled his collar up over his neck. He found a place behind a large boulder that jutted against the face of a cliff, forming a space that was almost completely walled off except for the front. He sat at the back of the space and settled in for the night.

The next morning had come quickly, bringing with it a strong, cold wind and a dark cloud cover. *Rain?* Jake looked at the sky and shook his head. It hadn't rained since the witnesses appeared, and they promised that it wouldn't rain until the Lord's return.

But now the clouds seemed to threaten to burst wide open making travel difficult for those that were escaping from Israel. The multitude of refugees of the day before had been reduced to just a handful, and the landscape was littered with cars that had been abandoned by those that had taken the same path as Yitzhak and his family. Jake stood and brushed the dust off of himself and made his way to the mouth of the pathway that led into the mountain. He observed a man and his family approaching. The man was young, no older than thirty, and was carrying a young baby strapped to his back and holding a walking staff in his right hand. His wife, not much younger than her husband, was pulling a child's wagon, red with rusted sides and a long black handle, containing supplies for the trip. To the woman's right was a young boy, no more than ten years old, with short hair and a smudged face, struggling to keep up with his parents. Following behind the wagon, the family dog, a tan, short-haired terrier, fell behind to investigate something of interest, then catching up again to avoid being left behind.

"Any news from Jerusalem?" Jake asked.

The man stopped and looked at Jake. Tugging at his black beard the man turned and looked in the direction of Jerusalem then back at Jake.

"The president has ordered that all roads out of Jerusalem and Israel be closed." The man turned and gestured to his family. His wife had her mouth and nose covered with a white scarf protecting herself from the blowing dust. "We barely made it past the road blocks. The only ones allowed out are those who are not Jews. President Christos' officials are going house-to-house and pulling people from their homes and arresting anyone who refuses his mark."

"What? He said that he would wait until six tonight."

"He has doublecrossed us. He started his persecution before the sun rose and has put to death a number of rabbis already and will stop at nothing to destroy the Jewish people."

"You were some of the last to get out of Israel?"

"Yes." The young Jew motioned to his family to resume their trek. "The only ones left there are those that received the mark or those who will be executed for not receiving it." Jake watched as the young family disappeared in the distance. He looked back toward Jerusalem. He could see no one coming.

On the east side of the mountain, Yitzhak and his family continued their journey after camping for the night. They traveled along the mountain's base for three miles before starting the ascent to Petra. The face of the mountain was barren with occasional outcroppings of large boulders of granite interspersed with tufts of camel's grass and acacias. The trail was steep and narrow with loose gray and brown rock, which made it difficult to get a good foothold. Hannah slowed the progress with her inability to keep up, stopping periodically to catch her breath. Yitzhak would sit with her until she was ready to continue. Ze'ev seemed unbothered by the difficulty of climbing such a steep grade, the strength of his youth exuding itself with a nervous restlessness as he refused to sit and rest. He journeyed forward a few yards then returned to where his parents were sitting. Anna kept stride with Hannah, occasionally taking turns holding Randy Jr.

"Just a little farther." Yitzhak nodded his head to the east. "At the top of this grade is a rocky ridge path that travels along the face of the mountain and to Petra. We will make camp at the top. Petra will be another day's journey; we should be there by sundown tomorrow."

"Let me rest a little longer." Hannah wiped the moisture from her brow. "I'll be all right in a few moments."

Hannah and Yitzhak sat and watched the stream of refugees pass by. The line of people was single file with most of the refugees abandoning the heavy supplies that they had at the outset. The rugged terrain made it to difficult to carry anything other than water and food; all else was a burden. The cool weather was a blessing, normal conditions of more than one hundred degrees would have made the trip virtually impossible, with heat stroke and dehydration causing some to die on the path.

"We must continue." Yitzhak stood and held his hand out to Hannah. "I want to make the top of the grade by sundown."

They started the final stretch to the top of the mountain. Ze'ev in his youthful enthusiasm took the lead and passed those that were ahead of him. He would have to wait periodically to allow the others to catch up. Two hours had past, the scenery unchanging with each step, except for an occasional outcrop of granite or a snake creeping its way across the path. But the top was in sight, and Ze'ev could see the ridge and ran back to tell his parents.

"I can see the path!" Ze'ev screamed out. "It's just ahead, Mother, and we can rest."

"Thank God." Hannah let out a sigh. "I wasn't sure that I could take much more."

"We will set up camp-" Yitzhak added, "-and prepare our meal."

"We have just enough food for tonight." Hannah said, "After today the Lord will have to supply our needs. I hope He does not forget us here in the wilderness."

"Have faith, Hannah." Yitzhak responded quickly. He was surprised at his wife's comment. "The Lord has told us through the Scriptures that he will take care of our needs."

At the top was a dusty clearing. Some, like Yitzhak and his family, made camp; others continued onward, taking the narrow ridge path that led to Petra. From the ridge the entire land of Edom lay before them as far as their eyes could see in all directions. A barren desert, made of sand dunes that are pushed by the wind that blew down from the mountain, gave it the appearance of waves moving upon the ocean and to the sea shore. It was a land in which only lizards and snakes could survive and only crossed by nomads and camel caravans. But Yitzhak was troubled by what he saw as he looked out over the ridge. A massive army, with tank brigades and artillery, covered the entire land and was advancing toward the mountain. The quickness of the advance and the fluidness of its motion made it appear like a mighty river rushing uncontrollably toward the sea-a flood of humanity with murderous intentions to kill the refugees that were fleeing from the Anti-Christ. The army advanced closer and Yitzhak knew that he could do nothing but hope for a miracle.

At the other side of the mountain Jake stood waiting. He had not seen anyone pass since the young family earlier in the morning. The entire day he waited and watched for any sign of his friends' arrival, pacing nervously on occasion to break the monotony. And, except for the howling wind that swirled dust and sand into the air, there was silence. The sky had threatened rain, but not a drop had fallen, and the sky was darkened by the raging clouds that blocked the light of the sun. Not since the Rapture had Jake felt this alone; even the scorpions and lizards abandoned Jake's company, hiding themselves under rocks and crevasses in the cliff, protected until the sun revealed itself again.

In the distance, Jake observed an approaching car kicking up dust in its wake and speeding closer along the highway. The car was a large white, early model Ford, with a crack in the windshield that extended from the center passenger side to the middle of the glass then curving upward to just above the driver. The white paint was darkened by the dirt that covered it, giving it a reddish-black hue from the color of the dust. The right front headlight was shattered and the bumper hung loosely and rattled loudly as the car stopped in front of Jake. Mary was driving and Steve in the passenger seat. Walking closer to the car, Jake sensed that something was not right. Steve sat motionless except for the moving of his head to and fro, motioning Jake not to come closer. Neither Steve nor Mary tried to exit the vehicle. Jake reached the driver's side and looked at Mary. She did not look back but continued to stare forward, ignoring Jake's presence. Jake looked at Steve, his hands were restrained behind his back and his feet were tied together with a rope.

"What's going on?" Jake screamed out to be heard above the howling wind.

The back doors of the car opened and two men in U.S.E. military uniforms, sand-colored camouflage khakis with "MP" sewn on the sleeve, quickly exited, holding pistols.

"Put your hands up-" the soldier nearer to Jake shouted, "-or I'll shoot."

Jake put his hands above his head. The soldier was tall and broad, a large man that towered over Jake. He had chiseled facial features with his high cheeks narrowing to a strong chin that jutted slightly, and sandy blonde hair that was cut short at the top of his head and shaved clean on each side to just above his ears. His dark brown eyes stared down the barrel of the pistol that was pointed at Jake, and the mark of the beast was displayed proudly on his forehead. The other soldier was not quite as large as the first. Except for his black hair and trimmed mustache, he was similar in appearance and was also pointing his pistol at Jake. The mark of the beast was not on his forehead, as it was on his partner, but on his right hand, the hand that held the pistol.

"Jacob Fredricks?" the large MP with the name Peterson hemmed into his shirt pocket pointed at Jake. "We've been looking for you a long time."

Jake stood there, saying nothing. He glanced at Mary and Steve in the car then back at the soldier. A squadron of U.S.E. fighter jets flew overhead in an eastwardly direction, and Jake took a prolonged look at the planes.

"It has begun," Peterson smiled. "Our planes are going to attack the refugees fleeing to Petra and our army is going to follow to kill anyone who survives."

"But you won't die such a merciful death." the short soldier added, "A helicopter will be here shortly to take you and your friend to Jerusalem. From there we have orders to bring you back to Rome to face execution in the arena." The soldier looked at Mary. "You have her to thank for that." Jake glanced at Mary who lowered her head to hide her eyes from him.

The wind stopped, and the two soldiers looked at each other in bewilderment. For the first time in the entire day there was complete silence. The howl of the wind and the swirling debris that it picked up was gone. The silence did not last long, broken by a low rumble in the west that slowly became louder as it advanced. Looking in the distance, Jake saw dust slowly rise into the air and ripples upon the land that moved fluidly towards them, as if it were ripples in the water after a stone had been tossed in. The soldiers turned to look to the west and noticing their distraction, Jake kicked the pistol out of the hand of the large soldier and in the same instant rushed the other soldier, knocking him to the ground. Taking advantage, Jake ran to the cliffs of the mountain to escape.

"Get up!" Peterson yelled to his partner and picked up his pistol from the ground. "Let's go after him!"

"There he is!" Both soldiers pointed their pistols at Jake. Jake had hid himself in a hollowed-out space in the rock.

"You're not as smart as I thought you were." Peterson stared at

Jake. "Did you honestly think that you could escape? I'm not going to waste my time with you any longer. I'll just kill you myself." The soldier raised his pistol and took aim.

The earth shook, disrupting the soldier's aim, the shot deflecting off the rock just above Jake's head. The intensity of the earthquake increased, causing the soldiers to fall to the ground and boulders to break loose from the face of the cliff, and the mountain began to crumble.

"God has done this!" the smaller soldier shouted, covering his head to protect himself from the falling rock.

"Your God has done this to us!" Peterson stared at Jake. "But in His wrath He will crush you as well. I'd rather the rocks fall on us than to worship your God." The three men disappeared in the dust and rubble of the rock and sand stone.

Untouched from the falling rocks, Mary and Steve watched in amazement. The cliff had fallen, raising into the air a large dust cloud that began to settle onto the car. Mary sat and smiled.

"He's dead." Mary stared with a smile as the dust settled. "My revenge is complete."

"Your revenge?" Steve shook his head.

"Jake was the reason that Randy was executed. If it weren't for him, Randy would have never accepted Christ as Savior and he would be alive today."

"Randy accepted Christ because he saw through the Anti-Christ's lies." Steve sighed and stared at Mary. "He understood what Revelation said to him. He's in Heaven now with the Lord, and if you ever want to see him again you will have to accept Christ in your life."

"My God!" Mary pointed toward the rocks that had just tumbled to the ground, "Look."

"What is it?" Steve struggled to get a glimpse. He was still bound to the seat and had difficulty getting a view.

Jake emerged from the rubble and walked toward the car, his complexion now the color of the dust that covered him.

"It's a miracle from God." Steve said, "The same God that Randy died for."

Jake opened the door and untied Steve. Steve stepped out of the car and the two men walked to the front of the car.

"Mary-" Jake reached out his hand in the direction of the car, "-come with us. It's not too late."

Jake heard the loud roar of helicopter blades and looked up to see the approaching aircraft, a military helicopter in the standard khaki green color and large fuselage that narrowed at the cockpit then widened along the center and tail sections. The tail projected from the back and was half as long as the fuselage.

"We have to leave now." Steve yelled at Mary. "The helicopter will be here in a few moments."

Mary opened the door and stepped out. She turned to look at the approaching helicopter then back at Jake and Steve.

"Mary, come with us." Jake reached his hand out toward Mary.

"No. You killed Randy … you and your God. I'll never forgive you and I will hunt you down until the day you die." Mary turned and ran in the direction of the helicopter.

"Mary, no!" Jake stepped toward her but Steve held him from going any further.

"We have to leave now." Steve said, "Let her go."

The two men turned and ran to what was left of the mountain and disappeared into a canyon that had been spared by the earthquake.

The earthquake caused Yitzhak to fall to the ground. So great was the shaking of the earth that the ground in front of the advancing army opened up, causing them to be swallowed up by the huge chasm. But the jets were undisturbed by the earthquake below and continued on to their target. Yitzhak could hear the jets advancing closer and he looked up to watch them approach. The stars began to fall to the earth knocking the planes out of the sky and killing the surviving soldiers that were not swallowed up by the chasm. The tremendous explosions from the impact of the falling objects caused the clouds in the sky to recede as a scroll being rolled up, and the debris that it released into the air turned the sun black as sackcloth and the moon to blood red. When it was finished the chasm remained, and the army had been destroyed.

"We shall not see Jake again until the Lord returns." Yitzhak spoke, unable to take his eyes away from the destruction that he had just witnessed. "The chasm will remain to protect us from the Anti-Christ-but it will also keep Jake from coming to us. Come, Hannah ... let's set up camp."

Chapter 14

From an ancient ruin at the time of the Rapture five years earlier, Babylon had once again become a thriving metropolis, rebuilt to the splendor that it had not known since the time of Nebuchadnezzar six hundred years before the birth of Christ. Stone walls extended fourteen miles on each side and were laid out in the form of a huge square surrounding the city. The walls were twenty feet high and eighty-five feet thick, each containing twenty-five brass gates for entering and exiting the city. Cylindrical watch towers, fifty on each side, rose another twenty-five feet above the top of the wall. The Euphrates River, long considered the lifeline of the desert, flowed diagonally from the northwest, dissecting the city into two equal parts. Babylon had become the trade capital of the world and a great industrial power producing a wide range of merchandise-gold and silver, precious stones and pearls, fine linen and silk, all manners of ivory and of brass and iron and marble. Cinnamon and ointments, wine and oil, fine flour and wheat, and livestock of sheep, cattle and poultry, along with products of technology, medical and scientific as well as electronic, and transportation made Babylon the envy of the world and a magnet of immigration and commerce.

However, Babylon was not a reflection of world affairs. Global drought brought on by the witnesses in Jerusalem caused increasing crop failures in every country. That, combined with the massive, worldwide earthquake eighteen months earlier, had caused severe famine. Rising inflation made what little food available too expensive to buy and many were dying of hunger daily. Wars against the U.S.E. and Alexander Christos were springing up throughout the world from discontented countries whose people were dying from malnutrition and disease. The resulting firestorms from bombs and weapons of war destroyed homes, forcing many from their shelters to face the elements. Lack of water prevented firefighters from extinguishing the flames, which spread to any existing food sources, adding to the shortage of food. Food cakes were rationed, two daily for a family of four, and only to those that had the mark of Alexander Christos. Those that did not accept the mark were left to starve or were transported to "labor" camps to be separated into groups; Christians and Jews were separated from those that were not Christian or Jewish. The former were sent to face execution in the Coliseum and other cities around the world or forced to perform hard labor for the "betterment of the government." The latter were sent to be "reprogrammed," failures of reprogramming would be treated as a Christian or Jew.

But the threat of death by execution did not stop the spread of the Gospel. Secret Christian organizations were formed. Underground structures, similar to the catacombs of ancient Rome, were constructed to hide the growing population of believers in Jesus Christ. Under the westernmost wall of Babylon was one such structure, a maze of tunnels hidden and unknown to government authorities. The tunnels were illuminated by torches affixed to its damp stone walls, and the air, insulated by the thick rock from the outside temperature, maintained a constant climate and temperature of sixty degrees. The entrances to the tunnels were hidden, some up to one mile or more from the wall. Similar to the way rodents would construct their homes with more than one entrance, so too were the tunnels of these "catacombs." Guards were placed at every entrance, each possessing an elaborate warning system to warn others deep inside the cave of intrusion from unfriendly visitors. The warning would allow those inside to escape capture from Alexander Christos' forces by escaping through other openings.

The opening to the main tunnel was found at the northern most wall of the city, hidden in a small patch of reeds at the point where the Euphrates River enters; a large boulder at the edge of the patch of reeds marked the spot of entry. At the base of the boulder was a trap door, camouflaged by artificial reeds that had been adhered to the top, opened outward leading to a stairway just below. The stairway descended eight feet to a small chamber and to a steel door that was bolted to the compression beams that kept the tunnel from caving in on itself. The steel door had a small opening, or window, at its center for communication and visual confirmation. Anyone wanting to enter the door would have to give the "password" to be allowed in. Just behind the steel door was a guard, relieved of duty every four hours, stood ready to sound the warning if needed. The warning system, an elaborate networking of alarm bells through out the entire underground tunnels, tapped into the electricity supplied to Babylon's wall. The guard need only to push a button located at the steel door to sound the bells. Heeding the warning all those inside could escape through hundreds of exits located within and without the city. Fortunately, the need to sound the alarm had not yet come to pass.

The guard at present, a small man of Nigerian ancestry, looked as though years of hunger had visibly taken its toll on him. His dark brown skin appeared tightly wrapped around his bones with each rib extruding. His lips and cheeks were sunken around his teeth. Daily, he ate only enough to keep him alive as rationed by the Christian community living in the tunnel. He had not been on watch for more than fifteen minutes when he heard the trap door open and the squeaking of the stairway with each of the newcomer's steps as he drew closer. There was a knock at the steel door.

"What's the password?" the guard with his finger on the alarm button asked.

"King of Kings," the voice at the other side responded.

"Have you forgotten the rest?" the guard tested the newcomer. He slid the small sash that was at the center of the door to take a look at who was on the other side.

"Luther-" the voice responded, "-there is no more."

"Jake-" Luther replied, opening the door, "-you can't be too safe. Have you come back from the meeting place?"

"Yes, and I have news from Jerusalem." Jake responded. A strange fate had found Jake here, a year and one-half after his and Steve's escape from the military police at Mount Seir. The chasm that had protected the Jews fleeing to Petra from the army of Alexander Christos had also prevented Jake and Steve from entering the rock fortress. Knowing that their lives would be in danger in Jerusalem, Jake and Steve decided to take their chances in the desert. Joining a nomadic group shortly after their escape, they traveled to Babylon. Six months earlier, Steve had decided to take his chances in Jerusalem and had found shelter with a Christian community there. Communication between the community in Jerusalem and the community in Babylon was done through messengers sent to a secret location, or meeting place, halfway between the two cities. Jake had lost weight, not to the extent of his Nigerian friend, but he was considerably thinner then he was when he lived in Jerusalem. His beard had grown to his chest and his once dark hair, almost completely gray now, flowed over his shoulders.

"Daily there are attempts on the lives of the two witnesses, and with each attempt they devour the would-be assassins with fire. They have inflicted all kinds of plagues against the people who have accepted the mark. They have turned water to blood and have not allowed it to rain since their first appearance. Locusts, large locusts, the biggest I've ever heard of, have destroyed most of the remaining crops, and gnats have infested any food products that are left. The latest reports are of flies-" Jake lifted his arm and clenched his hand making a fist, "-as large as a man's fist. Billions of them have swarmed on Israel and Jerusalem. You can't take a step without stepping on one or go outside without hundreds landing on you. The hatred towards the witnesses by the unbelievers grows daily with each new judgment. Yet the unbelievers still do not repent of their wicked ways, as is predicted in Revelation."

"And the witnesses will deliver more pestilence-" Luther locked the door behind them, "-before they die."

"I brought you a food cake." Jake opened his backpack and pulled the loaf out. "The driver of a food wagon was throwing loaves out to some people that had gathered in the city. Lucky for me he did not take the time to check to see if any of us had the mark. Take it; you need this more then I do."

"No. I will give it to the community to be rationed."

"You eat it, Luther ... the community here in the tunnel won't be able to ration one food cake. Take it-no one will miss it. Have you heard if there will be a meeting tonight?"

"Yes." Luther reached to grab the cake, "Tonight at seven o'clock."

"Good. I have more news to tell everyone. The witnesses have predicted that more judgments from God are coming soon. We must prepare."

The meeting place was a circular area large enough to hold a hundred or more people and was ideal for gatherings, such as the meeting that had been scheduled, and for worship. The entry to every tunnel within the catacomb had this area as the starting point and, if visible from above, the entire structure would resemble a starfish, with the meeting area as the body and the tunnels as its lanky arms. The arms would branch out farther into other tunnels that ended with exits, dead ends, or living chambers for the occupants.

The meeting had come to order, most of those attending were sitting on the floor, and others leaned against the rock walls. Attached to the ceiling at the center of the room hung a lamp; its power, like the alarm system, tapped into the electricity supplied to the wall. The speaker would stand in this spot to allow easy visibility to everyone that was in attendance. The weekly meetings were used as a platform to express concerns, criticism, and to settle differences within the community.

"Your attention, please," a brown-skinned man stood under the lamp. "Let us start the meeting." Ishmael Hassan had been given charge of the weekly meetings. A native of Iraq, he had come to the Lord after the war with the U.S.E. that resulted in the destruction of the American fleet in the Gulf. He was a tall man and, like most of those there, thin from lack of proper nutrition. A white turban covered his head; his black beard flowed over his chest and his voice, deep and distinctive, could be heard clearly. After saying a prayer of thanks, Ishmael addressed the gathering.

"My dear friends." He continued in broken English, "Our dear brother Jake Fredricks has returned today from our information outpost to the north. He has received word from our brothers in Jerusalem and would like to deliver that message to us."

"Thank you, brother Ishmael." Jake took his place at the center of the room. "As you all know, I have arrived back today from the meeting place in the desert where I met with some of our brothers from Jerusalem. They have a very important message that they want me to deliver to you. The two witnesses have warned them that the Trumpet judgments predicted in Revelation are going to take place soon."

"Did they give a day that these judgments are to pass?" Ishmael asked.

"No. That is why we need to prepare now. The first Trumpet judgment will destroy a third of the earth, burning up of a third of the trees and green grass."

"How can we prepare for such an event?" an elderly woman screamed out. "How can we protect ourselves from the judgment of God?"

"We have been eating dates and other fruits from the trees in the area, as well as from the cactus of the desert. We must go out and collect as much of this food as we can and store it for later use. After the first Trumpet, there may not be any trees or cactus left to live on."

"But can we collect enough to last the next two years?" Ishmael asked.

"Probably not. But what else can we do? We can either collect food or not, but if we don't, then we definitely won't have enough." Jake looked around the room and then continued. "The witnesses say that the second Trumpet will not sound immediately after the first. God will allow a short time for the unbelievers to turn to him for salvation. After this short time, the second Trumpet will sound, and as we all know, a third of the seas will be destroyed. God again will wait a short time for unbelievers to turn to Him. It will be the same with the third and fourth Trumpet judgment as well. But the witnesses say that starting with the fifth Trumpet judgment, God will not allow a time period for the unbelievers to come to Him. They will have to accept His salvation during this terrible time

So we must prepare, first by storing as much food as possible and then by storing as much water as possible. If God wills it, He will spare the Euphrates from the third Trumpet judgment-the poisoning of a third of the world's fresh water, but we must store as much of the water as we can in case the river is turned bitter."

"We must assemble teams to collect the food that we need." Ishmael stood next to Jake. "Everyone should team up in groups of five or six. It will be safer to collect food at night when darkness will hide us from the police. We will start tonight as soon as the sun sets and work in shifts. Only two or three teams out in the field at a time. When the first shift returns the second shift will go out. If the sun rises before all teams have their shifts, then those teams that have not had their opportunity to gather food will do so on the following night. After the food is collected, bring it here to this room. Gather as much as you can, be it fruit from the groves nearby, or fish or clams from the river. Many insects and reptiles are also edible; collect anything that can be used for food. If God wills it, He shall provide for us."

A cool breeze blew to the south and the sun shone brightly the day the hail and fire came. The large hailstones seemed to magically appear out of the blue sky, dropping to the earth and bursting into flames. As one stone fell, another would take its place to fall to the earth and deliver its destructive firestorm. Black smoke rose high into the air, replacing the bright, clear morning that had begun the day. Jake and the others had taken shelter in the tunnels, gathering in the meeting area to wait out the storm in safety. The ground below their feet shook with each impact of the stones on the earth's surface. They caused a constant low rumble that vibrated the walls and swung the hanging lamp like a pendulum. Seven hours had elapsed before the constant rumble of the falling hail had stopped, the ensuing silence came as suddenly as the beginning of the storm.

"Let's take a look outside." Jake glanced at Luther.

"Do you think it's safe yet?"

"The hail has stopped; it's safe now."

Jake opened the trap door, just enough to allow light to enter, and peered outside. The once bright, clear day had been darkened by the dust and smoke that had been thrown into the air by the impact of the hailstones and the ensuing fire. Jake and Luther stepped out of the tunnel and gazed in every direction. The fruit orchard and date trees were burning and in the horizon black smoke billowed high above the earth.

"The first Trumpet has sounded," Jake said. "Just as the witnesses said it would."

In a small room in Jerusalem, Mary, alone and shaking with fright, huddled in a dark corner opposite the window. The hailstorm had ended, but the fear that it had generated within her soul left her too weak to stand. She sat there with her head down, and she knew. As soon as the storm ended, she knew. God was bringing judgment to the world, and it angered her. With a blank look she stared across the room, seeing nothing but the images in her memory of the last five years. She thought of Randy and of his cruel death and of Jake and his fanatical faith. She thought, also, of her son and how his mind probably is being poisoned by Jake's faith and by those that had him now. How she hated Jake and with every breath she took she vowed to avenge Randy's murder with Jake's death. She would find Jake, if it took the rest of her life; she would find him and watch him suffer. Where Jake was, she did not know. The witnesses, she thought, surely Jake would be a follower of them. Mary wiped a tear from her eye and glanced at the mark on her right hand. "They will lead me to you," she whispered to herself. "Vengeance is mine, says the Lord? Yes, vengeance will be mine. With my dying breath I will avenge Randy's death and watch you die, Jake."

The following day, in front of the Wailing Wall, the two witnesses continued their message of impending doom. An angry crowd gathered around them, cursing and blaming them for the hail that had fallen from the sky.

"Repent!" the elder witness screamed out. "The wrath of God has only begun. Who will save you from the coming destruction?

Repent and receive the Lord Jesus as your Savior."

"Alexander Christos will save us!" a voice in the crowd shouted. "We will never worship your God. He has brought nothing but destruction."

"Reject Alexander Christos, the Anti-Christ," the younger witness responded, "or you will share with him eternal punishment in the fires of hell."

Mary stood in the crowd, not really listening for she had heard it all before. She just watched and waited for any sign of Jake. She knew that if she were to find him it would be here where the two witnesses were preaching. She noticed a young man, no more then twenty, picking up stones. He was not native to the region, European, she thought, by his pale complexion, blonde hair, and blue eyes. He had not shaved in a few days; the light stubble on his face was sparse at best. His lips were pressed tightly against each other, and his furrowed brow could not hide the anger that was within him. He did not take his gaze off of the witnesses, but stared at them intently-almost afraid that they would disappear if he lost eye contact. Satisfied with the stones, he broke through the crowd and lunged at the witnesses.

"Die!" he shouted, hurling the stones at the two men. "You and your God bring only pain and suffering!"

The younger witness raised his staff and pointed it in the young man's direction. Fire proceeded from the tip of the staff and consumed the young man instantly. Fear spread within the crowd, and they fled for their lives as the body of the young man smoldered with the stench of burning flesh. Mary took a position behind a tree and watched. The incident only heightened her anger and hatred toward God, but she would be patient. She would come daily, if she must, to find any sign of Jake or of any clue to his whereabouts. Taking one last look at the smoldering corpse, Mary turned and walked away. She would come back tomorrow.

Chapter 15

"You have to help us or we'll never survive!" Governor Santini of Italy stared down the long table towards Alexander Christos, the tone of his voice desperate and on the verge of panic. President Christos sat motionless, the 666 on his forehead shining in the light, unmoved by the plea offered by Italy's leader he himself had appointed to the office. Prophet Gallo, sitting to the right of President Christos, also sat motionless. Governor Santini was not alone in his feelings. The other nine governors of the European Unity were sitting at the same table and all shared his fears. "We have no food or water," he continued. "For over a year we have lived on the verge of destruction."

"Ask any of us," Governor Guibord of France added. "It has been over a year since the hailstorm and the great global earthquake and still a third of the worlds crops, trees, and grass lands are nothing but waste lands. Thousands die daily in my country alone of hunger and disease. I'm not sure how much longer my citizens can endure the plagues that have tormented us."

"The people are starting to rebel." Governor Santini sat back into his chair. "They're hungry and tired. They're watching their children go without food for days at a time, and there is no promise that any food will come soon. Our crops have been decimated.

Whatever was in those hailstones have destroyed the soil. Nothing will grow; the land seems to have been poisoned."

"Livestock has also suffered." Governor Kohl of Germany leaned on the table. "With no crops or hay to feed the livestock, they die of starvation or disease. With livestock dying there is no meat to eat. That, coupled with the destruction of the fishing industry caused by the meteorite that has destroyed a third of the earth's oceans, has caused many in my country to starve. The witnesses in Jerusalem called the meteorite God's second Trumpet judgment."

"I witnessed it fall to the earth and into the Mediterranean." Santini pointed to his brown eyes; "With my own two eyes I saw it fall with a streak of fire trailing behind it. The waves that it produced destroyed every city along the coast. I can still smell the stench of fish and other sea animals that died-too many to clean before that awful smell started to invade my nostrils. It made my eyes water."

"But the Mediterranean was not the only ocean that has been destroyed." Guibord added, stroking his gray beard, "Japan has been decimated. The country's entire source of food other than imported fruits and vegetables was destroyed. China has also suffered, and many starve to death daily. The people of China are rebelling. They are calling on their government to take military action against you."

"The second meteorite that fell has destroyed a third of the earth's fresh water." Governor Van Beak of Austria stood from his chair, "In my country, snow runoff from our Alps have been turned bitter. 'Wormwood' is the name that Christians gave to the meteorite because it made the water foul and undrinkable. Unbearable thirst has forced many to drink the water, even when they know it will kill them. Their thirst is too powerful to stop them from taking a drink. The water is deadly even after sanitizing it by boiling, and what adds to the misery is that it hasn't rained in two and one-half years since the witnesses in Jerusalem started preaching. Many are dying and-"

"But now the darkness that has consumed the earth is too much for any of us to take." Santini leaned onto the table as if his movement could, somehow, put emphasis on his words, "A third of the light of the sun, moon, and stars have been taken away by what Christians say is the fourth-" he held up four fingers gesturing to President Christos, "-Trumpet judgment. One-third less of sunlight has further harmed what little crop foods we have. The people in my country have grown impatient. And I have spoken to my colleagues seated here with us, and they agree that their people have also grown impatient."

Prophet Gallo stood up slowly. No one said a word as he walked around the president to the other side of the table before continuing along the entire length of the table.

"You say that your people are growing impatient." Prophet Gallo broke the silence, "What would they have us do? It is God that is bringing these judgments."

"Yes, Your Excellency." Governor Santini answered, "But my people think that President Christos is-" Santini trembled as he searched for the correct words and glance briefly at the president, "-how do you say ... dragging his feet in these matters. They want him to do something now."

"What would you have President Christos do?" Prophet Gallo questioned everyone, "How would you fight the God of the Christians?"

"We need to kill all the Christians," Guibord answered quickly. "As long as there are Christians in the world, their God is going to protect them."

"That will only bring more judgments." Santini stood from his table. "I think that we should offer peace to the Christians. Offer them land as was the case with Israel after World War Two. Give them land so they can live in peace, and God will protect them and let us live in peace as well."

"You fool!" Prophet Gallo answered angrily. He pointed his index finger at the governor. "No longer shall you have a place at this table."

Governor Santini started to choke, grabbing at his neck in a panic, trying in vain to open his airway. His face was a bright red and his eyes, the blood vessels breaking, began to bulge exposing half the orbit. Blood trickled from his ears and his nose. With one last gasp, he fell to the floor and died.

Prophet Gallo stood, looking at everyone at the table. There was complete silence. All eyes were on him.

"Is there anyone here-" Prophet Gallo asked, "-who would agree with their colleague, Governor Santini, that we should make peace with the Christians?" The governors sat quietly with their heads lowered not wanting to make eye contact with Prophet Gallo. "Good," he added breaking the silence, "Shall we continue with our discussion?"

"Prophet Gallo?" President Christos gestured to Prophet Gallo's chair. "Please, be seated."

"Yes, Your Holiness."

President Christos stood slowly and took a position behind his chair facing the wall; his back was to the table, and he held his hands behind him. He did not say a word and the men at the table were nervous and were glancing at each other, hoping to find an answer to what was happening from the face of the man who sat next to them.

Finally he turned and spoke, "We will wage a more intensive war against the Christians. Security has been lax. I have been hearing reports that food has been given to citizens that do not bear my mark. From this time forward, I will leave it in your hands to stop this incompetence. Anyone caught giving food to a person without the mark will be sentenced to death. Also, all food products shall be moved to military bases. No longer can it be obtained from merchants or vendors. To get on the base, the mark must be presented. If the person does not have the mark, he will be detained and questioned. Use torture if necessary to get any information to the location of others that do not have the mark. Most likely these individuals will be Christian. When we find the whereabouts of the others, they are to be executed immediately and their bodies hung on the gallows as a reminder of their crime. I hold you responsible for the proper implementation of this policy. Do not disappoint me. Take a good look at your friend from Italy." President Christos pointed to the body on the floor, "That heap that you see could have as easily been any one of you."

"But the witnesses in Jerusalem." Governor Kohl voice was soft and conceding; his hand trembled as he pushed back his blonde hair.

He lowered his blue eyes not wanting to even give the appearance of challenging the president. "The witnesses-" he continued, "-they are converting thousands to Christ daily and are bringing many against you. They have brought all kinds of pestilence that affect your loyal citizens around the world. I hesitate to repeat it, but the people have grown weary. They think that you should do something about those two men."

"Insects." Governor Cox of Great Britain spoke for the first time. "First it was the gnats, billions of them. They covered every living animal and man. Then the flies. The witnesses have brought all types of plagues to cause your people to suffer. They brought a plague to all our livestock, most of them dying. Locust ate most of our decimated crops, reducing further the food supply. The latest plague was of boils. Every man that had your mark got boils that covered the entire body. The witnesses are openly defying you and attacking your loyal citizens that bear your mark. It's as if they are repeating the plagues of Moses when he brought the Israelites out of Egypt."

"Then we shall kill them," President Christos stared at Prophet Gallo.

"No one can kill the witnesses," Governor Kohl answered. "Everyone who has tried to lay a hand on them has been consumed by fire. They have the power to bring fire from the sky and burn the flesh of men. It would take more than-"

"That is because you fools try to kill them with stones or by wrestling them to the ground." Prophet Gallo interrupted, "Leave it to me, Your Holiness. I will fly to Jerusalem tomorrow and meet with Governor Peron and we will devise a plan to kill the witnesses."

Mary Johnson remained steadfast in her vow to find Jake Fredricks. Every day for the last year she had come out to see the witnesses in the hope of finding him. The hatred that she harbored toward God and Jake had hardened her heart to the message that she would have heard from the witnesses. But every plague or pestilence that the witnesses brought meant that, somehow, Jake was to blame and, instead of heeding the warnings to repent, her anger grew.

Today would be no different. She leaned against a tree in an olive grove near the Garden of Gethsemane, shading herself from the hot sun and listened to the witnesses and watched the crowd for any sign of Jake. As she watched she noticed a short man with dark hair and a thick beard at the far end of the group that had gathered to listen. It was not Jake, she could tell by the man's stature, but he looked familiar. She could not be certain but *could it be?* She moved closer to get a better look. The beard had thrown her off but she recognized the eyes. It was Steve Anderson. At last she had found someone that could lead her to Jake. She kept herself at a distance so that Steve would not see her. For an hour she watched and waited, not hearing a word preached by the witnesses, her mind so wrapped up with not losing sight of Steve. Finally, Steve was leaving and started to walk away. From a distance Mary followed-never allowing herself to be noticed. She followed Steve past the Wailing Wall southward then eastward along a small trail. Reaching the southeasternmost part of the Temple Mount, Steve came to an opening in the wall camouflaged by a hyssop bush and a large stone. Mary stayed back, still unnoticed, and hid behind a small boulder just off of the trail. Raising her head slightly over the stone, she watched and listened.

"What's the password?" Mary could barely hear a voice coming from the opening.

"King of Kings." Steve replied to the voice within.

Mary saw a steel door open and watched Steve enter. For the first time in over a year she allowed herself to smile. She was on Jake's trail and would get revenge for her husband's death. *But how? Should I go to the authorities?* she thought. *No.* she answered her own question, her mind racing. *Prophet Gallo. I have to tell Prophet Gallo.*

The newspaper had reported that Prophet Gallo was coming to Jerusalem to meet with Governor Peron the following morning to discuss a way to solve the "Christian problem" and the witnesses. The Jerusalem headquarters of President Christos was located within the temple, and meetings with officials and world leaders were held in the conference room that had been added to the northern most side. A crowd of people had been waiting outside the temple when Prophet Gallo's motorcade pulled up. The police had formed a barrier along the path to the entrance, allowing Prophet Gallo and his entourage to enter unabated. Mary struggled to the front. As Prophet Gallo approached, she screamed out his name but he did not hear her; the murmuring of crowd drowned out her call. *If he enters the temple, I'll lose my chance.* With one last effort she broke through the barrier just in front of Prophet Gallo and fell at his feet.

"Have mercy on me, Prophet Gallo." Mary bowed her head, not allowing herself to make eye contact.

Prophet Gallo stared at the woman kneeling in front of him. The guards had reached for her but Prophet Gallo gestured to leave her be.

"Mercy?" Prophet Gallo asked. "What crime have you committed?"

"I have committed no crime." Mary answered. "I humbly request an audience with you. I have made a discovery that I trust only you to hear."

Prophet Gallo stared at her wearily. "Look at me." Mary lifted her head and stared at the gray haired man. "I recognize you from the Coliseum. You are the wife of the traitor that was executed for treason. How can I be sure this isn't a trick to get me alone to kill me for revenge of your husband's execution?"

"See." Mary lifted her right hand. "I have the mark. If I wanted to cause you harm, would I accept the mark of those I wanted to kill? Would I be throwing myself before you, begging for mercy? But you are correct. I do want to avenge my husband's death. But I do not blame you. The person I blame is a Christian, and if you allow, I shall tell you where he and many other Christians are hiding."

"Very well, I shall grant you an audience. If what you tell me is true, I shall reward you greatly. But if it is a trick, you will not live long enough to see the sun set. Guard, escort her inside."

Mary was led to Governor Peron's office. It was a small rectangular room with only an oak desk and two chairs. There were no windows to allow sunlight in to illuminate the room, only a small ceiling light and fan that hung above the desk and two standing lamps placed in the two corners of the room just behind the desk. A door to the left of the desk was left ajar and Mary could see that it was a restroom and shower area for the governor. On the walls hung photos of President Christos. One photo showed the president with the governor, shaking hands in what appeared to be a ceremony of some type. Time had passed slowly. Mary sat for what seemed hours, but glancing at her watch she realized that it had only been forty minutes. She had wondered if she had made a mistake by coming here. She thought of Prophet Gallo's last words to her: *"If this is a trick you won't live to see the sun set,"* and she hoped that the information about the Christians would satisfy him. But at this point, she didn't care. Her hatred for Jake and the chance that she could find him was worth the risk. She was not sure any more if she received the mark, the mark of the beast as Christians called it, because she worshiped Alexander Christos, or if she received it only to rebel against Jake's God. It didn't matter either way; she was lost in her hatred, lost in her last memory of Randy and of the cruelty by which Jake's God let him die. If Alexander Christos was just a puppet in God's eternal plan, a mere man controlled by a fallen angel named Satan, a being far less powerful than his Creator, then God could have stopped the execution of Randy. *How could God have let this happen to Randy? He accepted Jesus as his Savior and yet He refused to save him.* Hatred had been her undoing. It is a powerful emotion that clouds the mind and obscures the vision, allowing its victim to see only that which will feed its desire to do harm, and it had its tight grip on Mary. She need only to turn it over to God and her hatred would be healed.

The door creaking behind her broke her thought; Prophet Gallo entered the room and sat at the desk in front of Mary. He sat back into his chair and stared at the woman in front of him. Leaning forward with his elbows resting on the desk, he broke the silence.

"How fortunate that you have come, Miss Johnson. Governor Peron and I have been discussing, shall I say … our Christian problem. Their numbers have been growing, a horrible trend that President Christos and I feel must be stopped. I am intrigued by your knowledge of where some Christians are hiding. I think that we can work out a mutual agreement."

"An agreement?" Mary responded.

"Yes, an agreement." Prophet Gallo sat back in his chair placing his hands in his lap. "You said that you blame a certain Christian for your husband's death."

"Yes. A certain Christian I'm sure you would be interested in finding."

"Oh? And why would I be interested in this Christian more so than any other Christian?"

"His name is Jake Fredricks. I think you recognize the name."

Prophet Gallo stared at Mary before responding. "Yes, I know the name. He's wanted for harboring your husband, a proven traitor who was responsible for the deaths of thousands."

Mary's anger stirred within. She knew that Randy had been set up to take the fall for the American fleet. But she said nothing. Her goal was to avenge Randy's death with Jake's. Challenging Prophet Gallo now on that issue would not serve her purpose.

"Yes." She said, "But it was Jake who brainwashed Randy into becoming a Christian. I had worked out a deal that would have let Randy live. President Christos had even offered to spare his life if he accepted the mark. But he refused because Jake Fredricks had convinced him that President Christos was the Anti-Christ."

"And you? Your husband could not convince you?"

"No. I saw you perform miracles in New York. You have powers that I have never seen before."

"The powers that I have come from President Christos. You have proven yourself to be a loyal servant to the president. I will let you avenge your husband's death."

"How?" Mary sat up in her chair. "What can I do to help you find him?"

"You said that you know where some Christians are hiding."

"Yes. They're hiding in a cave at the southeasternmost side of the Temple Mount."

"You saw them there?"

"One of them I knew many years ago; his name is Steve

Anderson. I was looking for Fredricks when I found him as he was listening to the witnesses. He was with Jake during the failed capture at Mount Seir. I followed him from a distance to the cave's mouth. I even heard the password to get in."

"The password?" Prophet Gallo's brows rose with interest then narrowed. "What is it?"

"King of Kings."

"Very well." Prophet Gallo walked to the front of the desk and sat on the edge. "I have a plan and I need your help. When we catch Jake Fredricks, you can avenge your husband's death. Yours will be the hands that will end his life."

"I would enjoy that very much." Mary smiled. "I want him to suffer the way that Randy suffered. What is it that you want me to do?"

"Join them." Prophet Gallo stood and positioned himself behind Mary.

"Join them?" Mary asked.

"That's right. Find this Steve Anderson and tell them you have become a Christian. Once you join them, report back to Governor Peron every two or three days. Find out as much as you can about them and if they have any ties with any other Christian groups."

"But they will know that I am not a Christian. My mark, surely they will see it."

"Hold out your hand." He reached out his hand to Mary. Mary held up her hand showing the mark to Prophet Gallo. Taking her hand, he touched the mark and it disappeared.

"There-" he said, "-I have removed the mark. Go and join the Christian group and report to us. When we have found enough information about them and the location of other groups, we will destroy them, and you shall get your revenge." Prophet Gallo opened the door and summoned the guard. "Guard … escort Miss Johnson out and send Governor Peron in."

A few minutes had passed before the governor entered. A tall and slender man, he had, as most other Jews, long awaited the coming of their Messiah. He was a lover of his faith, and he believed that President Christos was the answer to his prayers and the fulfillment of Messianic prophecy. A zealot now for the new ruler, he had frequently said that he would lay down his life for that of his "Messiah." Both President Christos and Prophet Gallo trusted him.

"You summoned me, Your Excellency?" Governor Peron asked.

"Yes, please have a seat." Prophet Gallo gestured to one of the two chairs in front of the desk. "I have just had a conversation with a Mary Johnson. Her husband was executed in Rome for treason and for being a Christian. She says that she wants to take revenge for the execution on a Christian named Jake Fredricks, who she feels is responsible for her husband's death. She has knowledge of a community of Christians who are in hiding, and she thinks that she will be able to find this Fredricks there. She has agreed to join this Christian community and to bring back information to you every two or three days regarding the community's everyday life and to the whereabouts of other Christian communities."

"That would help us greatly in our mission to kill the Christians."

"Yes, but I want her under constant surveillance. I want you to report to me daily on her activities and where she goes. When she reports to you, I want you to immediately inform me of the information that she has given. Leave no stone unturned in finding these Christians, but let her infiltrate the community without any interference from you. We have known that these communities exist and that they have been communicating with other communities as far as Northern Africa and Babylon. I think that Mrs. Johnson can lead us to all of these Christian communities, and then we will destroy them all."

Mary was relieved as she sat at her desk in her apartment. She did not know, up to the time that she left Governor Peron's office, if Prophet Gallo would be satisfied with their meeting or whether she would come out of it alive. But she knew now that she would find Jake with the help of Prophet Gallo. Tonight she would plan, and tomorrow morning she would put that plan into action.

The sun had barely showed itself over the mountains the following day, and there was a brisk early morning chill to the air when Mary left her apartment. Walking quickly along the trail that led to the entrance of the cave, Mary felt uneasy. *Someone's following me,* she thought, then looked behind her, but saw nothing. She passed it off as nervousness attributed to what she was about to do. Reaching the entrance to the cave, she stood there; again a feeling of uneasiness overcame her. She turned to survey the area but found nothing. She shook her head and faced the steel door and knocked.

"What's the password?" a voice from within asked.

Mary took a deep breath. *King of Kings;* she heard Steve say just the other day. *But was that still the password? Would they change the password periodically to keep one step ahead of anyone that would try and do what she was doing?* She could not think about it any longer; she had to answer.

"The password please," the voice asked again.

"King of Kings," Mary replied.

At the center of the door was a small opening covered from the inside by a veil. Mary could see a pair of brown eyes staring at her.

"I don't recognize you."

"I don't belong to the group. I have recently become a Christian and need shelter."

"How do I know you're telling the truth?"

"I am a friend of Steve Anderson. He knows who I am. Tell him that Mary Johnson is here."

"I'll be back. I'll get him."

Mary stood outside the door tightening her cloak to protect her from the chill. The uneasy feeling that she experienced earlier had returned. Again she surveyed the area. *Is someone following me?*

"Mary?" Steve Anderson opened the door. "Mary, are you all right?"

"Steve. How can I tell you how sorry I am for what happened at Mount Seir? But I've become a Christian now, and I don't blame anyone for Randy's death."

"But how did you find me?"

"I spotted you as you watched the witnesses two days ago then followed you here. I didn't approach you then because I didn't know how you would react. But I won't be able to survive without help. That's why I'm here now."

"Bless you, Mary. We have all found out the hard way the cost of not being a Christian. Come inside where we can offer you protection."

Steve and Mary entered the cave and closed the door.

Mary had been correct, someone had been following her. Hiding behind the same stone that Mary had hid two days earlier, a police official observed what had happened and was ready to report his findings to Governor Peron.

———————

Hannah Benziman had missed Jake. Two and one-half years had passed since she last saw him, and daily she mourned for him as a mother mourns for her own son. The chasm that remained around Mount Seir and Petra had protected her and her family, but it had also kept Jake from joining them. She felt guilty, even unworthy. Her life was protected by God's mighty hand while Jake's life, if he was still alive, surely was one of hardship and strife. Word from the outside world had not come since the first months that they were at Petra. After the chasm had been put in place, the only ones that could come to the rock fortress had to be flown in by helicopter, "the wings of an eagle," as Yitzhak had described it. The last group to arrive had told of horror and murder by U.S.E. forces that were acted upon the Jews that had stayed. Up to two-thirds of the population was killed. Was Jake among those killed? She did not know and would not know until the Lord's return. By now famine and drought was taking its toll on the world, as prophecy had predicted, and Hannah was thankful for the manna and springs of water that God was giving to his people at Petra. But with each meal, her thoughts returned to Jake and the plight that he was suffering. Was he hungry or thirsty? Was he in prison, facing daily torture at the hands of his captors? She could only pray that God would protect him.

Randy Jr. had been a blessing and had grown strong. He had dark blue eyes and blonde hair like his mother and a tall stature and big bones like his father. He was as a grandson to both Hannah and Yitzhak, and they loved him as much as their granddaughter. Rachel had been born to Anna and Ze'ev six months earlier and was the first child to be born at Petra. Yitzhak had never been more proud save for the birth of his son Ze'ev. "Rachel looks just like me," he would brag; "One look and you know she is my grand-daughter." Rachel's brown eyes were strikingly those of Yitzhak, but other than that, she looked more like Anna than Yitzhak, but no one dared tell him that. Anna nursed Rachel while the others sat at the table preparing to eat. Food was plentiful and the water was crystal clear. God had provided manna, as He did with Moses and the Israelites when they came out of Egypt and had provided all the needs of those living there. But even with the blessings before them, Hannah mourned inside for Jake. She was unusually quiet this evening and seemed to be daydreaming.

"Hannah-" Yitzhak said, "-your mind is wandering again. What are you thinking about?"

"Jake," Hannah replied. "I hope he is well. God has provided us with manna and water. While we have plenty to eat and drink, he goes hungry."

"Yes, it is a sad thing. But the Lord provides strength to all our Christian brothers and sisters who are not with us here. You should not worry about things you cannot control. If Jake is still alive, then he is living for Christ; and if he is not alive, then he is with the Lord. We will be with Jake again, and in a year's time, the Tribulation will be over and the Lord will have returned. Whether Jake has survived the Tribulation or not, he will be in Heaven with us to worship the Lord."

"A long year," Hannah replied, comforted little by her husband's words. "I wish the Lord would come now and we would all be together again."

"He will come again soon enough, Hannah. Have courage and accept what the Lord has for us in this final year. In the meantime I am going to the spot that overlooks the chasm. Give me a few minutes there to pray then come join me."

Yitzhak loved the place that he privately called the "view of God's protection." From there he could see the entire Edom Valley and the chasm that had surrounded Mount Seir and Petra. Every day he would come here to pray and offer thanks for God's blessings. But he also mourned for Jake, although he would not allow his emotions to show it. He considered his emotional strength to be a blessing to Hannah. She would not want a man that showed a weakness, and she would gain strength through Yitzhak's courage. He was thankful that his wife and son were safe, but he would gladly trade places with Jake. Jake was stronger than he, an old man that could offer not much than emotional strength to his wife. But that is what Hannah needed and he praised God. Yitzhak finished praying and lifted his head to the sky. From the east came a bright object, as a star, a burning ball of red, yellow and orange flame and trailing behind it was a plume of black smoke. Getting larger as it approached the earth, the star filled the air with the smell of sulfur, and the heat radiated toward Yitzhak, turning the skin on his face red. Falling into the chasm and hitting the earth, the star exploded. The earth shook as black smoke billowed into the air, darkening the sun and sky.

Then they came. Out of the black smoke came creatures, nothing like Yitzhak had ever seen. Thousands upon thousands came up out of the chasm like horses prepared for battle with wings resembling locusts. Their faces were like the face of a man with long wooly hair; their teeth were large and sharp, and saliva foamed at their mouths. Breastplates, like iron, made up the front of the creature before turning into coat of horse-like hair at the midsection. Their tails, long enough to flick a fly off of their head, ended in a stinger which delivered agonizing torment to those that did not have the seal of the true God. They made a loud sound, as chariots in battle and the rumbling of horses' hoofs. Their motion was quick and their turns were sharp, like those when roaches scatter when a light is turned on. They had the stench of death, of decaying flesh, noticeable even to Yitzhak high on the mountain. Quickly they covered the entire valley before heading off in every direction to inflict their torture.

Yitzhak stood in awe. There was no confusion with him as to what this was. The fifth Trumpet had sounded and the Abyss had been opened, allowing these demons to roam the earth and bring pain for five months. *Apollyon*, Yitzhak thought, *they have come to destroy.*

Chapter 16

J ake was standing along the bank of the Euphrates when the screaming started. He enjoyed praying along the river where there was a quiet calm and few others, if any, allowing him to be alone to reflect upon his life. Often he would think of his wife, Tracey, and his son. He missed them dearly and wished that he had listened to her about Jesus and His salvation prior to the Rapture. He'd be with them now in the presence of the Lord if he had. Although the tears had stopped, the years had not eased his pain of separation from them, and the persecution that he faced daily did not help; it just added to his loneliness. *Not much longer Tracey*, he thought, *and we'll be together again-you, me and John.* She would have made life easier for him in the Tribulation, but he was happy that she did not have to live through it. It was the anticipation of Christ's imminent return and that Tracey and John would be coming with Him that gave Jake strength and the courage to continue on. His thoughts, and the quiet calm, were broken by the screams, few and barely audible at first, then becoming more frequent and louder as time passed. He had never heard screams like this. Even with the last six years of murder and death, of famine and disease, he had never quite heard the type of screams that were coming from Babylon. They began as a high-pitch screech, a sound that he knew was one mingled with fear and of surprise, then suddenly becoming dull in volume, the severe pain taking the strength to scream any louder from its victim. Looking toward Babylon, Jake's mind was invaded by thoughts of doom. Did the Anti-Christ's forces find the community? Were they under some kind of attack? Were the screams coming from his friends, his brothers and sisters in Christ?

Jake ran toward the main entrance of the underground tunnels. Prepared to die if he had to, he would fight to protect his friends. Breaking through a patch of thick reeds, he saw that three of the demons that had come out of the Abyss had surrounded him. Slowly they closed in on him, getting to within a foot. Their backs were arched, which allowed their scorpion-like tails to be positioned just above their heads, posed to inflict their tormenting sting. They stood there watching Jake and examining him, appearing to be looking for something on his body. One reached out and grabbed Jake's right hand with its locust-like wing and stared at it intently. Another came to within two inches of his forehead and appeared to be looking for something. The stench was nauseating, and Jake wanted to cover his nose and mouth with his hands but did not move a muscle other than his eyes following their every motion. His heart was pounding, and beads of sweat poured from his face and dripped onto his shirt, soaking it with the salty fluid. He could hear them breathing with a high-pitch wheeze and felt the air on his face as they exhaled. A thick, mucous saliva fell from their mouths and onto his shoes. Then, as suddenly as they appeared, they disappeared, scurrying away quickly and with purpose.

Jake took a deep breath then continued his run to the tunnel. He reached the entrance and started pounding on its steel door. There was no response from inside, and Jake pounded on the door again.

"What's the password." Luther's voice emanated from within.

"King of Kings!" Jake yelled out in frustration. "For God's sake, Luther, open the door!"

"What's going on?" Luther opened the door. Jake hurried in, closing the door behind him.

"I'm not sure. I saw some ... some type of creature or something. They looked like what was described in the Book of Revelation. Apollyon the destroyer."

"What?"

"The Book of Revelation, Luther. The demons that were released at the fifth Trumpet judgment from the Abyss. And the screams-did you hear them? I thought that they were coming from here."

"Yes, I heard them. But they have been coming from the city."

"My God. They must be attacking the unsaved. I want to gather everyone together at the meeting place tonight. We need to discuss what has happened and make everybody aware that the demons of the fifth Trumpet have been loosed."

"Can I do anything to help?"

"Tell anyone who enters that there will be a meeting tonight and that it is important that they be there. They may already be aware of the demons, but I feel that it is important to have a plan set up for our protection, and everyone's input will be appreciated. I'll start spreading the word within. We'll start the meeting at seven P.M."

"A plan for our protection? Do you think that the demons will harm us?"

"No. If they wanted to hurt me, they definitely had a chance about ten minutes ago. They are only interested in unbelievers, those that do not have the seal of God. But there may be some of us who don't know what these demons are. If these demons are the fulfillment of the fifth Trumpet judgment, then they are going to inflict their torment for five months."

"Five months?" Luther looked confused, "We're going to have these things killing people for five months?"

"That's just it, Luther. They don't have the power to kill, not just yet anyway. They can only inflict pain for five months, and their victims will not be allowed to die. The Bible says that the people, the ones that do not have God's seal, will "seek death but will not find it." For five months, Luther, they will be tormented."

"I'll just stay in the tunnel for the next five months ... thank you very much."

"No, Luther. That's one of the reasons I want to meet tonight. This is our opportunity to be out there spreading the Word of Christ."

"What? We'll be attacked by those demons."

"Luther, haven't you heard a word I said? They will only attack those people that do not have the seal of God. We are sealed by our faith in Christ. But I can't imagine that there will be a lot of people who aren't Christian having the courage to step out of their homes or hiding places in fear of the demons. If we can show ourselves and convince them that accepting Christ will protect us from the demons, then they may turn from the Anti-Christ. It still won't be risk free, but it will be safer then the way we've been witnessing thus far."

"I understand what you're saying, my brother, but it may also inflame the people's anger seeing that God is protecting us and not them. They may just want to kill us rather than accept Christ's mercy."

"That is true. The Bible says that most will refuse to repent and accept Christ. But we need to be there for those few that will accept Christ. We just can't hide ourselves in the tunnels."

"Agreed. I'll inform anyone who comes that there will be a meeting tonight at seven P.M."

"Thank you, Luther, I'll see you then."

Steve Anderson led Mary down a long, narrow tunnel that was barely illuminated by flaming torches that hung upon the damp walls and set every ten to fifteen feet. Steve also carried a torch that he held in front of him to guide the way and occasionally waved his hand in front of his face in an attempt to remove the smoke that drifted into his eyes. Large rats crossed the pathway and scurried quickly to escape their steps. Steve seemed not to notice, keeping his quick pace, but Mary would let out a low screech then purposely step to one side to avoid the rodent. The air was warm and humid with a musty smell. Droplets of fluid formed on their faces, and their clothes were damp, but Mary was unsure whether it was due to perspiration or the wet climate within the tunnel. *Where was he leading her-to Jake? Was he even here?* Her stomach was churning with anticipation and with the hope that Jake was there. Steve glanced behind himself to make sure that he hadn't lost Mary with his quick pace. Finally he spoke.

"We've prayed for you, Mary. Every day we would remember you."

"We?"

"Yes. Jake and I continually petitioned the Lord for your soul and for your safety. I'm thankful that He has answered our prayer."

"Jake is all right, then?"

"He is alive and well. He will be happy to hear that you have accepted Christ as your Savior."

"Jake is here then? I look forward to seeing him."

"No." Steve took a deep breath and continued down the tunnel. "He's not here. There is another Christian community in Babylon-he is there. After our escape at Mount Seir, we were prohibited from going into Petra by the chasm that surrounds it. We escaped to Babylon where we helped form the Christian community. I came to Jerusalem to help set up the community here. But weekly we send messengers to communicate with our brothers and sisters in Babylon."

Mary could barely hide her disappointment that Jake was not in Jerusalem, but she knew that if she bided her time, she would meet up with him again. In the meantime, she would gather information about the community and give the details to Governor Peron. She hoped that Prophet Gallo was a man of his word and that he would allow her to avenge Randy's death. Steve led Mary to the end of the tunnel and to a wooden door made from the trees of the once vast cedar forests of Lebanon. Knocking on the door, he turned to Mary, "You don't know how thrilled I am that you are here. I know it's been a hard road for you, but you'll see Randy again. Your first step to seeing him again was when you accepted Christ-"

"What's the password?" a voice on the other side of the door interrupted.

"Lord of Lords." Steve replied then turned to Mary. "We changed the password at the inner door just in case the first barrier had been found out."

The door swung open revealing a large room. *A sanctuary?* was Mary's first thought. An altar, made of smooth stone taken from the Jordan River and held together by mortar, had been set at the far wall and unlit candles were place on top at either side.

There were no chairs to sit on, and the entire room was illuminated only by the torches that hung along all four walls.

"Come, Mary. I will show you our home until the Lord returns. This room is where we come to worship. Each Sunday those who want to share their testimony of Christ and what He has done for them comes here and shares their story. Then we study Scripture and prophecy that tells us what lies ahead for us. All of us here agree that the Lord will return at the end of the Tribulation-less than a year from now."

"Scripture tells you when the Lord will return?"

"Not exactly. But it gives us what events will happen before he comes. We know that the treaty that President Christos agreed upon with Israel marks the beginning of the seven-year Tribulation. As you may remember, that was over six years ago. We also know that after three and one-half years that he will turn his back on Israel and persecute all Jews and Christians. That was almost three years ago. There are many other events that give us clues to Christ's return. The Seal judgments-which we feel are past, and now the Trumpet judgments. We know of four that have passed and we believe that the fifth trumpet has sounded and that the release of the demons has already taken place."

"The release of the demons? Steve, there's a lot that I have to learn."

"You are new in Christ." Steve let out a chuckle, "Like a newborn still feeding on mother's milk. I will not overwhelm you with all the details now. The point I'm trying to make is that the Bible gives us clues to Christ's return and we are close to that time."

"The Bible predicts all of this?"

"Every event that has taken place since the Rapture has been predicted by the prophets. First the Rapture itself. Then the treaty with Israel and the rise of a world leader and the false prophet. We know them as President Christos and Prophet Gallo-the Anti-Christ forcing people to accept his mark or to face death. Wars, famine, drought and death have all been predicted. The witnesses prophesying here in Jerusalem and the one hundred and forty-four thousand Jews that are evangelizing the world, all were predicted thousands of years before they happened. All we need to do is read what the Bible says about what lies ahead from this point on and we can be assured, as God lives, that those predictions will come true. Randy came to believe, too, in what the Bible told him. He knew it was true and he was willing to die for the truth. You can say that the truth had set him free."

Mary was silent, lost in the thought of what Steve had just said to her. *Was it true?* Two and one-half years she was witnessed by Randy when he lived in the cave and never had she looked at it that way. He and Jake constantly tried to explain to her the meaning of the four horsemen of the apocalypse and of the trumpet and bowl judgments that were to come. Why was it now making sense to her? Why couldn't she have seen it at the time when Randy was living in the cave in Denver? The spell that Prophet Gallo had on her blinded her to what Randy and Jake had been trying to tell her. But she knew her husband well, better than anyone, and he would never have given his life for something he didn't believe in with his whole heart. *President Christos and Prophet Gallo. Are they really the Anti-Christ and False Prophet that the Bible predicted?* She could never get Randy to buy into the fact that Prophet Gallo had done miracles in New York when she saw him there and that he was of God. *Why? Did he know something that she didn't? Was she so blind and hell bent on getting Randy to believe as she did that she failed to see the signs that he was giving her from the Bible? Could Satan, so evil as to mislead the multitudes, perform good deeds such as the healing of the sick and the raising of the dead? The great deceiver. Only a great deceiver with an ulterior motive could perform such feats.*

For the first time since Randy's death, Mary started to doubt the reasons why she was hunting Jake. If what Steve was saying is true, then it was President Christos that let everything happen. It was he that allowed Randy to be executed and to suffer for the name of Christ. Steve was correct in that Randy would have never allowed himself to die for something that wasn't true or, at least, believed wasn't the truth. And Mary had let Randy down for not believing and by blaming Jake for what had happened. It all came flooding in on her-the predictions, the death and destruction of the last six years, the hatred toward Jews and Christians, which she was guilty of, and the rise of President Christos and Prophet Gallo.

Only by the power of Satan could they be performing supernatural deeds, but none hit her as hard as the truth. The truth had opened her eyes and had set her free. The truth was that Jesus died on the cross and rose from the dead and that He was coming back at the end of the Tribulation to collect His own. The truth had lifted the blindness of hatred from her eyes and the thought of vengeance from her heart. *It's too late for me. I could never allow myself to accept Christ.* She had accepted the mark of the Anti-Christ and bore it on her right hand; at least she did prior to Prophet Gallo removing it so that she could infiltrate the Christian community and expose it to the authorities. *Christ would never accept her now*, she thought, *a person full of hatred and anger, and a woman who willingly accepted the mark of the beast.* Shame overwhelmed her and she hung her head and cried.

The spy that had watched Mary enter the tunnel had left Governor Peron's office. He had given the governor the location of the entrance to the Christian hideaway. Now it was the governor's turn to relay the message to Prophet Gallo who had ordered that all information obtained regarding the Christian community to be passed on to him immediately.

"Miss Hayden?" The governor spoke into the intercom.

"Yes, Mr. Peron?"

"Call Rome and see if Prophet Gallo will take my call. Tell his secretary that it is regarding Miss Johnson and the Christian community."

"I'll call him right away."

A few minutes later, the governor's secretary buzzed the intercom. "Mr. Peron?-Prophet Gallo's secretary on line one."

Governor Peron picked up the phone, "This is Governor Peron."

"Governor Peron-" the soft voice at the other end of the line said, "-please hold for Prophet Gallo."

A few more moments had passed before Prophet Gallo picked up the line, "Governor Peron, have you something to report regarding Miss Johnson?"

"Yes, Sir. One of my spies has confirmed the location of the Christian hideaway and the password *King of Kings*. He has reported that Miss Johnson had entered after giving the password. He waited for two hours but she did not come out. However, he observed two others enter, both giving the password. My spy is under the impression that this hideaway may be larger than we first thought. Would you like us to take action against them now?"

"Not yet. Keep the entrance under surveillance for now. Try to get as many spies as you can to follow anyone who comes out. I want to know where they go and what they do. I want to find out where they are getting food and supplies. I do not want anyone to approach them lest they start getting suspicious, nor do I want them to have any clue that they are probably being watched. The more information we can obtain, the more likely that we will be able to find other Christians."

"And what about Miss Johnson?"

"I don't trust her. Collect any information that you can from her of course, but we really do not need her now. We know where they are, and all we need to do is be patient. Call me back when you have more information."

"Yes, Sir."

Governor Peron placed the phone down then was startled by the scream that came from the front office. It was a blood-curdling scream that shook him to the core. Opening the door, he stood motionless, paralyzed by what he was witnessing. Fear had left him powerless and took away the strength to scream. He had never seen anything like it. A creature so hideous with its human-like face and horse-like body that it left him so powerless that he could not even look away as he watched the scorpion-like stinger of the demon imbed itself into his secretary's chest. Dropping the still screaming secretary to the floor, the creature turned to the governor and advanced quickly with its back arched and its tail ready. The governor could only watch as the creature moved closer.

_____

"It's not very large, but you will find everything that you need," Steve said, showing Mary her living quarters. "There's a cot to sleep on and a small table in the corner to write or study. Is there anything that you need from the outside? Any personal belongings that you need to get? If there is, I can get someone to help you get it."

"No." Mary answered quietly, her thought still pondering what Steve had told her earlier, "I have nothing left."

"Oh, but you do. You have Christ, and soon we will all be with Him, and you will see Randy again and together you will eat from the tree of life in the paradise of God."

It seemed so perfect to Mary. How she would love to be with Randy again in paradise. *But I'll never be allowed in*, she wanted to say, *not after what I have done.* "Thank you, Steve, you make me feel better. It's just been hard for me, especially since I was the one who tried to get you and Jake captured at Mount Seir. I don't know how you could ever forgive me."

"If I didn't have Christ, I could have never forgiven you. But that was then and this is now. You are my sister in Christ, and if He can forgive you, then so can I. Now rest up. I want to introduce you at the meeting that we will be having tonight at seven. I'll come get you."

"All right. I'll see you then."

Mary lay on the cot, tears welling in her eyes and trickling down the side of her face. She had tricked Steve about her having accepted Christ as her Savior. How she wished she had accepted Him, but in her mind she was past saving. But one thing that she did know was that she would not report to Governor Peron. Here, in these musty quarters she would have refuge and friends, something that her hardened heart had not allowed her to have for the past three years. Not wanting to think any longer, she closed her eyes and fell asleep.

Steve's voice startled Mary and she lurched out of bed quickly. Mary staggered to the door and let Steve in.

"Mary," Steve said. "Come quickly, it has sounded."

"What has sounded?" Mary replied still in a sleepy daze.

"The fifth Trumpet."

"The fifth what?"

"Trumpet. Remember I told you earlier of the Trumpet judgments? The fifth one has sounded, and demons have been let loose to torment those that do not have the seal of God."

"How do you know? Have they attacked the community?"

"No. They can only harm non-believers. All Christians have the seal of God so that gives us protection from them."

Mary was nervous. She hadn't accepted Christ. "Are they going to kill all non-believers?" she asked.

"They don't have the power to kill. They can only cause pain, tremendous pain as the Bible puts it. For five months they can inflict their sting, and Revelation says that the pain will be so great that its victims will prefer to die and actually seek death. But God won't allow them to die; they must suffer the pain for five months."

"How can God allow that to happen?"

"The ironic thing about it is that He allows it to happen because He loves us."

"That's a strange way to show it."

"Mary, His judgments are sort of a last resort. He's not necessarily doing it to just punish the wicked but to turn their hearts around. Many will come to accept Christ as Savior as a result of the judgments. Many more will not and will only have their anger fueled by them. But it is because God does not want to see any soul lost but that all should turn to Him that He sends judgment."

In Babylon, Jake had formed a small group of Christians with a goal of witnessing to the unsaved on the streets of the city. In the four weeks since the release of the demons, he and his group had shared the Good News, converting many to Christ, but he was frustrated because many more had not heeded his plea to accept God's forgiveness. Jake had not gotten used to the cries that reverberated throughout the city. Four weeks had passed and still the demons inflicted their tormenting touch. At night he would lie awake listening to the screams that echoed through the walls of the tunnels as if they were made of paper and not of stone. The screams seemed the loudest at night when darkness, made even darker by the fourth Trumpet judgment's blackening a third of the sun, stars and moon shrouding the country side. Jake never understood why sound traveled more swiftly at night, if it did so, or whether sound was heard because of the decrease in the urban hustle and bustle of daily life. But whatever the reason, the howling screams kept him awake, and he would pray for the souls that not had accepted Christ and for those that were tormented by the sting of the demons. Although horrible, Jake knew that all the judgments meted out upon the earth were God's way of getting the unsaved to turn to Him. With this in mind he formed the group to witness to any unsaved souls that would brave the streets and accept and believe the Gospel. Today the group prepared to preach in the market square. Jake had come a long way in his walk with Christ. He had become a persuasive speaker and gained courage, not unlike the Apostle Peter did at Pentecost. His compatriots had nicknamed him "Rock," in honor and reference to the Apostle. Whether he gained courage from the Holy Spirit, or the knowledge that time was short, or that it didn't really matter in the end if he lived or died, as long as he did it in Christ his Savior, it was worth doing. All he knew is that, what ever the reason, he was no longer afraid.

Jake stood at the center of the market square where there was a small outdoor stage or amphitheater. Before the release of the demons, actors would perform in plays and mini-concerts were held there, but fear had gripped the city since and all performances were postponed. Only when hunger forced the unsaved to venture out of their homes or apartments to get food and other supplies would anyone brave the streets. It was mostly the men that would try and provide for their families by chancing the attacks of the demons while their families were safe at home. Only a small crowd had gathered today.

"Accept Christ!" Jake started, "And He will protect you from the demons that inflict their tormenting stings. We are an example of how God has protected us from them, and an example to you that He will protect you as well. All you need to do is accept his forgiveness through His Son Jesus Christ."

"But it is your God that has inflicted this on us. How can you say that he will protect us?" an angry listener yelled out.

"Because of what I have just told you. We do not fear the demons because they can do us no harm. I have come face to face with them, on more than one occasion, and they can not touch me. Accept Christ and you can have this protection as well."

"You're lying!" a young man raced to the edge of the stage. His brown, blood-shot eyes stared directly at Jake and tears cascaded down his cheek. "My mother lies in bed with excruciating pain compliments of a demon's sting that your so-called loving God has released. She tries to commit suicide daily, but she fails. She has even drunk cyanide, but it does not work. I have many friends who suffer daily, but your God will not let them or my mother die in peace. It is He that torments them, not the demons."

"That is because she does not know Christ." Jake replied. "Nor your friends. If they accept Christ, their pain will be healed."

Suddenly a demon appeared, approaching the small crowd, and they scattered from the stage. But the young man was unable to escape and seemed trapped at the foot of the platform. Jake grabbed the man under his armpits and pulled him onto the stage.

"Surround him!" Jake yelled to his Christian friends. "We can protect him from the demon."

Immediately Jake and the others surrounded the young man. The demon approached the human circle but could not get through.

"The demons have been commanded that they can not hurt anyone with the seal of God." Jake looked back at the young man. His skin was ashen and his heart was pounding. Beads of sweat dripped from his forehead, and he fell to the stage too weak to stand. "He can't hurt us so don't try anything stupid like trying to run," Jake screamed "As soon as you leave this circle of Christians, he will pounce on you."

"But wh ... what can I do?" the young man stuttered, "You can't stay here forever."

"No, we can't stay here forever, but you can accept Christ in your heart and be forgiven."

"What?"

"Accept Christ. The demons cannot hurt those with God's seal. Can't you see that he cannot hurt us? It is not because of anything that we did, but because we have accepted Christ as our Savior. Fear God and give him glory. It's your only choice if you want to be protected from the demons."

"Okay, I'll do it. But how?"

"Ask Christ to come into your life now." Jake replied, "You're a sinner, and He died for your sins. Admit that you are a sinner and tell Him that you accept his sacrifice on the cross and that He rose from the dead to give us eternal life. Do it now and He will forgive you, and God the father will put His seal upon your forehead. Only then will He protect you from the demon."

"I accept Him. Protect me, Lord, from the demon," he prayed. "I accept You Jesus, as Lord and Savior. I accept the sacrifice that You made for me. I believe that You died for the forgiveness of my sins and that You rose again so that I may have eternal life."

The demon stared at Jake then turned and walked away. The invisible seal of God had been placed on the young man and he collapsed face down, praising God.

Jake and the others returned to the underground tunnels later that evening. Steve Anderson had come to Babylon to deliver a message to Jake and had been waiting in the meeting room for the past four hours. He wanted to personally bring the message that Mary Johnson had received Christ and that she had found shelter in the tunnels of Jerusalem. It had been a long trek across the desert and Steve, dusty and tired, welcomed the rest that the four-hour wait had given him. Jake entered the room and Steve met him at the door.

"My brother Jake, the Rock." Steve greeted Jake with a smile and grabbed hold of his shoulders, "It is good to see you."

"And you, Steve." Jake replied, embracing his long-time friend and former copilot. "You look good; God has taken care of you."

"And you, Jake. I have some good news to tell you. I found Mary, or should I say she found me. She has accepted Christ as her Savior."

"Praise God. Did she come with you?" Jake smiled broadly. Daily he had prayed for Mary. Until today he was not even sure that she was still alive.

"No. She is still a babe in the faith and the demons have left her feeling uneasy. She wanted to see you, but she has been hiding in the tunnels since she arrived. She refuses to leave until the demons are gone. Can you come back with me? She says she would like to talk to you."

"Did she say what about?"

"No, she wouldn't tell me. I assume that she wanted to make things right with you with everything that had happened at Mount Seir."

"I've forgiven her a long time ago for that. Nothing needs to be said. But to answer your question, I don't think that it would be good for me to leave here just yet. I've formed a group with the goal to witness to those here in Babylon who have yet to accept Christ. I felt the Lord telling me that with the demons loose for five months that it would be a good time to spread the Good News of the Gospel. I can't leave here until that goal is achieved, another four months at least."

Steve caught Jake up on how Mary had seen him as he watched the witnesses at the Wailing Wall and had followed him to the tunnel entrance. Jake had told him of the incredible story of how the Lord had protected the young man from the demon at the market square and that he had accepted Christ as a result.

"How long will you be staying before you head back to Jerusalem?" Jake asked.

"We will leave tomorrow morning, I'd like to get an early start. But I hoped that we could break bread tonight and pray together. I feel that we should lift Mary up in prayer."

"By all means. I would be honored to sup with you. But I don't know how quiet it will be tonight. The screams have not stopped since they started; we should also pray for them."

———

Five months had passed since the demons were loosed from the abyss. But as suddenly as they appeared, they disappeared, leaving only memories of the tormenting pain that they had inflicted to the unsaved. None were more excited about that than Mary Johnson.

For five months she feared the demons and stayed inside the Christian hideaway in Jerusalem-never venturing outside for fear of the demons. Steve had worried about her lack of faith and her mental health. He thought it odd that she would not go outside not once in that time. But he was unaware that her fear was because she never accepted Christ in her heart because she felt unworthy of God's forgiveness. She did not have the seal of God, and the demons, no doubt, would have inflicted their sting on her. Her fear had subsided when the demons disappeared, and she began to leave the hideaway for hours at a time. Steve began to feel better about her turnabout and thought it a good idea to take her on his next trip to Babylon the following week. She agreed to go. She longed to talk to Jake and set the record straight with him.

President Christos was angry. He wanted the Christian hideaway destroyed, and he thought that Prophet Gallo was waiting too long to do so. Five months of planning and still there was no move to invade the Christians.

"I want to know why you haven't made a move on the Christian hiding place?" President Christos glared at Prophet Gallo.

"We wanted to wait to see if they would give us clues to other hideouts," Prophet Gallo answered. "We do have some evidence that Jerusalem Christians are communicating with Christians located somewhere in Babylon. We were hoping that this Mary Johnson would lead us to them. I have ordered surveillance, but the demons had attacked every spy that we had sent and, as far as we know, Miss Johnson has not come out of the hideaway since she entered."

"When she does, I want her arrested and executed like her husband."

"Yes, Your Holiness. Now that the demons are gone, I don't think it will be long until she and the others that are hiding will lead us to Babylon's Christians. When that happens, we'll make our move."

"Good. Now then, what do you have planned for the two witnesses? They are making me look foolish and I want them dead."

"I have a plan that will take care of them. I will send a battalion of soldiers to open fire on them with automatic weapons. Previous attacks on them have been made by anywhere from one person to a handful of people. It is easy for the witnesses to burn them with fire because of the attackers' numbers. They may be able to kill some of our men but they will not be able to kill all of them before they are killed. Leave it to me. They shall be dead within a month's time."

Mary was exhausted when she and Steve Anderson had reached the outskirts of Babylon. She couldn't wait to get inside and rest but was also nervous about seeing Jake Fredricks again. What would he say to her? Had he really forgiven her for what she tried to do at Mount Seir? Could he ever trust her again? She thought that the answer to all those questions would be an emphatic no. Approaching the Euphrates River from the west, Steve heard the roar of armored vehicles and saw dust rising high into the sky from the river's east side. Taking a pair of binoculars from his bag, he looked at what was causing the disturbance. The Chinese were mobilizing and setting camp along the river bank and extended to the far north, as far as his eyes could see. The army of two hundred million had arrived and were preparing to invade the Middle East.

China had tired of the living conditions that they were forced to live under. Famine and drought had left millions of her citizens dead, and millions more were not expected to live through the coming months. A third of the fresh water and lakes that had not dried up by the drought were made poisonous by the star that the Jews and Christians named "wormwood," and many died at the water's edge after taking a drink. Violence and fighting among China's citizens for the last bit of food or a chance to get drinkable water escalated, leaving many lying in the streets bleeding or dead. Her citizens dying and the civil uprising that resulted from it had left the government no choice but to march against the United States of Europe and Alexander Christos.

The Soviet Union, once a premier world power, had weakened from their failed attack on Israel and had suffered a similar fate as their neighbors from the East. One-time enemies, the Soviet Union and China had become allies in order to survive. Together they now planned an attack on the U.S.E. For years, the Soviet Union had dams placed along the Euphrates north of the Middle East. Stopping the flow of water from these dams would take away the only barrier that China had on her way to Israel and then Rome. The Soviets and Chinese would not carry out their plans just yet. They had allied with the countries of Northern Africa and would wait for their move before stopping the flow of the Euphrates.

The Northern African Alliance was formed a year and a half earlier. Led by Egypt and Libya, the countries joined to share resources and manpower to survive the famine and drought that had devastated their homelands. After suffering at the will of the demons, the Alliance conspired with China and the Soviet Union to invade Israel. The plan was to have the Northern African Alliance invade first through Egypt and the Sinai, hopefully diverting U.S.E forces to the south. When this was accomplished, China would attack from the east and the Soviets from the north. Their plan was foolproof, so they thought, and Alexander Christos' reign would end.

Chapter 17

"We've finally found Mary Johnson, Your Holiness-" Governor Peron sat opposite Prophet Gallo, just in front of the prophet's desk. The Governor was relieved that he could finally report the long-awaited news to his superior. "And she's traveling east with a group of Christians. I'm having them followed as we speak. We think they are going to Babylon."

"She has deceived me-" Prophet Gallo responded, "-and I will make her pay dearly for her treason. But I have fooled her as well. Remember that I told you how I made Alexander Christos' mark on her right hand disappear?" Governor Peron nodded, "I merely made it disappear; I did not remove it. It will reappear again, soon."

"And then her friends will see that she has the mark."

"That's right." Prophet Gallo allowed himself to smile. "And when they see the mark, she will be rejected by them. In the meantime, continue to monitor the group; see if they lead you to the Christians in Babylon. Then destroy their hiding places and bring Miss Johnson and as many of the Christians back alive as you can. I will send them back to Rome to face execution as a gift to President Christos.

"And what will become of Mary Johnson?" Governor Peron asked.

"Mary Johnson?" Prophet Gallo stood from the desk and took a deep breath. With a smirk on his face he asked, "What is it that we do to traitors, Governor? She will face the same death as her wretched husband. I want you to go to Babylon and personally oversee the operation. Are you well enough to go?"

"Yes, Your Holiness, I am well. The demon's sting has healed and I feel strong."

"Good." Prophet Gallo stood and walked to the front of his desk and sat on the edge. "Then, if you are well enough, I want you to travel to Babylon immediately."

"I am well enough to travel, Your Holiness. I am at your disposal, and at the disposal of our Lord Christos."

Mary Johnson and Steve Anderson were happy to reach Babylon. The journey from Jerusalem had taken longer then they would have liked. Traveling only in the cool morning hours, they were forced to stop in the early afternoon to rest the animals and refresh themselves. An unusual heat pattern had developed in the afternoon that carried with it a strong, hot wind that blew the dry, dusty sand into the air, reducing visibility to almost zero. Steve could not recall such a strong wind along the trail, or a time when visibility was so limited that it forced them to camp for most of the day. Also unusual, he thought, was that this wind was not the cool breeze that he had grown accustomed to, but a hot wind that reminded him of the air that is pushed through a furnace to warm a room. He longed for a cool breeze-one that would, at least, stop the perspiration from soaking their clothes and causing the dust to adhere to their skin. Finally reaching Babylon, Steve bowed his head and thanked God for their safe arrival. Little did he know that he and his group were followed.

Mary was glad to get out of the Jerusalem hiding place. Five months she spent inside not so much as to step outside and go for a walk. But life, for her, had been the best it had for a long time. The camaraderie and sharing, the daily Bible studies and loving friend-ships had impressed her. Every person within the Christian hideout had been assigned a responsibility or role for the betterment of the community and the uplifting of each other. Because she was new in Christ, or so the community thought, she was assigned to read the Bible to those that could not read. Mary resisted at first, but as time passed, she looked forward to the time that she could read to another. She could read to her audience for hours at a time. She was known to end a marathon reading session then go to her room and read some more. For the first time since Randy's death, she felt loved and was able to show love. Five months in the community had changed her from a hatred-filled woman seeking revenge to a woman who wanted to show that she could still love another. She had not seen her son in three years and longed to hold him and to tell him that she loved him. She hoped that he was alive and well. Steve had told her that Randy Jr. was living in Petra with Yitzhak and Hannah. There he would be well taken care of until Christ's return to bring in the Millennial Kingdom. That was little consolation for her broken heart; she knew that she was not going to be there. Even with the changes in her life, she could never get herself to accept Christ in her life. She felt unworthy and undeserving. In her mind she committed the unforgivable. She had accepted the mark of the beast which had reappeared slowly over the past couple of days. Mary was unsure how long she could hide the mark from the rest of the group. She had read enough of the Book of Revelation to know that those that had the mark and worshipped the Anti-Christ were sentenced already and going to receive eternal punishment. Though she did not worship the Anti-Christ nor wanted the mark any longer, she did accept the mark of her free will.

Jake Fredricks anxiously anticipated Steve and Mary's arrival. He was disappointed that he would not be in the tunnels when they arrived, but the group that he had formed when the demons were released from the abyss were still witnessing in the city, and he had planned to witness at the market square today. God had protected Jake's ministry and, God willing, he would be back later that night to meet with Steve and Mary. He wasn't sure how he would react when he and Mary would finally meet again; all he knew was that he couldn't wait to see her and to welcome her into the Christian family. Usually groups from both the Jerusalem and Babylon communities would meet somewhere in the desert halfway between both cities. But Steve wanted to personally bring Mary to meet with Jake in Babylon instead of the desert. It turned out, as Steve reflected back on the poor weather, that it was for the better that they had not met at the usual place. Steve turned to Mary and pointed toward the large boulder that marked the main entrance to the tunnels. Mary lifted her head, straining to look and shielded her eyes from the glaring sun then turned to Steve.

"Steve, I'm so nervous." She stopped for a moment and stared in the direction of the boulder. "I'm not sure how Jake will react when he sees me."

"Don't worry." Steve responded, "Jake is just as anxious to see you. He has prayed daily for you and has forgiven you. He's longed for this day."

"How do I look?"

"Considering that we have traveled in a sand storm and haven't washed since we left Jerusalem, you look good. But it looks like the blowing sand has given you some marks on your left cheek and mouth."

Mary touched her cheek, and it was painful to the touch. She pulled her hand away quickly.

"Oh, don't worry about it." Steve said, "He won't even notice."

"You did." she responded and they both smiled.

Steve and Mary entered the main entrance hidden by the reeds at the base of the large boulder.

"King of Kings," Steve said. The door opened and Steve and Mary entered.

"I'm looking for Jake Fredricks." Steve asked, not recognizing the guard. "Is he here?"

The guard, a short and dark man missing one leg, sat on an old wooden chair. His crutches lay against the wall next to the chair. Looking up at Steve with his brown eyes he answered, "He just left here maybe a half hour ago. He said that he would be back later tonight."

"Did he say where he was going?"

"He has been witnessing at the market square in town every day. It's amazing that he hasn't been arrested. No one even attempts to arrest him. He shows no fear when he is there. God has been protecting him like no other that I have ever heard of."

"Can you see that she gets to Jake's quarters?" Steve gestured to Mary. "I want to go find Jake and bring him back. Also if you have some antiseptic or ointment that you can get her I would appreciate it. We traveled through a tremendous sand storm and I think that the stand may have broken the skin on her face."

"I'd be happy to." The guard responded, "I'm off duty in fifteen minutes and will take care of her myself."

———

Governor Peron had flown to Babylon that morning to meet with the spies that had been following Steve Anderson and his group. Although a short flight, Governor Peron was glad to be on the ground and at President Christos' Babylon headquarters located in the middle of the city. From his window, he could see a man standing on a stage at the center of the market square speaking, almost yelling it appeared, with his flowing salt and pepper beard moving with every word that he spoke. He was surrounded by a crowd of people; some seemed agitated while others sat calmly listening to what the man had to say. He couldn't help but think of the two witnesses in Jerusalem; the man on the stage seemed to carry the same strength of character and courage. Interestingly enough, another man walked onto the stage and knelt in front of the orator. Putting his hand on the man kneeling in front of him, the speaker yelled out and looked to Heaven. "Today salvation has come to you. Receive eternal life that the Lord Jesus has bought for you with his crucifixion at Calvary." The governor chuckled then shook his head.

The door to the office opened and the governor turned to see who had opened it.

"Two gentlemen to see you, Sir," The secretary peeked her head just inside. "They didn't give me their names. Should I let them in?"

"Yes, I'll see them. Send them in."

———

Jake had finished preaching from the stage when Steve found

him. They greeted each other with a hug and a kiss on each cheek.

"Good to see you, my brother." Steve said.

"And you, Steve. I have anticipated your arrival. Did Mary come with you?"

"Mary is at the tunnel. She is resting in your quarters."

"She is well, then?"

"Yes. We encountered severe sand storms on the trip and she suffered some minor skin abrasions as a result, but other than that she is fine."

"Steve, the second vial of God's wrath has been poured out. I've been seeing its effects for the last couple of days."

"That's the vial that causes the outbreak of sores on the worshippers of the Anti-Christ?" Steve replied.

Jake shook his head in acknowledgement. He was saddened that he had not reached as many of the unsaved as he could have and knowing that there were more judgments coming that the unsaved were going to have to endure. "The Nebuchadnezzar Memorial Hospital has been inundated with people seeking medical treatment for sores that are developing over their entire bodies. The sores develop slowly, but in a matter of just hours can develop to be very serious, even deadly if not treated. They are very painful and ooze a milky fluid. Maggots have infected larger wounds, which are usually found in advanced cases just before death occurs. And still those that worshiped the Anti-Christ refused to turn from their sins. I have been witnessing about the sores and the other judgments that are to come, but the unbelievers just don't want to turn their lives to God."

"Let's go, Jake." Steve placed his arm around Jake's shoulder. "We knew this was going to happen and we know everything that will happen until the Lord's return. No need to get down, you're doing everything that you can. Besides, Mary is waiting for us."

"They have just left me." Governor Peron spoke to Prophet Gallo on the phone, "Miss Johnson and the group she is with has led us straight to the Christians' hiding place."

"Good." Prophet Gallo replied, "I have also received some

reports that the Christians may be tapping into the power supply at the westernmost wall of the city. That's where we'll strike first."

"Strike first, Your Holiness?"

"President Christos has given orders to destroy the wall?"

"Yes, Your Holiness, but when? How?"

"As you know we have a small number of our troops in the region to monitor the Chinese that have mobilized along the Euphrates. I have ordered them to seek out and find the Christian tunnels. We believe that the tunnels are below the western wall of Babylon and that they are even using the wall as a source of power and shelter. And now that we know where the main entrance is to the tunnel-thanks to your spies-we will also be able to go into them and capture any Christians that may be inside."

"But, Your Holiness-" Governor Peron interrupted, "-won't the troops be needed to hold back the Chinese troops along the Euphrates?"

"No," Prophet Gallo responded. "The Chinese are there by design; it has been arranged as was predicted thousands of years ago. President Christos knows; he's been waiting for this very moment. The Chinese will be fighting on our side in a short time, they just don't know it yet."

"What? But how? Why?"

"President Christos has powers that you cannot understand. Soon, not only will the Chinese invade the Middle East, but what's left of the Soviet Union and the countries allied with the Northern African Alliance will all be converging on Israel. There they will turn their weapons on the God of the Christians when He returns and we will wage war on Him."

"But-"

"Governor Peron-" Prophet Gallo cut the governor off. He grew weary of the interruptions, "-just follow the orders that I give you. Don't worry about the Chinese; that will take care of itself."

"Yes, Your Holiness." Governor Peron conceded humbly.

"At midnight tonight I have ordered that the western most wall of the city be destroyed. The outlying areas up to a three mile diameter will be saturated with our troops to capture any Christians that try and escape through any other openings in the desert. After the wall is destroyed, the soldiers will enter the tunnel through the main entrance. That will force the Christians inside to either fight and die or to escape through the other exits. I suspect most will run and try to escape into the desert. But that's where they will be ambushed by the soldiers that are guarding the desert exits. I want Jake Fredricks and Mary Johnson alive, if possible."

Luther waited impatiently in the doorway of Jake's quarters. His skin was pale, and he was overwhelmed with nausea every time he glanced into Jake's room. He had done everything that he could but it was not enough. He only wanted to keep Mary company until Jake's return, but within just a couple of hours the sores on Mary's face had worsened. He had tried applying some medicinal ointments and salves in an attempt to stop the sores progression, but the ones available to him were old and ineffective. He was relieved to finally see Jake and Steve at the far end of the tunnel. Luther ran to greet them.

"Jake, come quickly!"

"What is it, Luther?"

"Come-It's your friend Mary."

Jake and Steve rushed into the room then as quickly as they entered they stopped just inside unable to move any closer, paralyzed by the hideous sight. Steve turned away and, like Luther, was nauseated by what he saw. The stench of rotting flesh filled the room and it took all of Jake's strength to get closer. Tears filled his eyes as he looked down at his friend and one time co-worker. She was not the beautiful woman that he once knew. Her beauty was replaced by three large ulcerating sores on her face that dropped maggots onto his pillow. The deepest sore exposed the entire cheek bone and her bottom lip was entirely gone, exposing her teeth, which were loosened by her grossly receded gums. A large hole in the middle of her face was all that was left of her nose. Mary looked up at Jake and tried to speak. Her voice was barely audible as Jake sat on the bed next to her and leaned his head closer to hear.

"For years-" Mary strained to get the words out. Her speech

was raspy and slow. She labored to speak and breathed deeply as if the breath that she took would give her the strength to finish. "For years I hated you. I blamed you for Randy's death and swore that I would get revenge."

"Don't talk, Mary," Jake interrupted, his voice cracking, "Save your strength."

"No, Jake. I have to say this. I wanted to see you suffer-like Randy suffered. I vowed that I would see you die and that I would be the one responsible to see that it happened. I even spoke with Prophet Gallo and planned to capture you."

"But you accepted Christ as your Savior and you changed your mind?"

"No." Mary's tears rolled down what was left of her face, mingling with the maggots that fell on the pillow case. "I felt so unworthy. After I took refuge with Steve in the tunnels of Jerusalem, I was given the responsibility to read the Bible to those that could not read. I read the Bible every day and realized that what you had been telling me since the Rapture was all true. I realized that I was wrong and that you were right."

"That doesn't matter now, Mary."

"But it does matter. I've accepted the Anti-Christ's mark. Prophet Gallo made it disappear when we planned that I should seek you out. But that was only temporary." Mary lifted her right hand to show Jake. The mark had returned. "I read the Bible enough to know that there is no place in heaven for those that accept the mark and worship the beast."

"Mary, you don't worship the Anti-Christ."

"But I have the mark."

"That doesn't matter if you accept Christ in you life. Many will come to Christ during the tribulation. Mary, whoever calls on the Lord will be saved, even those who may not have known better at first. Many who thought that the Anti-Christ was God but discovered the truth will be saved. The Gospel of Matthew says that the only sin that shall not be forgiven is blasphemy against the Holy Spirit and continual rejection of His urging. Mary, if you ever want to see Randy again, then you have to accept Christ as your Savior."

"But I am so unworthy. How can Jesus ever forgive me?"

"Just ask." Jake took Mary's hand. "Just ask, Mary, and He will forgive you. Everything is possible with God."

"I accept Him." Mary's words were labored, "He is my Savior."

"Good, Mary. Jesus is the Son of God and died for your sins. He came back to life on the third day. Do you believe that?"

"Yes, I believe." Mary took a deep breath. "The Lord Jesus is my Savior." Mary doubled over in pain, placing her head in Jake's lap. Maggots and bloody fluid from Mary's sores drenched Jake's pants but he didn't seem to notice. He could only feel love for his friend, and her physical condition didn't matter. He placed his arms around her shoulder trying to comfort her.

"Mary-" he said, "-don't be afraid. Soon you will be with the Lord and Randy." There was no response. "Mary?" Jake turned Mary to her back. She was dead, and the mark of the Anti-Christ that was on her hand was gone.

Jake lowered his head and sobbed. Mary was with the Lord now, yet he felt that he had let her down. She had suffered needlessly and Jake felt responsible. He wondered what else he could have done differently to have convinced her to accept the Lord earlier. He was the one who felt unworthy now. He couldn't understand why the Lord had spared him thus far yet has taken everyone that ever mattered to him. Was this his punishment for not listening to Tracey sooner and for not accepting Christ as his Savior before the Rapture? Tracey had tried to warn him, but he didn't listen. Of the other four, Randy, Mary, Sam and Joyce, he was closet to Tracey and should have known. But to see his friends die of horrible deaths was worse than being killed himself. He would have gladly changed places with any of them, to suffer the way that they had. It would be over for him if he could just change places with them, and he would be with the Lord and with his family. As usually occurred when Jake felt like giving up, the white dove appeared. The first time, Jake remembered, was just after the Rapture when he realized that his wife Tracey and son John were gone, then on the window sill at the home of his friend Yitzhak Benziman. Now, after losing yet another friend, the dove appeared. How it got into the tunnels he did not know, but he was uplifted that it did. Landing on his shoulder, the dove seemed to stare Jake in the eyes and as usual Jake grew strong.

"There's still work to be done, I know," Jake said as if he knew the dove understood. "I will be strong."

The dove took flight and exited the room. "Did you see the dove, Steve?"

"What's that?" Steve squinted his eyes.

Jake shook his head. "Oh-nothing."

"Come on, Jake." Steve said. "You can sleep in my quarters tonight. Luther and I will take Mary and prepare her for burial."

"I could use a little rest. Come get me when it's time to bury her. I want to be there."

"We'll get you. Try and get some sleep."

Surprisingly, Jake drifted off quickly but was asleep for only an hour before he was awakened by the alarm bells sounding. He sat straight up in bed taking a few moments to gather his senses. The loud roar of an explosion shook the bed and dust fell from the ceiling. He could hear screams coming from the tunnels. Then Steve opened the door.

"Jake, get up!" he screamed. "We have an intrusion alarm from the main entrance and a large explosion has come from the direction of the wall."

Jake and Steve ran down the tunnel with Steve in the lead. As they turned a corner they saw U.S.E. soldiers coming towards them. Stopping for a moment, they turned back in the opposite direction. Shots rang out as they started to run. Jake reached an exit corridor then turned to see if Steve was behind him. Steve wasn't there. Poking his head around the entrance of the corridor, Jake could see Steve on the floor. He had been shot but was still alive. A soldier stood over him with his rifle pointed at him. Jake could hear the soldier ask Steve who he was.

"Are you Jake Fredricks?" The soldier asked.

"No." Steve answered, breathing heavily. He groaned from the pain of the bullet wound in his leg.

The soldier reached down to see if Steve had any identification. Not finding any, he questioned Steve again.

"So, you're not Jake Fredricks. Do you know where he is?"

"He's dead," Steve answered. "He's been dead for over a year now."

"You're lying," The soldier said, kicking Steve in the head. Motioning to his colleagues, he continued, "Stand back."

Raising his rifle to Steve's head, the soldier fired one shot, killing him instantly. Jake stood there quietly, stunned by what had just happened. *I have to get out of here.* He turned back into the exit corridor and ran to the opening. Turning the bolt lock to open, Jake opened the trap door. He peeked through the small opening that he had made and saw nothing but darkness. The night air was quiet, revealing nothing of the carnage and invasion in the tunnels below. Stepping out, he was immediately surrounded by four soldiers. Jake had been captured.

Chapter 18

—⧓———⧓—

Two months in a damp and cold jail cell within the bowels of the Roman Coliseum had become unbearable for Jake. The stone walls seemed to close in on him more and more every day, making the already small area a claustrophobic's nightmare. The cold floor was just long enough for Jake to lie down on when he slept at night, and the width, barely enough to sit against the wall and stretch his legs, was slightly over half the room's length. There was no artificial lighting to illuminate the room after the day's end. The only light came from the sun during the shortened days, its rays filtering through a lattice-like ceiling that was made from iron rods that criss-crossed to form square openings. Along the roof, guards paced the catwalk looking in on the prisoners from above through the openings in the ceiling. Nothing was hidden from them. The toilet, if it could be called that, was just a small hole in the floor that opened to a long and narrow aqueduct-type structure that would carry away human waste. The stench was nauseating, especially on the hottest and sweltering days. Jake's only visitors, other than a fellow inmate that was allowed to deliver his food, were two or three large rats that would enter through the hole in the floor looking for food. At night, Jake would sleep with his foot on the hole's cover to keep the rats from entering, but there was nothing he could do about the huge cockroaches and the biting centipedes that crawled on him at night, keeping him awake.

The moans of other prisoners who were sick or dying constantly echoed through the prison's corridors. As time passed, the moans became less noticeable, not because the sound became less frequent but because one's ability to tune out the noise became more acute in an attempt to remain sane. The food, or *gruel* as the prisoners called it, was a soupy mixture of unknown ingredients. Not even the guards knew what was in it, but it was served once every two days, barely enough to keep the prisoners alive for a short time let alone for years at a time. The *gruel* resembled the appearance of oatmeal but was never served warm and at times would have mold growing on the top. When hunger became too much to bear, Jake would supplement his diet, and he suspected that other prisoners had as well, with the roaches and centipedes that invaded his cell. Eating the insects was difficult at first but became easier as his hunger grew, and they actually tasted better than the concoction that was given to him. A lesser man would have died within the first weeks, but Jake's strength came in knowing that the time was short and that the Lord was coming soon. He did what he had to do to survive, and he prayed that he could hold out just a little longer.

Jake spent most of his time in prayer, and, when possible, he would witness to a fellow inmate that he knew only as Max. Max was an elderly man, bald on the top of his head with short gray hair along the sides of his temple and a distinctive scar that extended from his bottom right eye lid to across his nose and to the upper left corner of his lips. He had found favor with the guards and, as a reward, would be allowed out of his cell to deliver the *gruel* to the other inmates. He was also allowed to read the newspaper and had, on numerous occasions, shared with Jake the events from the outside world. Jake looked forward to the short encounters with Max and had felt that he had made progress with convincing Max of the Lordship of Jesus Christ. Jake had told Max of everything that had happened to him in the almost seven years since the Rapture and of the prophecies that had been fulfilled in that time. But he had fallen short of convincing

Max completely and hoped that he could do so before it was too late.

Jake heard the approaching foot steps just outside the steel door and the metal sash slide open. It was Max, and Jake assumed that he would soon be receiving his soupy gruel.

"Hello, Jake." Max said, "I have a surprise for you and the other prisoners today."

"What is it?" Jake replied.

"We have been given real meat today and warm bread to eat."

Jake's curiosity rose. "What's the occasion? Has President Christos grown soft?"

"No," Max replied. "The witnesses in Jerusalem have been killed today."

"What? How?"

"The paper said that U.S.E. forces had gathered around from a distance and opened fire on them. The witness were able to kill a few of the soldiers but were overpowered by the number of troops. Their bodies lie in the street as we speak. Everybody is celebrating and exchanging gifts. And as you can see, even prisoners have been given a chance to celebrate with real food."

"Max, remember what I'm about to say. In three days the witnesses will come back to life and ascend into heaven."

Max chuckled. "Jake, you're a dreamer."

"No, Max, it's true. I tell you before it happens so that when it does you will know that it happens by the power of God."

"Jake, if that is true, then you will probably not live to hear about it." Max's voice became almost a whisper. He had grown quite fond of Jake and found it difficult to give Jake the bad news.

"What do you mean?"

Max looked down at the floor unable to make eye contact with Jake. "The paper also reported that you are to be executed in three days. To face the same execution as your 'co-conspirator Randy Johnson' as the paper put it."

"I haven't even had a trial. How can they do that?"

"When Alexander Christos gives an order, it doesn't matter if it is right or wrong. The order is obeyed."

"Max, I thought when the time came, and in my mind I guess I knew that it would come, that I would have more fear. But right now all I feel is relief. If what the paper is reporting is true, then I will be with my Lord very soon." Jake looked down at the floor and took a deep breath. "I need to be alone, Max. I'll talk to you in a couple of days."

"I understand, Jake. If the God that you worship is as powerful as you say I hope that he protects you."

"He is as powerful as I have told you. Whether He chooses to save my life or allows me to be executed will not change that. Just remember what I have told you. You will be forced to make the decision to either accept or deny Christ; I hope when you see everything happen the way that the Bible tells you it will, that you will decide for Christ."

"If the witnesses come back to life as you say they will, then we'll see. Take the newspaper ... I'll see you in two days."

Jake sat on the floor and seemed to stare into space. The images of Randy's execution were as clear to him today as they were the day that it happened. He hoped that he would be as brave as Randy was. But anything was better-even death-than living in the conditions that he was living.

According to the paper his execution was an event worth seeing, billed as the biggest execution since the "traitor Randy Johnson's" three years earlier. Rome officials expected a capacity crowd in the Coliseum to view the execution. The paper went on to report that many see Jake's execution as a continuation of the frenzy and anti-Christian sentiment that has gained momentum since the two witnesses first appeared in Jerusalem just after Alexander Christos' assassination and resurrection. "The witnesses are dead." Alexander Christos was quoted in the paper. "And Christianity has died with them. Now is time to eliminate all Christians from the face of the planet, and we will renew our fight against them, starting with the execution of Jake Fredricks."

The people still worship him, Jake thought; after everything that has happened, they do not turn to God. Jake could not eat. It had been years since he had a meal like the one that Max had just given him, but he was not hungry.

"You better eat it, Fredricks," The voice of the guard on the catwalk echoed. "In three days you'll be dead so you better enjoy the meat while you can." The guard walked away laughing. Not saying a word, Jake sat against the wall and closed his eyes.

———

Two days had passed and Jake, deep in prayer, had barely moved from the spot that he had been sitting. A light touch on his shoulder interrupted his thought as a white dove landed on his shoulder. As in other times of despair, as Jake remembered, a white dove appeared to him giving him strength and the courage to continue on. The first time was just after Tracey and John were Raptured, the second time on the window sill just after Randy's execution, and then again after Mary had died. It was almost mid-day when Max slid open the sash on the door of Jake's cell and stared inside. He looked down on the floor where he had placed the meat and warm bread two days earlier. What little food that wasn't eaten by the rats was covered with the roaches and centipedes, and Max reached inside and banged the plate against the wall to knock off the insects.

"Did you eat any of it?" Max asked, slapping a roach off of his hand.

Jake shook his head, "No. I'm just not hungry. I've been in prayer."

"Praying to your God to spare your life?"

"No, Max, I've been praying for you."

"For me? I'm not the one facing execution tomorrow."

"No, you're not, but I've been praying for your soul and that in the time that I have left that I can convince you of the Lordship of Jesus. I've already told you that three days after the witnesses are killed that they will be brought back to life and ascend into Heaven."

"I remember. You honestly believe that they will come back to life?"

"Oh, they will come back to life, Max. The book of Revelation also predicts that the remaining water on earth will be turned to blood and that the remaining light sources-the sun, moon and stars-will be made dark. There will be no more light. Armies from the east and west and from the south will converge on Israel. The Chinese have been positioned and ready for an offensive for months now. And, at that time, the Lord Jesus will return with legions of angels and destroy the Anti-Christ and his kingdom. Babylon will fall and if not for the Lord shortening the days, no life would remain on earth. I'll be dead by then, but I wanted you to know now so that when it does happen you will have been warned beforehand."

"And your Bible tells you this?"

"Yes."

"Well, if the witnesses come back to life tomorrow, then I will have to give it some consideration."

"Don't wait too long, Max. Your soul depends on it."

"I'm going to miss you, Jake. You have always thought of others before yourself." There was an awkward silence. Max reached behind himself and grabbed today's edition of the newspaper then handed it to Jake. "Your execution is scheduled at ten in the morning. This will be the last time we speak before they take you away. May your God have mercy on you."

The next morning came quickly. At 9:30 A.M. the door to Jake's cell opened, and he was ordered to exit the room. A guard tied Jake's hands behind him while two other guards, one at each side, escorted Jake down the long corridor that led to the place of execution. At the end of the corridor was Max's cell, and Jake could see Max holding up a newspaper and yelling, "They've come back to life! The witnesses. Jake, you were right, they've come back to life!"

"Accept Christ!" Jake screamed, looking back as they passed. Max lowered his head and started to cry.

"Quiet!" the guard shouted, striking Jake in the ribs. Jake doubled over, trying to catch his breath and would have fallen to the ground if not for the guards holding him. Yanking Jake forward and not allowing him to regain his feet, the guards dragged Jake to the post that was set at the middle of the arena. The roar of the frenzied crowd was deafening as the guards dragged Jake to the gallows where the execution was to take place. *Am I to be hanged or killed the way Randy was*? But that was part of the plan. A victim can gain courage in the face of death when he knows how death will occur thus robbing the spectators of witnessing complete suffering of the one who is about to die. Thousands of executions had taught the executioner that fear is increased when the knowing how death is to come is taken away, leaving victims unable to prepare for death. So it was with Jake, he had prepared to die the way Randy had, but now the uncertainty of how he was to be executed weighed heavily on his mind.

At the gallows, the guards bound his feet together and tightened the rope that held his hands behind him. Above him a noose was lowered but didn't stop at his neck but continued to his waist. Jake was not going to be the first to die on this day, nor would he be the last, but his execution was the most anticipated. The crowd's anger about the witnesses being raised to life would now be directed toward Jake, and their angry cries for a slow, torturous death did not escape President Christos' attention.

The guards tied Jake's hands, which were already fastened behind his back, to the rope that was lowered moments earlier. The executioner turned to President Christos and waited for his order to start the execution. With a wave of the Anti-Christ's hand the rope became taut and lifted Jake off of his feet. The weight of Jake's body forced his arms upward and hyper-extended his shoulders opposite their natural rotation causing excruciating pain that radiated from Jake's shoulders and down his sides past his rib cage. He was hoisted to ten feet above the platform and held there momentarily to allow the crowd to witness the suffering, before dropping him uncontrollably. The rope was made taut again just short of the platform causing his arms to be ripped upward with a force that pulled his joints out of place with a loud cracking sound. Jake screamed in agony. He was hoisted up a second time to hang precariously above the platform, then as before was dropped again and, as before, stopped abruptly just prior to reaching the platform. This time his arms ripped upward to almost vertical over his head and shoulders.

Jake was in and out of consciousness from the pain that surged through his body. With every bout of unconsciousness, the executioner would place smelling salts under Jake's nose so that he would awaken again to endure the excruciating pain. The coliseum was vibrating with the tremendous roar of the audience that screamed their approval of the torture that was delivered to Jake. The executioner stepped down from the gallows and grabbed his bow and positioned himself just in front of the platform. Jake was hoisted once again to above the platform and hung there. This is it, he thought, looking down at his executioner; soon it will be over. Jake stared down at the executioner as he lifted his bow and pointed it at Jake. The roar of the crowd continued to vibrate throughout the coliseum. Jake closed his eyes and waited to die.

In and out of consciousness, Jake could hear Tracey's voice calling his name and a warm, peaceful feeling overcame him.

"Jake! Jake, can you hear me?" He heard her voice. He could feel her presence and knew that he would be with her soon. Her voice called to him again, and Jake opened his eyes. He was staring at the ceiling of his Boston home, and Tracey was looking down on him.

"Jake, wake up. You're having a nightmare."

Jake sat straight up in bed and looked around the room. He was soaking wet with perspiration; his heart was racing, and his breathing was rapid.

"My God," he said, grabbing Tracey's arm. "It was all a dream. I didn't miss it. I didn't miss the Rapture."

"Jake, what are you talking about? Are you okay?"

"You're here. Thank God you're still here. And John, where's John?"

Jake ran quickly to John's room with Tracey following closely behind. John, sitting in his crib, smiled brightly at seeing his father. He hadn't seen his father in almost three and one-half weeks since Jake had left on his latest flight overseas. Jake lifted John out of the crib and hugged and kissed his son repeatedly.

"Jake, what's going on? Have you completely lost it?"

"No, Tracey. I've found it. Last night when I went to bed, I was angry with you. But I had a dream-no, a nightmare-that you and John were Raptured and that I was left behind. But it was a dream. Thank God it was only a dream."

"But, Jake-"

"Just listen." Jake interrupted, "I dreamed that I was living through the Tribulation and that ... that the Anti-Christ, you called him Alexander Christos was taking over the world. Randy was executed and Mary was trying to have me captured. Millions upon millions died as the result of the plagues and God's judgments. Then I was captured and was going to be executed." Jake was short of breath, "Then I woke up to find you."

"Jake, it was only a dream."

"No, Tracey, not just a dream but a second chance. You told me before that I should accept Christ, that I shouldn't wait because there would not be any second chances. But God has given me a second chance. In my dream, God caused me to live through the Tribulation. And now I'm here with you and John. I didn't miss the Rapture. He has given me a second chance to accept Him as Lord."

"Jake." Tears flowed from Tracey's eyes. "What are you saying?"

Jake grabbed Tracey and held her in his arms. John sandwiched between them. "Tracey, I'm saying that I believe in Jesus and I accept him as Christ the Savior who died for my sins that I might have eternal life. He's given me a second chance."

Tears ran down Jake's face mingling with Tracey's tears. They praised God as they huddled together. Over Tracey's shoulder Jake could see a white dove through the bedroom window as it landed on the railing of the deck. Jake stared at the dove and mouthed a thank you before putting his head back down on Tracey's shoulder. As the dove took flight it looked back through the window of the home and Jake and his family were no more. A few miles to the east there was a large explosion at the airport that rocked the house, dropping the picture frames from the wall and to the floor. In the distance, toward Logan International Airport, black smoke rose into the sky.